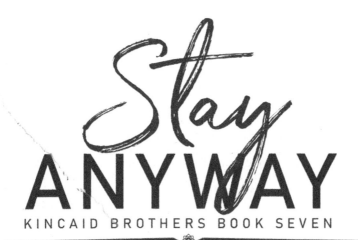

ANYWAY

KINCAID BROTHERS BOOK SEVEN

NEW YORK TIMES BESTSELLING AUTHOR
KAYLEE RYAN

Cover Design: Book Cover Boutique
Cover Photography: Sara Eirew
Editing: Hot Tree Editing
Proofreading: Deaton Author Services, Jo Thompson, Jess Hodge
Paperback Formatting: Integrity Formatting

ANYWAY

KINCAID BROTHERS BOOK SEVEN

NEW YORK TIMES BESTSELLING AUTHOR

KAYLEE RYAN

Maverick

I HATE WORKING SATURDAYS. WHAT I hate even worse is working when I know my entire family is gathered, and I'm not there. I'm used to working long hours, but we usually do it all through the week and try to avoid weekends. However, the weather rained us out two days this week, hence the reason we worked on Saturday.

Yeah, I fucking hate working the weekends.

Not because I go out and party. That's something I used to do with my brothers, but now that they're all married, well, all except for me and my twin, Merrick, our nights out look a whole lot different. Not that I mind. I love spending time with my family, and my brothers' wives and kids are cool as hell.

I'm speed walking to my truck, knowing that my family is waiting for me, and I know that my mom and my sisters-in-law have more food than we can eat waiting for us, and I'm starving.

My phone rings, halting my stride. Fishing it out of my pocket, I grin when I see my brother Ryder's name on the screen. I'm sure he's wondering when I'm going to be there. Today is the grand opening of his wife's boutique. "Yo," I answer.

"Hey, man. You headed home?" Ryder asks.

"Yeah, I'm walking to my truck now."

"All right, be safe. Come straight to the boutique."

"I will. Aw, shit," I mumble, seeing a car broken down on the side of the road just outside the parking lot. There appears to be a woman standing outside the car, and even from here, I can see the worried expression on her face.

"What's up?" Ryder asks.

"Nothing. It looks like a woman might be broken down. Flat tire from the looks of it now that I'm closer. I will handle this, and then I'll be on my way."

"Be safe."

"Always." I end the call and shove my phone back into my pocket. When I reach my truck, I unlock the door and toss my lunch box inside before closing and locking it. Instead of driving to the woman and her broken-down car, I walk. I figure I'll be less intimidating. However, that still might not be the case. I'm a strange man approaching her. At least I'm still in my uniform shirt, even if the sleeves are cut off. I have a clean one to change into in the back seat of my truck. I knew I'd be heading straight to the boutique opening from work today.

"Hi." I raise both hands in the air as if I'm being arrested. "My name's Maverick. Do you need help?"

The woman stops and stares at me. The worry is written all over her face. She opens her mouth, then quickly closes it again.

"I work here." I nod toward the parking lot and point to the logo on my T-shirt. "I was just getting off work and saw you might need some help."

She sighs, her body visibly relaxing. "I have a flat tire."

I nod. "I can see that. Can you pop the trunk? I'll have the spare put on in no time." I approach her slowly.

"That is the spare." She pulls open the back door, and that's when I notice a baby sleeping in a car seat. "The windows were down," she explains.

I nod. "I have nieces and nephews; they're always a bear if you wake them up before they're ready."

She exhales, and her shoulders drop, apparently relieved I'm not judging her. It's not like the baby was locked inside the hot car. All four windows are down.

"I don't have air conditioning, so the windows were already down, or else I would have had to wake her up. I wouldn't leave my baby in a hot car." She lifts the slumbering little girl into her arms. "This is Ada," she whispers. She looks up and smiles softly. "She can't resist a car ride."

"Yeah, my nieces and nephews can't either. I didn't catch your name?"

"Oh." She blushes. "My name's Stella."

"It's nice to meet you both. Why don't you go around to the other side of the road, on the sidewalk, and I'll take a look." I don't know what in the hell I'm looking for. The tire is flat, and if that's the spare, I'm positive she doesn't have another in her trunk. It's not like the spare from my truck will work.

"The keys are in it," she says before doing as I ask and moving to the sidewalk. "I appreciate you stopping to help. I was starting to panic."

"Did you call anyone for help?" I ask.

"No." I glance up and see a look of shame cross her face. "The only person I could call would be my grandparents. They live in Willow River. Grandpa still works, and my grandma, she doesn't get around so well these days. I didn't want to bother her. I was getting ready to look for a tow company, but they're so expensive." She presses a kiss to her daughter's head.

I don't pry into her life, but it's apparent that she's hit rough times. I couldn't imagine not having anyone to call to rely on. I think about my brothers and their wives—my now sisters by marriage—and I would jump to help any one of them at the drop of a hat. My chest constricts when I think about Stella and baby Ada not having that.

Kneeling, I look at the tires, and they're bald. They're almost slick; they're so bald. I stand back up and break the news that I can tell Stella already knows is coming. "It's going to have to be towed without a spare."

She nods. Tears well in her eyes as she holds her baby girl close to her chest.

"My brother Declan, he owns an auto repair shop in Willow River. I can call the shop and have one of his guys tow you there, and they can get you taken care of."

"I—do you know how much?"

"Family discount." I wink at her. I know once Declan hears her story, he's going to be fine with writing it off, and if not, I'll pay the bill. I'm not a millionaire, but I'm not living paycheck to paycheck either. Something tells me that Miss Stella and baby Ada could use a guardian angel in their lives. It's something small, but I hope it helps.

"I can pay. Maybe I can work out payments or something?"

I wave my hand in the air. "Trust me, it's taken care of." Pulling my phone out of my pocket, I call the number for Declan's after-hours tow service. I give them all the information, giving them my name instead of Stella's. "All set," I tell her, sliding my phone back into my pocket.

"Thank you, Maverick."

"You're welcome. Why don't you grab anything you might need out of your car, and we'll lock it up? I'll give you a lift."

"Oh, you don't have to do that," she says.

"It's fine. Besides, we're going to need the car seat for Ada, and tow trucks aren't really equipped for that." Reaching into my back pocket, I pull my wallet out and retrieve my license. Walking toward her, I stop and hand her my license. "Take a picture. You can even keep it until we get where we're going. Send it to whoever. That way, they know you're safe."

"Okay." She fumbles to get her phone and takes a picture of my license, which I still hold out for her. Her fingers tap the screen before she pushes her phone back into her pocket.

"I'm going to grab her car seat for my truck. Is that okay?" I know I'm a complete stranger to her. I need to proceed with caution.

She hesitates but eventually nods. "Okay."

As I pull open the back door, the hinges squeak, and I make a mental note to have Declan or one of his guys take care of that as well. I quickly unlatch the car seat and roll up the hand crank window.

"You're fast at that."

"Nieces and nephews." I grin. "I have eight brothers, but I'm the favorite uncle."

"Eight brothers?" Her eyes widen.

"Yep. I'm a twin, and even though we're identical, I'm the more handsome."

She giggles, and my shoulders relax.

"I bet they all say that they're the favorite."

"Oh, they do, but everyone knows that Uncle Mav is the man." I tap my chest, and she giggles again. "I'm going to go put this in the back seat of my truck. Stay on the sidewalk. I'll be right back to help you carry anything you might need from your car."

Relief crosses her face. "Thank you, Maverick Kincaid."

"You're welcome, Stella." Once I reach my truck, I have the car seat installed in record time. I grab my lunch box and toss it in the back. Thankfully, I have a tonneau cover, so I don't have to worry about it flying out.

"All set. What else do we need?" I ask. Ada lifts her head and blinks at me. "Hey, little lady. Did you have a nice nap?"

She grins and buries her head in her momma's neck.

"She's shy," Stella explains. "I need my purse and her diaper bag, and that should be fine for now."

"Great. May I?" I point to the car. She nods, and I reach inside, grabbing both bags, and rolling up all the windows. I'm finishing up when the tow truck arrives. "Hey, Jerry," I greet the driver.

"Maverick, good to see you."

"You too. Can you tow this back to the shop? I'll see Declan later and touch base with him about what's going on."

"Sure thing. Miss, do you have everything you need?"

"I do. Thank you."

Jerry nods before getting to work and loading the car.

"This way, ladies. Your chariot awaits."

Stella smiles and shakes her head. "Are you always this... upbeat?" she asks as we walk slowly, side by side, toward my truck.

I shrug, even though she's not looking at me. "Mostly." We reach my truck, and I pull open the back door. Stella is short, so she's going to have to climb up inside to place Ada in her seat. "I can strap her in. You can check my work when I'm done."

"Are you sure?"

"Positive. Hand her over, Momma. You can double-check my seat installation before we get Miss Ada settled in her seat."

She exhales in relief. "Thank you, Maverick. I don't know why you're being so kind, but I appreciate your generosity. I appreciate you taking the steps to make me feel comfortable. I know trusting a complete stranger is a gamble, but my gut tells me you're a good man."

"Your gut is right. If one of my sisters-in-law were in your position, I would want someone like me to stop and help them." I nod toward the seat. "Climb on in and check my work."

She kisses her baby girl on the cheek and reluctantly hands her over. I'm prepared for Ada to cry because I'm a stranger, but she does the exact opposite. She offers me a toothy grin and nestles her head on my shoulder.

"She's not really used to men or strangers," Stella says.

With one arm holding Ada tightly, the other strokes up and down her tiny back. "We're best buds." I flash Stella a grin. "I'll be right here, I promise." I nod for her to check my work. She returns my nod and turns back to the truck.

I watch her as she grabs ahold of the oh-shit handle, or whatever that handle is called, places her foot on the running board, and hops up into the back seat of my truck. I can't help but check out her ass in those cute little cutoff shorts she's wearing.

Ada places her hand on my cheek, her tiny fingers rubbing over my stubble, but her head remains on my shoulder. "Mommy's making sure your seat is safe." I don't know if she understands what I'm telling her, but I find myself explaining what's going on, anyway.

"You did a good job," Stella says. She's sitting beside the car seat in my truck.

"You hear that, baby girl? Your momma said I passed." Stella holds her arms out for Ada, but instead of handing her to her mom, I place her in her car seat, and, like the expert favorite uncle that I am, strap her in without incident. "Safe and sound." I bop Ada on the nose, and she covers her nose with her tiny hands as she giggles. "Come on, Momma." I hold my hand out for Stella, and she hesitates but places hers in mine. I hold her hand, but she has to let go to reach for the handle. Instinctively, I grab her by the hips and lift her out of the truck.

"Thank you," she says softly once her feet are firmly planted on the ground.

"You're welcome." I close the door, and with my hand on the small of her back, I guide her to the passenger side and open that door for her.

"Are you always a gentleman?"

Her tone tells me she's having a hard time believing I don't have an ulterior motive.

"Yep. My momma would skin me alive if not." I wink and make sure she's all in before closing the door. "So, where are we headed?" I ask once I'm in the driver's seat.

"I live with my grandparents in Willow River."

"I've lived in this town my entire life, and I've never seen you around." I know damn well I would have remembered her.

"I just moved here. I was in school, but—" She glances back at Ada. "—life happens."

"What about your parents?" I ask her.

"They're—not helpful. They disowned me when I refused to end my pregnancy. They said that I was ruining my life." Her eyes break away from her daughter and come back to me. "My daughter is the best thing that's ever happened to me. I withdrew from school and got a cheap apartment, but I was struggling to make ends meet. My grandparents insisted Ada and I come and stay with them. A fresh start, I think they said." I see her eyes go wide before she turns to the window, realizing she just revealed her family history. I have a feeling she didn't mean to blurt all of that out. Something inside her must have wanted me to know that she's trying. That she may seem helpless, but she's doing the best that she can. She also more than likely doesn't want me to think she's taking advantage of her grandparents.

"Who are your grandparents?" I ignore the other part, because the anger I feel on her behalf is brewing inside my chest.

"George and Harriette Gunderson. They own—"

"Gunderson's Hardware," I finish for her.

"Yeah. You know them?"

"I do." She seems to relax even further in her seat at the realization. "Good people."

"The best," she says, emotion filling her voice.

Glancing at the clock on the dash, I see that I'm really late. "Hey, I have a small thing I was supposed to be at for my sister-in-law Jordyn. She's opening a boutique. Do you mind if we stop there before I take you home?" The offer is out of my mouth before I can take it back. I could drop her off at her grandparents'. Their place is at the other end of town, but it's maybe ten extra minutes. However, I think Stella needs some happy in her life, and today is definitely about the happiness with the boutique opening. Besides, I'll introduce her to my sisters-in-law. She's new in town, and I'm only helping her meet new people.

"I don't want to intrude."

"No intrusion. I promise. There are a lot of us. The more, the merrier."

"What about Ada?"

"Are you kidding? I have lots of nieces and nephews, and don't be shocked if someone steals her away for some baby snuggles. There are a lot of us, and not enough littles for all of us to get snuggles at the same time." I hope that the smile I give her eases some of her worry.

"We're at your mercy, Maverick Kincaid."

My cock twitches. I know that's not what she means, but damn, this sexy siren and her words and that fine ass of hers is all kinds of temptation.

It's been an hour since Ryder called, but I'm finally pulling into Kincaid Central. It's a huge building where we will now have family get-togethers with a table big enough for all of us and more. It's something that my sister-in-law Jordyn insisted on when she recently came into an inheritance. It's also the location of her boutique. Today is the soft opening for family only, even though we've all spent a lot of time here during the build, helping out where we could.

"Ready?" I look over at Stella.

"You sure about this? Won't they think we're—together?" she asks.

Her cheeks are the lightest shade of pink, as if she's thinking about the two of us together. I have to fight to hide my smirk.

"Nope. They would already know if you were mine." With that, I grab my keys and slide out of the truck. I open the back door and unbuckle Ada from her car seat, just as Stella rounds the back of the truck.

"I'll take her so you can spend time with your family."

"You're hogging the baby snuggles, darlin'. That's not going to work in there." I point over my shoulder to the massive building. I quickly transfer Ada into her arms. "Come on." Reaching in, I pick up the diaper bag and toss it over my shoulder. With my hand on the small of her back, I lead them inside.

"Hey, everyone." I wave. "This is Stella, and this little cutie is Ada. Their car broke down, and I gave them a ride into town after calling Dec's shop to tow their car. I told her the more, the merrier." I rattle off an explanation, partly so that Stella will feel more comfortable and partly because my family is all looking at me like I've grown a third arm since the last time they saw me. It's not like they've never seen me with a beautiful woman before.

"Of course," Kennedy speaks up. "How old is your daughter?"

"She just turned one," Stella answers.

"Come on in. Let's get you something to eat." I guide her further into the room, ignoring the curious looks of my brothers. I see Jordyn and walk toward her, lifting her into my arms and spinning her around. She laughs and swats at me as I place her back on her feet. She motions to the table of food before her eyes lock on something across the room. No doubt it's Ryder she's looking at. Absently, she pats my arm and walks away.

"How about I take her while you make a plate? I'll help you get settled." I offer her the smile my mom calls charming.

"Oh, you don't have to do that." She brushes off my offer.

"It's no trouble. We're buds, right, Ada?" I ask the baby, offering her my index finger.

She latches on and giggles.

"Are you sure?" Stella bites down on her lip. Her facial expression tells me she's not nervous to let me hold her daughter. It feels more like guilt. As if only she can take responsibility for her.

"Come to Mav, baby girl." I hold my arms out for Ada, and she comes to me willingly with a smile on her sweet face. "Mommy's going to get you both some food." I bounce her in my arms, and she laughs.

"She likes you."

"All the ladies like me," I reply. Stella rolls her eyes playfully.

Stella makes herself a plate, and a smaller one for Ada. I lead them to a table and wait for her to get settled before handing Ada to her. "What do you want to drink?"

"Um, anything. I'm not picky."

"We have pretty much everything."

"Root beer?"

"Coming right up." I tickle Ada's belly before making a beeline for the table, making my own plate before grabbing us both a drink. By the time I get back to the table, Alyssa and my mom are talking to Stella, and sure enough, my mom has Ada in her arms. I take the seat next to Stella and dig in, letting the ladies get to know each other.

I can still feel the stares of my brothers, but I ignore them. I know what they see. Stella is a dime all day long. With her platinum blonde hair, those big baby blue eyes, and her curves, it's a distracting combination.

They think I'm hitting on her, but I'm really not.

Yes, I can appreciate her beauty, but I seriously am just trying to help her. My momma raised me right. Besides, I can be nice to a woman and her daughter and not expect anything in return. I glance over at Stella, and she blushes. It's cute as hell. I wink at her, because that's who I am, and she quickly turns away.

Yeah, the ladies love me.

Chapter 2

Stella

GETTING RESCUED BY A HANDSOME stranger was not on my bingo card today. Who am I kidding? Nothing about today has gone the way it was supposed to. I wasn't supposed to be driving home from Atlanta today. However, Ada's dad refused to come and pick her up. What makes matters worse is when I got there, he wasn't home. I had to call his cell five times before he answered, and he claimed he forgot.

Forgot.

How do you forget that it's your weekend to see your daughter? How did he forget when we talked right before I left the house to drop her off because he didn't have gas money to come to Willow River? How is that normal? It's not. *He's* not. But those are the cards my baby girl and I have been dealt.

Speaking of normal, Maverick Kincaid is unlike any man I've ever met. He's kind, and he's good with kids. He's gorgeous and not at all what I was expecting when he approached my car earlier today. Sure, I barely know the guy, but from what I've seen, Maverick is one of the good ones.

As an only child, I don't know what it's like to have a large family, but the Kincaids seem to have it down to a science. Kids are passed around, and everyone is talking and laughing, and it makes me yearn for something like this for Ada.

She doesn't know either set of her grandparents. My grandparents are her great-grandparents. They're so good with her, but it's just not the same. I know that they are getting up there in age. They can't run and play with her as my parents could have. I swallow back the emotion when I think about losing either one of my grandparents. They're the only family we have since my parents disowned me.

Well, I guess that's not completely true. We have Ada's sperm donor, but that's all he was good for. The minute I told him I was pregnant, he informed me he didn't want to be a dad. Since then, he's done everything in his power not to have to help support our daughter. He can't hold down a job. It's more like he refuses to hold down a job, so child support is nonexistent. I'm doing this on my own, and that's okay, but sometimes... sometimes, I wish we had a support system like the one we've found ourselves sitting in the middle of today.

"Do you want me to take her?" I ask Carol Kincaid, Maverick's mother. She scooped Ada up in her arms as soon as we were introduced and has had her ever since.

"Oh, heavens no. She's a sweetheart." She holds Ada's hands while my little one bounces on her little legs on Carol's lap, laughing and having the time of her life.

"Just let me know." I watch the two of them as my chest fills with longing for all the things my baby girl is missing out on.

"She's fine. You eat and enjoy the break. I had nine; I know that breaks for mothers are few and far between."

I smile and nod. "Thank you for having us. I hope we're not intruding." Maverick insisted the more, the merrier, and well, I was at his mercy, so I agreed. I was also curious about the family of the man who went out of his way to be kind to me and my daughter.

"Nonsense," Carol tells me. "Our door is always open. You see this wild group, right?" she asks. "We're prepared to feed a small army, one bigger than ours." She laughs, which makes Ada laugh as well. Her eyes flash to her son, who is sitting next to me. She's smiling as if she has a secret the rest of us are not privy to.

"Told you." Maverick leans over, pressing his shoulder into mine. "Stella's grandparents are Harriette and George Gunderson," Maverick tells his mother.

"Oh, what a small world. Raymond and I, that's Maverick's father, were just in the hardware store the other day. George was telling us that his granddaughter and great-granddaughter were staying with them for a while. How are you liking Willow River?"

"We've only been here a couple of weeks, but I've always loved the town. My parents didn't bring me to visit often, but it holds a special place in my heart. They used to take me to a sunflower field."

"Yes!" Carol exclaims. "Sunflower Park. It's in Harris, just a twenty-minute drive from here."

I nod. "I want to take Ada there and get some pictures."

"You should talk to my sisters-in-law Palmer and Scarlett. They're both photographers and work at Palmer's studio, Captured Moments. I'm sure they'd be happy to help on that front," Maverick tells me.

"I was just going to snap a few with my phone." I smile kindly. I would love to afford a professional photographer, but right now, professional pictures are not a necessity, unlike diapers and other essentials that Ada needs.

Maverick turns to look at me, and he nods. He gives me a look, one I can't decipher, but I'm sure he sees a broke single mom.

Not that I take offense to him thinking that. That's exactly what I am. I'm struggling, and I'm so grateful for my grandparents taking us in so that I can save some money and get back on my feet.

"Who do we have here?" an older gentleman asks, stepping up to the table. He leans down and kisses Carol, which tells me this is Maverick's dad.

"Dad, this is Stella, and that cutie Mom is hogging is Ada. They had car trouble, and I had her car towed to Dec's shop. I was going to take them home, but I was already late, so I convinced the ladies to join me."

"I'm sorry," I whisper.

Maverick whips his head around. His intense gaze staring me down. "You have nothing to apologize for. I had to work today at the last minute— I was supposed to be off. If I didn't have to work, who knows how long you and Ada would have been sitting there on the side of the road? Everything happens for a reason, Stella."

"Is this the cool kid's table?"

I look up and do a double take. There is a replica of the man sitting next to me, smiling down at my daughter.

"There are two of you?" I whisper to Maverick. I mean he told me, but seeing it is surreal. I realize my question sounds stupid, but two Mavericks is a lot to take in. Not that it matters. He tosses his head back in laughter, drawing attention our way with the boisterous sound.

"Merrick, this is Stella, and that cutie our mom has been hogging, is her daughter, Ada. Stella, this is my twin, Merrick."

"Nice to meet you," I say politely.

"You too. Sorry about her." He nods toward his mother. "There just aren't enough babies to go around yet. Give us a few years. My brothers are working on it." He winks.

"I don't mind. I feel guilty. I should be looking after her."

Maverick's father laughs loudly. "As soon as the love of my life decides she's ready for a break, it will be my turn. I hope you don't plan on heading home anytime soon." He's smiling, and I know his words and his smile are to put me at ease, and it works.

"They're baby hogs. Literally. I have to run and hide whenever I get lucky and get one of our nieces or nephews. Well, all except for Blakely. She's the oldest by a few years, and she knows how to play us all." Maverick shrugs as if it's no consequence that the girl, Blakely, rules the roost.

"Uncle Mav!" A little girl comes bouncing over to us. "You have a baby?" she asks, her eyes wide.

"No, kiddo, this is my friend Stella. That is her baby girl, Ada." He points to where my daughter is living her best life with his mom. "Stella, this is my niece Blakely, the oldest of my nieces and nephews."

"It's nice to meet you, Blakely." I smile kindly. She tilts her head to the side, studying me. I try not to squirm under her gaze. She's a kid, for goodness sake. I should not let her scrutiny get to me. I grab my water and take a drink to give myself something to do other than stress about this little beauty approving of my presence among her family.

"Stella, do you like arm porn?" Blakely asks.

I choke on my drink of water. Maverick is laughing, and I can feel his shoulder shake next to me. I open my mouth to reply but then quickly close it. Did she ask me what I think she did?

"Blakely." Carol sighs. "Go find your daddy."

"He's drinking a beer over there." She points behind her. "My daddy and my uncles gots arm porn, Stella. If you are Uncle Mav's friend, you must like it, huh?"

Merrick is doubled over, his hands resting on the back of his dad's chair as he heaves with laughter.

"Declan!" Raymond calls out. "Come get your daughter," he says, barely containing his own laughter.

"What's so funny?" Blakely asks.

"Come here, you." Maverick snakes an arm around her waist and pulls her onto his lap. "You can't go around asking people if they like arm porn," he tells her. How he manages to keep a straight face, I'll never know.

"But my mommy and my aunts like the arm porn, Uncle Mav." As if she needs to demonstrate, she reaches out and squeezes his bicep. She nods her approval, and all I want to do is tell her, "Same."

Maverick definitely has some sexy arm porn. I cover my mouth because even thinking about it makes me want to laugh, and he's trying to discipline her, so I need to be a mature adult and keep a straight face. It's hard to do.

"Daddy." Blakely climbs off Maverick's lap and wraps her arms around the newcomer's waist.

"Are you being good?" he asks. He stares down at her like she's his world, and I feel my chest tighten with longing. Not for me, but for Ada. Will she ever know what it's like to have a male role model who looks at her like she's his little princess? My grandpa does a great job, but he's older, and by the time Ada is Blakely's age, who knows how well he will be getting around? A wave of sadness washes over me. I can't imagine a world where Gramps isn't working at the hardware store and rushing home to Grandma for dinner. I know I can't be selfish and keep them forever, but I can still wish for it.

"I'm always good, Daddy."

"Uh-huh." He laughs at his daughter before giving me his full attention. "Hi, I'm Declan."

I wave awkwardly. "Stella. Another brother?"

"Yeah. I'm the mechanic. We'll get your car fixed up. Make sure you give Mav your contact info."

"My daddy works on cars. When I help, I have to wear my wiener pants. That's how he's gots all the arm porn, right, Daddy? Working on the cars?" Blakely asks.

I slap my hand over my mouth and watch as Declan smashes his lips together to contain his laughter. He eventually gets himself under control. "Blake," he warns, in what I'm assuming is his dad voice.

"Uh-oh." She wiggles away from him and backs away slowly. "I better go see my mommy and my aunts." With that, she turns on her heel and darts across the room.

Several voices, including Maverick, Merrick, Declan, and their parents, call out—hell, I think every adult in the room gives her the warning simultaneously: "Don't run," making her giggle.

"Sorry about that," Declan says, running his fingers through his hair.

"Nothing to be sorry for. She's adorable." I'm not exactly sure what wiener pants are, but I can only imagine what that sweet girl has made up in her mind.

"She is." He nods. "She's also a handful. She was the only grandchild for a few years, and well, my brothers spoiled her, and she's... a character." The smile on his face tells me that he adores his little girl. "My wife and I, we've been trying to teach her, but she's got a mind of her own."

"She's perfect," I tell him.

He smiles over at Ada, who is laughing at their father as he makes funny faces at her. "They grow up way too fast."

A beautiful woman walks up, and he immediately slides his arm around her shoulders, pulling her into his chest. "Our daughter is talking about arm porn again." She bites down on her lip, hiding her smile.

"She's your daughter when she talks about arm porn," he tells her. "That's you and the Kincaid ladies all day long."

"He's right," Merrick chimes in. "You can't blame us for that."

"Fine. I'll take the blame for the arm porn. Lord knows this family has it an abundance." She smiles up at her husband.

I want what they have.

I want a man to love me so openly that everyone around will know it without him saying a word.

"Hi, I'm Kennedy. This one is mine." She pokes Declan gently in the belly.

"I'm Stella. Nice to meet you. I met your daughter. She's adorable."

"Thank you. We have a son too. Beckham, he's one."

"The same age as Ada." I nod toward my daughter.

"Oh, we should schedule a playdate." She rattles off a bunch of names and ages. "Blakely is the odd woman out." She laughs. "The rest of them are really close in age."

"I'd like that," I tell her, and we exchange numbers. Mentally, I'm fist bumping myself for making friends with other moms, even though I know it wouldn't be happening if the handsome stranger sitting next to me didn't offer to help me and then insisted my daughter and I join him today.

As the day passes, I meet several more brothers, wives, and kids. Ada is passed around, and my baby girl soaks up all the attention. What started out as a shit-tastic day turned out to be one of the best I've had in a really long time.

"You about ready to go?" Maverick asks me.

"Yes. I'll just go get Ada," I say, nodding to where Merrick is holding her in a chair. They both look as though they're on the verge of falling asleep.

"I'll get her." He gives my shoulder a gentle squeeze, and he leaves to take my daughter from his brother.

I watch him as he gently lifts her into his arms and settles her against his chest. Ada lays her head on his shoulder, and Maverick rubs her back soothingly. He says something to Merrick that makes his twin laugh. With a nod, he heads my way. "Ready?"

"I can take her." I reach for Ada.

"Nah, she's comfy. Aren't you, baby girl?" She's content to be snuggled in his arms.

"Don't you need to say goodbye to everyone?" I ask him.

"Nah, I see them all the time. Besides, they're also wrangling up their littles to head home."

Not knowing what else to do, I grab the diaper bag and follow him out to his truck. He straps Ada in with quick efficiency before softly closing the door. With his hand on the small of my back, he opens the front passenger door for me. Once I'm settled, he closes the door and rushes to slide behind the wheel.

"Do you want me to drive you by Declan's shop so that you know where it is?"

"You don't have to do that. Willow River is a small town. I'm sure I can figure it out."

"Your grandparents know as well. Dec does all of their maintenance and repair work."

The knowledge makes me feel better. Silence fills the cab as Maverick pulls out on the road. We're getting close to my grandparents' place, and I need to get out my thank-yous for today so that when we get there, I can grab Ada and we can get out of his hair. I know I need to, but doing so means today is over, and well, I'm sad about that.

"Thank you for today, Maverick. For stopping to help and including us in your day. You didn't have to do that."

"You're welcome. It was nothing, and you met the fam. They were happy to have you there. I'm sorry they hogged your daughter all day."

"No. Don't be. She loved all of the attention. It was nice to feel like we were a part of something more. Something bigger than what's our reality."

"Well, I'll loan them to you anytime. Don't get me wrong, I love them, but I'm more than happy to share. There are plenty of Kincaids to go around." He glances over and winks, and my face heats, so I turn to look out the window.

We're both quiet until Maverick pulls into the driveway and turns off the truck. "I'll carry her in for you."

"Oh, you don't have to do that. I'm used to doing it."

"I know I don't have to. I want to." Something crosses his face, but it's gone before I can name it.

Speaking of being gone, Maverick is out of the truck, snuggling my sleeping daughter to his chest before I can unbuckle my seat belt and climb out of his truck.

"Lead the way," he says, stroking his gigantic hand over Ada's back.

I nod and turn, walking toward the front door. The house is quiet, and that's when I remember Grams telling me they were going to visit friends for dinner. Suddenly, my day, tagging along with Maverick and his family is even more of a blessing. We would have spent the day alone. Don't get that twisted. I love quality time with my daughter, but I can also admit I'm lonely, and the adult interaction was nice.

"Back here," I tell Maverick. I lead him to the small bedroom I'm sharing with my daughter. "I can put her down," I tell him.

"Nah, we have a better chance of her not waking up if we don't transfer her."

I stand by and watch as he lowers her gently into her crib and brushes her hair back from her eyes before standing to his full height. He reaches into his pocket and pulls out his phone. Unlocking the screen, he hands it to me. "Put your number in," he tells me. "I'll make sure to get it to Declan. Do you need a ride to work or anything?"

"No. I've been looking for work, but nothing yet. I'm going to start at the store with Gramps tomorrow. I was hoping to avoid that."

"Why?" he asks, keeping his voice low, careful not to wake Ada.

"I already feel as though I'm taking advantage of them. We're living with them rent free. I don't need them to pay me too."

"That's what family is for, Stella. Let them help. I know them pretty well, and I'm sure they're happy to do it."

"Yeah," I reply. That's exactly what they've been telling me since I got here, but I still feel guilty.

"Declan will be in touch." His fingers fly across his screen, and I hear my phone. "I just texted you, so now you have my number. If you need me, you call me. You know, if you're stranded or need to borrow my crazy family for an afternoon."

"Not crazy."

"We are, but I love them because of it."

"I'll walk you out."

He nods and leads the way to the front door.

"Thank you again so much."

He turns and lifts his hand to brush my hair out of my eyes, much like he did my daughter's. "You're welcome, Stella." With that, he turns and walks away.

My heart pounds in my chest as I watch him leave. There isn't a doubt in my mind that everyone he knows, their life is better because he's in it.

Maverick

THE POUNDING OF RAIN AGAINST the window wakes me up. Rolling over, I glance at the alarm clock. I don't need to be up for work for another half hour. Chances are, we're going to get rained out again. Reaching for my phone, I check, and sure enough, there's a message from my foreman telling us to stay home today. I don't mind it too much. I make prevailing wage, and my bills are low. It helps that I'm still living with Merrick, and our rent is cheap. I also save most of what I make. One day, I'm going to want a house of my own, and the idea of living paycheck to paycheck to get it is not appealing to me at all.

Who knows, I might even find myself a woman and settle down and raise a few kids. I mean, I know it will happen eventually. At least, I hope it will. It would suck to be the only one of my brothers who doesn't find their wife. Merrick and I are the only two left standing. I'm not in a hurry to find her, but I do want to find her one day. In the meantime, I'll enjoy flirting with the ladies, and loving on my nieces and nephews.

Turning off my alarm, I pull the covers up to ward off the chill of the air conditioning and try to fall back to sleep. After twenty minutes of tossing and turning, I know it's not happening. My body is used to getting up early. I decide to go ahead and shower and make some breakfast. I'm certain that if I'm rained out, Merrick is too. He's a heavy equipment operator, whereas I work on a road construction crew. Both, depending on what stage we are in for the job, are not possible when it's raining as if you were pouring piss out of a boot.

I'm sliding my scrambled eggs onto a plate when Merrick walks into the kitchen. He's in his underwear, and his hair is a mess. "Rained out?" he asks.

"Yeah. You too?"

"Yep."

"Here." I glide the plate of scrambled eggs toward him on the island. "Toast is in the toaster." As if on command, the toast pops up.

"Thanks," he mumbles, grabbing the toast before pulling the gallon of milk out of the fridge.

I busy myself making another plate of eggs. "I think I'll go by Declan's shop today. Make sure everything is all set with Stella's car."

"She's cute."

I nod. She's not just cute. Stella is a knockout with her long blonde hair and big blue eyes. And those legs of hers—yeah, cute is not the word I would use to describe her. Gorgeous, beautiful, and stunning are way better descriptions.

"She's got a kid."

"Yep." Ada is adorable. She's close in age to most of our nieces and nephews. She seemed to have a blast yesterday with my family. Soaking up all the attention we rained down on her. She's a happy baby, and I'll admit, when she snuggled up to me, it pulled at that invisible string in my heart.

"You going to see her again?" he asks, pushing his now-empty plate away from him.

"I'm sure. She's living in Willow River." That's not what he's asking me. We both know that I'm evading the question. One that I don't have an answer to.

Am I attracted to Stella? Fuck yes. But it's not just her. She's a single mom. It's more than just Stella and me if I were to pursue her.

"Avoidance." Merrick grins, and I toss my napkin at him. His laughter fills the room. "Come on, man, you brought her to a family function."

"She was stranded, and I was already late. I didn't want to let Jordyn down."

"Is that your story?" My twin gives me a knowing look.

"It's not a story," I defend. "Besides, I knew she was new in town. I thought it might be nice for her to meet some people. I'm pretty sure our sisters are going to be including her on some outings with the kids."

"Our sisters hope that she's going to be their sister." He smirks.

"Fuck off." I chuckle. "You're making something out of nothing. I helped her out, drove her home, and that's that."

"Did you walk her to the door?"

"What?"

"You heard me. Did you walk her to the door?"

I roll my eyes. "You know I did. Mom would ream my ass if she found out otherwise."

"Oh, so now we're blaming this on our dear momma?" he asks, pretending to be appalled.

"Stop, Mer. You're projecting, and it's nothing."

"I'm your twin, Mav. You know I can feel what you feel. I know we don't talk about that shit much, but you can't deny it. I know you better than I know myself. At least, that's how it feels at times. I know you're interested in her."

"I never denied that."

"Yes, you did!" he exclaims, a smile lighting up his face.

"I thought you were tired," I grumble.

His shoulders shake with silent laughter. "I'm wide awake, brother."

"Fine. Yes, I'm attracted to her. But there are millions of beautiful women in the world that I'm attracted to."

He nods. "But none of them ended up at an event with our family. Stella did. Stella and her cute baby girl. Her cute baby girl, that, if my memory serves me correctly, was snuggled up to your chest as you carried her out of Kincaid Central yesterday."

"I was just being polite and giving her a break. She's a single mom doing it all on her own. You know how Dec struggled."

"I do. I also know he did a damn good job, just as I'm sure Stella is as well. Ada is a happy, healthy baby. Stella was perfectly capable of carrying her sleeping daughter out to your truck."

He's not wrong, but I also don't want to hear it. "Why the interrogation?"

"Just trying to get you to admit that you felt something different." He taps his hand over his chest. "I felt it, Maverick. That's why I made it a point to come over and introduce myself to her. My gut tells me she's different."

"What are your plans today?" I ask, changing the subject. I don't want to talk about Stella anymore. Every time I hear her name there's this unsettled feeling in my gut. It's an annoyance that everyone thinks that I want her. I mean, they're not wrong. In different circumstances, I'd have hit on her for sure, but this situation is different, and I was just being a nice guy.

"Laundry, probably. The pile in the corner of my room is getting out of control."

"Yeah, I need to do that too. I'll check the detergent and stuff before I leave and pick up more if we need it on my way home."

"Thanks. I've got this. Go check on your girl's car."

"She's not my girl," I mumble, even though the sound of it lights something inside me. I head to my room and grab my wallet before slipping into my shoes and heading out the door.

The parking lot of Declan's shop is packed. Seeing all the cars instantly puts a smile on my face. My brother is killing it. It makes me damn proud to see Declan thriving. Orrin is as well, and so is Palmer's photography studio. I'm certain Jordyn's boutique will do the same.

Reaching into the passenger seat, I grab the box of donuts I picked up at the bakery. I'm whistling when I enter the building. Alyssa looks up from her computer and smiles when she sees me. "Hey, sis," I greet her.

"What do you want?" she asks, laughing when I place the box of donuts on her desk. "Donuts, and a cheery greeting. What do you need?"

"Can I not visit my brother and my sister-in-law?" I ask.

"I'm watching you, Mav," she teases.

"How's your day?" I take a seat on the stool next to her desk.

"It's going. The phones have been slow, which is good. I have some invoicing I need to get caught up on."

"Business is good."

"Yeah, it's been busy."

I nod. "Is Dec busy?"

"I think he's out in the shop." She opens the box of donuts and plucks one out. "I don't care what you're buttering me up for; this is worth it." She takes a big bite and groans as if it's the best damn thing she's ever eaten, making me laugh.

I stand and point at her. "Save one of those for me."

"No promises." She grins before taking another hefty bite of her donut.

Pushing through the service door, I scan the bays, looking for my brother. I find him standing next to Stella's car, which is currently on the lift. Careful of where I'm going, I make my way over to him. "How bad is it?" I ask him.

"Her tires are bald, all four of them, and she needs brake pads."

I nod. "Have you looked it over completely?"

"Yeah. It's pretty sound otherwise. Just the regular maintenance that's been neglected."

"Go ahead and give her four new tires, the brakes, and change the oil and any other fluid and filter that it needs. Oh, and replace that spare. I have no idea how long she's been driving on it."

"I'm pretty sure she's not going to agree with that assessment."

"I don't care. She has a baby. She can't be driving around on bald tires with bad brakes."

"Mav, brother, I don't think she can afford that."

No shit. "I know, but I can."

"Maverick." He uses his dad voice that stops Blakely in her tracks.

"Declan." I use the same tone.

"Come with me." He tosses the rag he was using to wipe his hands on the hood of the car and heads toward the service door that I just passed through. I follow along behind him, ready for a speech from my big brother.

Once we're back in the waiting area, he freezes. "Who brought donuts?" he asks Alyssa.

"Mav, but I can't figure out what he's buttering me up for."

Declan turns to look at me over his shoulder. "Kiss ass." He laughs as he stalks toward Alyssa's desk and steals a donut. "My office, little brother." He nods toward the hall.

"Oh, Mav's in trouble," Alyssa sings.

I stick my tongue out at her like the mature adult that I am, shove my hands in my pockets, and follow Declan down the hall to his office. He's already sitting behind his desk with half his donut devoured. He nods for me to sit. I close the door before I do. I don't need his employees to hear this conversation.

"Talk."

"About what? The weather? How are my niece and nephew? Any plans for another?" I ramble. I know it's going to piss him off, but he's treating me like a damn kid.

"Stella."

I sigh, my shoulders slumping. "Look, man, she's having a rough go of it. Ada's dad is a deadbeat, and she's here staying with her grandparents. I don't know the entire story, but I know she's hit hard times, and I want to help."

"Why do you want to help a complete stranger?"

"Fuck, Declan, I don't know, okay? Because I can? Because if that were my sister, wife, or daughter and they fell on hard times and I wasn't there to help them stand, I'd want someone without an ulterior motive to step in and do it in my place."

"She's going to be pissed."

"I know." Leaning forward, I rest my elbows on my knees and run my fingers through my hair. "It's not safe, right? Would you let Kennedy drive around with those tires and brakes?"

"Kennedy is my wife."

"Answer the damn question, Declan."

"No. No, I wouldn't let Kennedy drive on those tires and brakes."

"She doesn't have a Declan. As far as I can tell, she has her grandparents, and I'm sure they would help her if she asked, but Stella's not going to ask. I got the impression she feels like she's imposing by staying with them."

"I'm sure George is aware."

"Maybe, maybe not. If he's never ridden with her or driven her car, how would he know about the brakes? And the tires? I'm sure he's not paying attention."

"You sure you want to do this? It's going to set you back several hundred dollars."

"I'm sure."

He nods. "Fine, I'll take care of it. You'll get the family discount, so everything at my cost, and free labor."

"I can pay for labor, Declan."

"No, instead, I want you to watch the kids so I can take my wife out to dinner, just the two of us."

"Done." I hold my hand out to him to shake. "Just tell me when." He takes my hand in a firm grip and grins. "She's cute, though, right?"

"Yeah, Ada is a cutie." Fuck, what's wrong with my brothers today? Cute? Do they really think Stella is *just* cute? Are they fucking blind?

Declan bursts into laughter. He's grinning like a fool. That's my cue to leave. I stand and he does the same. Before I can open his office door, he slaps his hand on my shoulder.

"Can I be there when you call her and tell her about this?"

"No." She's going to be pissed, but there is just a part of me that can't let her get back into that car unless I know that she and her baby girl are going to be safe.

"I'm pretty sure we have everything we need in stock. I should have it done for her today."

"Okay. I'll call her."

"Good luck, brother."

"Thanks." I follow him out of his office, wave to Alyssa, and make my way to my truck. I pull out of the lot, drive to the grocery store, and park. I didn't want to be at Declan's shop, and I didn't want to be at home where Merrick could hear this conversation either. Not that I keep things from my brothers, but something tells me I'm going to have to charm Stella into accepting this gift, and well, I don't need their commentary when I try to do it. I have no doubt that Declan will be sure the others know of my act of kindness.

Grabbing my phone, I dial her number.

"Hello?" she answers hesitantly.

"Morning, Stel."

"Maverick? Is everything okay?"

"Of course it is."

"Why are you calling me?" It's easy to hear the confusion in her voice.

I gasp as if I'm appalled. "Can a guy not call his friend?"

"Are we friends, Maverick?" The question is whispered as if she's almost afraid to hear my answer.

"We are."

She exhales softly.

Was that an exhale of relief? Yeah, that's what I'm going with. "I'm calling with good news. Declan should have your car all fixed up by the end of the day."

"Wait. No, I mean, I need to call him and talk about cost."

"It's taken care of."

"What do you mean it's taken care of?"

"I took care of it."

"You... took... care... of... it?" she asks slowly. "What does that mean?"

"It means a friend is helping a friend."

"Maverick. No. I mean, thank you, but no. I can't let you do that. I can't pay you back. I don't even have a job right now."

There's panic in her voice, and I rush to assure her. "It's a gift, Stella. I don't expect a single thing from you in return."

"There's a catch. What's the catch?"

"No catch."

"There is always a catch. I'm not sleeping with you." Her voice is stern and maybe a little guarded. I'm sure some asshole made her feel like that's all she's good for, making a name for the entire male population when there are still good guys out there.

"Whoa, hold up. That's not on the table. I'm just trying to help. I want to think that if it were one of my sisters or someone I'm close to and I wasn't there, that someone like me with no other motivation other than to help someone out would step up for them."

"I thought you only had brothers?"

"My sisters-in-law are my sisters. Not by blood, but by heart."

"Damn," she mutters. "Maverick, I appreciate you, but it's too much."

"It's not. Besides, I'm getting the family discount, and Declan is desperate for a kid-free night out with his wife. I volunteered to babysit for labor costs. It's all been taken care of. We even shook on it. Brothers can't take back a deal made with a handshake."

"That's ridiculous." She laughs.

My shoulders fall at the sound of her laugh. I was certain she was going to let me have it. "You can't go back on a handshake, Stel."

"It's too much."

"It's not."

"Yes, it is," she counters. There's less conviction in her tone. She wants to accept the help because she needs it. I don't know if it's pride or guilt. My guess is that a little of both are keeping her protesting.

"Someday, when you're able and have the time, you can pay it forward."

"That day will never be here, Maverick. I'm a single mom without a job, living with my grandparents because my parents kicked me out when I told them I was pregnant. My daughter's father is a deadbeat who reminds me daily he doesn't want to be a father. I can't see a time in my life that I'll ever be able to pay this forward."

"You can volunteer at a shelter, the church, or the town festival. Paying it forward doesn't have to be monetary."

"You can't."

"I already did. Declan is finishing up. He'll call me when he's done. I'll call you and take you to pick up your car."

I hear her sniff. "I don't know what to say. I want to keep fighting you, but I know this makes my car safer for Ada, and because of my daughter, I will let this go. For now. I will repay you in some way. Even if it takes me fifty years, I will repay you."

"You just did. I know what this means to you, and the fact that you are adamant that you need to repay me when I've said you don't, tells me how much you appreciate this."

"You are one of a kind, Maverick Kincaid." Her voice is raspy with her emotion and dripping with sincerity.

"Nope, I'm a twin, and I have seven other brothers outside of Merrick who would do the same thing. I'll call you soon. Maybe we can grab dinner while we're out."

"No. You've done too much."

"You know, I'm the baby, well, the other half of a pair of babies of the Kincaid family. We're spoiled and stubborn, and I've never done well with the word no. Merrick and I were Blakely." I laugh.

"She's adorable."

"Are you saying I'm adorable?"

"Thank you, Maverick," she says, avoiding my question.

"You're welcome, Stel. I'll see you soon." I end the call before she can decline. It feels good to do something nice for someone in need. That's why I'm smiling, not because I get to see her again in a few hours.

Definitely not that.

Stella

I'VE BEEN A NERVOUS WRECK since Maverick called this morning. I'm still stunned at what he's doing for me and Ada. We're strangers to him. I've never met a man like him, willing to give so much of himself and his hard-earned money to help someone in need. Part of me still feels like this is a dream. Maybe I'll wake up and realize the handsome stranger and his incredible family were all just a figment of my imagination.

It's too much like a fairy tale.

The last couple of years, my life has been more of a bad afterschool special than a happily ever after. This is not how I thought my life would turn out, but here I am, trying to make the best of the hand that I was dealt. Sure, I had an unplanned pregnancy at the end of my sophomore year of college, but never in my wildest dream did I think that my parents would disown me because of it.

I fought for my daughter.

I'm still fighting for her. For us. I smile down at her, where she's sleeping peacefully in my arms. It's comforting to know that there are still good men out there. I hope that when the time comes—many, many years from now—Ada will find a good man to love her unconditionally. Something she's never going to get from her father. Sadness and anger wash over me when I think about Derrick. He was able to cast us aside without a care in the world.

Honestly, I don't know why I bother. That's not true. I keep hoping he'll realize that he's missing his baby girl growing up. I keep holding out, thinking he's going to change his mind. I know that makes me a fool, but I want that for my little girl. I want her to have her father in her life.

With one hand, I scroll through the online job listings for today. I hope that I can find work soon. I hate the thought of Grandma and Grandpa adding a position for me at the hardware store just to get me back into the workforce. They've done enough for us as it is.

My phone rings in my hand, startling me and causing me to jump. Ada whines, but I'm able to answer before the ringing wakes her up. "Hello."

"How's your day, Stel?"

Maverick. "You mean other than a stranger paying to fix my car and make it safe, same old," I say with a sigh.

He chuckles, and the sound is deep and sexy. "Sounds like a damn fine day to me. Declan called, and your car is ready. I thought I'd swing by and pick you girls up and take you to dinner before we go and get your car."

"Maverick, you've already done so much. You really don't have to take us to dinner too." My heart warms because, without question, he automatically assumes that Ada will be with me. I could have Grandma watch her, but I don't want to lean on her any more than I already am. Besides, when I find employment, she volunteered to watch Ada for me. I'm going to pay her what

I can, but the guilt of that situation still weighs heavily on my shoulders.

"No way, woman. We made plans. I'm free, you're free, and we both know Ada misses me." I can hear the humor in his tone, and I can't resist a smile. Thankfully, he can't see me. "I'm on my way to pick you ladies up."

"Thank you, Maverick." I know he's not going to give up. I might as well have dinner with him and thank him again in person for all that he's done. It's not exactly a hardship to spend time with him. He's easy to be around, and I can admit he's just as easy on the eyes.

"See you soon." He ends the call, and I toss my phone next to me on the couch. Ada is still sleeping. Carefully, I stand and place her in her Pack 'N Play while I rush down the hall to my room to freshen up.

Ten minutes later, my hair is combed, and I have a diaper bag packed. I changed into a shirt without baby drool all over it, and that's as good as it's going to get. Besides, it's not like Maverick is interested in me. He's just a nice guy, one of the few in my experience, and he's out of my league. He could have anyone he wants. He's not going to set his sights on a single mom who can't afford to fix her car and is living with her grandparents.

A soft knock on the door tells me he's here. I'm thankful both of my grandparents are at the hardware store today. Something about inventory. Grandma doesn't go in often, but she always helps with inventory and if someone calls in sick. Grandma was giving me one of those smiles. You know the one who says they think they know more than what they do, or that they think they know more than you do? Yeah, she gave me one of those when I told her Maverick Kincaid dropped me off. When she heard about my day, how he helped, and then took me to a family event, well, let's just say I can see the wedding bells in her eyes.

Yeah, I'm glad she's not here.

When I open the door, I'm greeted with Maverick's cocky smile. "Hey, Stel," he says.

He's not the first person to shorten my name, but damn if every time he does it, my heart races in my chest. "Hi. Ada is sleeping, so give me a second."

"No." He rushes to reach out and grab my arm. "Don't wake her up. Babies hate that." The expression on his face is so intense that I almost laugh. Almost.

"I know. I was dreading it, to be honest."

"Why didn't you tell me she was napping?"

His hand is still on my arm, and the heat of his touch is like a bolt of lightning racing through my veins. I ignore it, pretending like his touch doesn't affect me. "Because you've done so much for me. I wasn't about to dictate when you take me to pick up my car that you're paying for."

"Stella." He sighs, shaking his head. His hand drops from my arm as he takes a step into the house and closes the door behind him. Keeping his voice low, being mindful of Ada sleeping, he says, "She's your little girl. She comes first. I could have waited. I got rained out of work today, and I've just been sitting at home with Merrick. I was going stir-crazy, but I could have waited."

"I couldn't ask you to do that."

"Yes, Stella, you can. From here on out, you tell me what you need. Hell, tell me what you want. Don't just go with what I say."

My heart is going crazy in my chest. Is it because he's standing so close, I can feel his hot breath against my cheek? Is it because he's putting us first? Putting Ada first? Honestly, I think it's a combination of all of it. Then his words register. "From here on out?" I ask, my voice barely audible.

"Yes, from here on out. You tell me what's up? Got it?"

I want to ask him what that means. Will I be seeing more of him? I assumed not. He's being a nice guy, but once I have my car, there's no need to see him again, right? I open my mouth to ask, but Ada's cry stops me. I turn toward the living room with Maverick hot on my heels.

"Hey, baby girl," he coos at my daughter. His long-ass legs beat me to the Pack 'N Play, where he lifts her into his arms and snuggles her close. "How was your nap?"

Ada instantly stops crying as she stares at him. Her little hand brushes against the stubble on his face, and she giggles at the feeling beneath her fingers.

"Are you ready to have some dinner with Mommy and me?" he asks.

She coos at him as if they're having their own little conversation.

"I should change her before we go."

"Sure." He bounces her in his arms before he hands her over to me. "What can I do?"

"Nothing. I'm all set. The diaper bag is packed, and you have a car seat, right?"

"Yep. We're all set there." He reaches out and tickles Ada's belly, making her laugh. "Damn, you're cute," he tells her.

Not sure what to say, I turn and walk down the hall to the bedroom to change her diaper. I could have done it there on the couch, but I needed a break, a breather from the sexy man who's inserted himself into my life. I'm grateful for everything he's done for me, but I still don't understand it. All I can do is make sure that I repay him in some way in the future, whether that's paying it forward as he's asked of me or to him directly.

I *will* make this right.

I hate the feeling of owing someone, but I'm struggling. I'm broke, with only the support of my grandparents, and the thought of asking them for the money for my car is worse than letting Maverick pay. I've taken too much from them staying here and invading their lives.

"Mommy's going to find a job, and we're going to get back on our feet," I tell my daughter. She reaches for the pack of wipes and tries to stick it into her mouth. I tap her nose before taking the wipes and replacing them with a small set of toy keys that she can chew on. She babbles and coos, and it fills my soul. She's growing and doing something new or making new sounds, and I cherish every second of it.

Once I'm finished, I place Ada on my hip and carry her back to the living room. Maverick looks up from his phone, which he slides back into his pocket.

"Ready, ladies?" he asks. Ada babbles and holds her hands out for him. Her easy acceptance of him helps me relax. Kids are a good judge of character, or that's what I've read.

"We really don't need to get dinner. Just taking me to get my car is more than enough. You've done so much for us, Maverick."

"Are you kidding me? I'm the luckiest man in Willow River. I get two beautiful ladies to have dinner with me." He winks.

That wink is powerful. It has a swarm of butterflies taking flight in my belly. "Thank you."

"Stop thanking me, Stel. Now, hand her over." He reaches for Ada, and she goes to him willingly, with a smile on her face. She was already leaning toward him with her arms out. I push the fact that she wanted him and not me to the back of my mind. My baby girl is just soaking up the attention. "What are we thinking for dinner?" he asks Ada, then turns to look at me. She babbles as if she's answering him, and I can't hold my smile.

"Just a drive-thru is fine." I shrug. I'm not picky.

"What? Two beautiful ladies as my guests, and you want me to take you to a drive-thru?"

"French fries." I nod toward Ada. "It's her favorite."

"Right, well, how about the diner in town? Dorothy's is the best. They have fries for this cutie and a lot of options for us."

I open my mouth to argue and quickly close it. "Okay. Thank you." If I keep arguing, he's going to think I'm ungrateful. I'm not. I'm just embarrassed he feels like he needs to take care of us.

"Ada, tell Mommy to stop thanking me." He raises Ada's hand and helps her point at me. My daughter laughs, loving all of his attention. She coos and babbles, doing as Maverick asks.

"Let's hit the road." He turns with Ada in his arms and carries her out to his truck. He bounces her on his hip, and her squeals of delight follow them.

I rush to grab the diaper bag, lock up the house, and follow them. By the time I reach them, Maverick has Ada in her seat, and he's buckling her in. I don't bother asking if he needs help. I know he doesn't. Instead, I climb into the passenger side and turn to glance at my daughter. It's the mother in me. He knows what he's doing. He's proven that but I can't help but check, anyway.

"How was your day?" Maverick asks once we're on the road.

"Good. I spent a good part of the day job hunting."

"No luck?"

"Not yet. I'm not exactly qualified for much. I'm a college dropout." Here I go again, blurting out the sad truths of my life. It's as if just being in Maverick's presence is a truth serum, causing me to word-vomit all of my issues.

"What were you going to college for?"

"I hadn't declared a major. I was working on getting all of my general classes out of the way."

"What do you want to do?" The tone of his voice tells me he's not being polite. I really think he wants to know the answer.

I glance back at Ada, who's happily chewing on her keys. "Something that lets me be home at night with my daughter. I don't want to miss sports, school plays, or anything else. She's my entire world."

"As she should be. My brother Brooks is a nurse, and he's always having to trade shifts to not miss stuff. Luckily, he works with a great group and they all pitch in to help each other out."

"And you work construction, right?" I ask him.

"Pretty much. Road construction. I work for a paving company. The job is hot as hell, but it pays well, and I'm usually laid off during the winter months."

He pulls into the parking lot of the diner in the center of town and turns off the truck. "Have you eaten here yet?" he asks.

"No. I've been trying to save money as much as possible." It's as if I can't help myself where he's concerned. My voice is low because it's embarrassing that I'm a single, unemployed mother, especially when this sexy man seems to have his life together.

"Understandable. I'm glad I get to be the one to bring you here. Their food is incredible. It's all home-cooking, and even the burgers taste like you're at a barbeque." With that, he climbs out of the truck and makes quick work of getting Ada out of the car seat.

I do what it seems that I always do where Maverick is concerned. I grab the diaper bag that has my wallet and phone shoved inside and follow him into the diner. With Ada on his hip, he opens the door for me. I step inside and survey the place, looking for somewhere to sit where a high chair won't be in the way.

"Right, back corner," Maverick says. His hand lands on the small of my back, and I shiver at the contact. He keeps his palm there, leading me to a booth. When we pass a small row of high chairs, he drops his hand from my back and snags one for us. He places it at the end of the booth before he slides in one side and places Ada on the table in front of him, making funny faces at her and making her laugh.

"I can take her."

"Nah, she's my little buddy, right, Ada girl?" He makes another face, and Ada belly laughs, placing her hands on his cheeks. I glance around, and we seem to have gained the attention of the entire diner. Not that I can blame them. Maverick is all muscles, five o'clock shadow, dark hair, and tall. And to see him talking and playing with my daughter as if she's his best friend... as if she was his, it's definitely something to see.

"Hey, Mav," a woman who looks like she's my age greets him. "What can I get for you?"

"Hi, Amy." He greets her cordially before his eyes find mine across the table. "Stel, do you know what you want to drink?"

"Just water for me."

"Water? Come on now. You need to experience Dorothy's sweet tea."

I can't help but smile at his enthusiasm. "I'll have a sweet tea."

"What about my little buddy here?" he asks me.

"I have a sippy cup of milk for her."

"All right, well, then a sweet tea for me, too, Amy. Thanks." He doesn't even look at her as he makes another silly face at Ada. "You better look at the menu, Stel."

"Do you know what you're getting?"

"Yep. Meatloaf dinner, with mashed potatoes and green beans, and some french fries for my girl here." He blows a raspberry on Ada's cheek, making her giggle and pull his hair.

"No, sweetie." I reach across the table to help free him from her grip.

"She's fine, Momma." He grins and continues to give her his full attention.

A few minutes later, Amy is back with our drinks, and we place our orders. I get the same thing as Maverick and order an applesauce, which I will share with Ada.

"So, you hung out with Merrick today? What's it like having a twin?"

He shrugs. "I don't know any different. He's my best friend, but I could say that about all my brothers, even with the age difference between us and the oldest, which is Orrin."

"I'll never keep them all straight." I internally cringe. It's not like I'll need to keep them straight. We're not dating.

"Nah, you'll get it."

"How do people tell you and Merrick apart?" I ask.

"I'm just a little taller than him. Other than that, we're exactly the same. I'm a little louder than him, but our personalities are also similar." He looks over Ada's head at me. "You're just going to have to spend some time with me so that you can tell us apart."

His confidence is sexy.

He's sexy.

"I'm sure you have better things to do than hang out with a single mom." The comment is out before I can think better of it.

"You're her mom, and you're single. I think we've already determined that I'm lucky to have the company of two beautiful ladies."

I want to ask him what that means. Is he interested? Am I? My life is a mess. I'm struggling each and every day. Do I have the time for a relationship? Do I want one? Ada's dad and I were never serious. We went on a few dates, and when I found out I was pregnant, he walked away.

I can admit that I'm scarred by his rejection. Not only of me, but of my daughter. I don't need her falling in love with him only for him to leave us. I have to be smart about who I let into her life, for fear of them walking right back out of it. However, Maverick, he's already inserted himself into our lives. He's helped me more than Ada's father ever has.

"Maverick Kincaid has game," I tease. It's easier than letting myself fall into running what-ifs through my mind.

"You hear that, Ada? Mommy thinks I've got game." He snuggles her close before placing her in the high chair, and suddenly, Amy appears with our food.

All through dinner, he engages me in conversation and helps with Ada. He offers her his mashed potatoes, which she prefers over her own french fries. I should have thought about getting Ada her own order, but being around Maverick scrambles my brain. By the time we leave Dorothy's Diner, our bellies are full, and my heart, well, let's just say my heart is full of hope.

For the first time in weeks, it feels as though this move to Willow River was not just the only option; it was the right one for me and my daughter.

Chapter 5

Maverick

"WE'RE DOING TWO TRIPS THIS year, right?" Orrin asks our dad.

My brothers, my cousin's husband, Deacon, and I are all sitting out on my parents' back patio with Dad talking about this year's camping trip. It's an annual event Dad started when we were little to give Mom a break. Now that we're older, and all but me and Merrick are married, my brothers convinced our dad to add a second annual trip.

"Yeah, one for us guys, and one for the families." Dad nods, and there's a smile playing on his lips. He loves that Mom is now included. Not just Mom, but the grandkids and my sisters-in-law—they're just his daughters in his eyes. The in-law added to the end is unnecessary.

"I think we should hold off until the fall for the family trip. Jordyn is pregnant and who knows who else will be by then." Brooks, the nurse in the family, laughs. "It will be easier for her if it's not so hot."

"Not a bad idea," Dad muses. "I'm sure the kids wouldn't mind, but a nice fire on a chilly night is the best."

"Maybe, but if we don't find Jordyn some help, we won't be going anywhere. My wife is stubborn," Ryder grumbles.

"What's going on?" Sterling asks.

"She's doing too much. She's pregnant, and she's dragging her feet at finding help at the boutique," Ryder explains.

"She's early in her pregnancy. As long as she's not walking around thinking she's Hercules lifting things she shouldn't be lifting, she should be fine. She'll rest when she needs to," Brooks tells him.

"Have you met my wife? She's determined to make this boutique a success. I get it, I really do, but I worry about her. She needs to give herself some downtime. She's convinced she doesn't need help yet."

"Have you discussed this with her?" Dad asks.

He nods. "I told her she needs help, so she doesn't work so much."

Dad laughs. "Son." He shakes his head. "Come on now. You know better than that. You can't tell her what she needs to do. You have to express your concerns with her. Have an actual conversation that's more than you telling her what she needs to do or can't do."

"Yeah," Declan chimes in. "Have you learned nothing from us?" He snickers.

"Right? There is no telling Crosby what to do." Rushton's eyes widen like he can imagine his wife being pissed off at him.

I'll say this about my brothers. They fell in love with kind, loving women, but they also aren't pushovers. They're not afraid to stand up to their husbands—as it should be. I'd say out of all my sisters-in-law, Palmer and Scarlett are the feistiest, but then again, Alyssa, Crosby, Kennedy, Jordyn, and Jade can also hold their own. It's actually fun to watch these tiny women put my brothers in their place.

"Happy wife, happy life," I say with a grin.

"Like you would know." Deacon chuckles.

Ryder turns to face me and smirks. "How's Stella?"

I shrug. "How would I know?" I dropped her off to get her car on Monday and texted to make sure she got home okay and didn't have any issues. I haven't heard from her since. Not that I really expected to.

"Come on now," Archer chimes in. "You two looked pretty cozy last weekend."

"She was in a bind. I helped her out. How is that cozy?"

"You stayed by her side the entire time," Rushton speaks up.

"She didn't know anyone. Besides, I was eating... she was eating." I shrug. It's not a big deal, but I should have known my brothers would make it so. I mean, Stella is a beautiful woman. Of course they would assume I'd want more from her. I really was just trying to be a nice guy and help her out.

Declan clears his throat and gives me a pointed look. I glare back at him. I know what's about to happen. There are no secrets in this family. "How's her car?"

"Fine. I dropped her off to pick it up, and that was that."

"Really?" Orrin asks. "I was certain a little birdy told me that you took her and her daughter out to dinner before you took her to get her car."

"Stupid small town," I mutter under my breath.

"And..." Sterling grins. "I heard she might have had some assistance with the bill."

"You know, now that you mention it," Merrick muses, "he's been on his phone a lot lately."

"What?" I turn to look at my twin. "I haven't been on my phone any more than usual." I glare at my brother, and he laughs.

"Let me rephrase that. You've been checking your phone more frequently." He holds his hands up in the air as if he needs a line of defense against my look.

"Just because I'm bored out of my mind sitting at home with you at night." Fucking twin. Everyone knows that Merrick and I are practically the same person, and if he makes a claim, when it comes to me—and me when it comes to him—it's ninety-nine percent fact. Most of the time.

"That's what we do. We go to work, come home and chill, hang with the fam, and hit the club sometimes. You've never been bored before," he challenges.

"Are you done?" I ask him.

He taps his index finger against his chin as if he needs to think about it. "I will be when you admit you're hoping to hear from Stella."

"I didn't expect to hear from her," I defend. "I didn't know you were monitoring how many times I looked at my phone."

"Leave him be." Dad comes to my defense. He's laughing, which tells me he's sided with my brothers. I'm annoyed, but I shouldn't be. I've been on the giving end of dishing out shit on my brothers my entire life. I guess it's only fair, I get my turn receiving as well.

"Yeah, leave me be," I tell Merrick. We may be fully functioning adults, living on our own, working full-time jobs, and paying our own bills, but we're also still the little boys who grew up together, and I hope like hell that will never change.

I fight the urge to stick my tongue out at him, but I like to think I've grown out of that stage, even if the will to do so is strong.

I love my brothers—all eight of them, including Deacon. I love them even when they're riding my ass about things that don't matter, like how often I look at my phone.

"So, it's settled then. A trip for us next month, and then with the entire family in the fall?" Dad asks, turning the conversation back in the right direction. After raising nine boys, he's a professional at deflecting an argument and rerouting a conversation. Not that we're arguing, really, but you get the point.

"Sounds good," Brooks says. "That's my weekend off, so we're all set. I need to go. Palmer has some photos she needs to edit. I told her I wouldn't stay long so that I could help with the kids while she gets her work done."

"You should have brought them with you," Sterling tells him.

"Get your own," Brooks fires back. There's no heat in his tone. It's common knowledge that we're all baby hogs. All of us. Currently, there are not enough babies to go around, which is why my mom snatched up baby Ada last Saturday to love on her.

"Working on it." Sterling grins.

It's not just an "I'm happy I'm having lots of sex with my hot wife" grin. It's an "I know something you don't know" grin.

"Spill it," I tell my brother. I probably shouldn't be calling him out, because if that grin means what I think it means, his wife will have his balls if she finds out he told us without her.

Sterling crosses his arms over his chest and smirks. "You tell us why you've been watching your phone like it might grow legs and walk off, and I might."

I hold his stare for several seconds and shrug. "Just checking to see if she'd reach out."

"And *she* would be?" Sterling asks.

I roll my eyes. He knows exactly who I'm talking about, but I get the game. I need to spell out my confession to them. "Stella. She's new in town, and I told her if she needed anything, she could reach out. She doesn't have a lot of support, and I know she's been looking for a job. I told her that if she needed insight on a local company or employer, she should let me know." I don't know why they're making such a big deal over this.

"Uh-huh," Sterling says. He doesn't believe me, but that's fine. They'll see it, eventually.

"Your turn, brother," I tell him. I make a show of crossing my arms over my chest and mimic his stance. My brothers and I are all muscular. Hence the "arm porn" my niece Blakely can't stop talking about.

Sterling makes a point of letting his eyes scan over all of us. "Not a single word," he threatens. We all nod because, with a warning like that and the smile he just gave us a few minutes ago, we all know what he's about to say. "We're pregnant." His smile is huge as he says the words. "Tink wanted to wait to tell everyone tomorrow at Sunday dinner. She's just passed her first trimester, so thirteen weeks." His smile is infectious.

"Congratulations." I rush him, wrapping my arms around him in a hug. I step away, letting my dad, brothers, and Deacon take turns congratulating him.

"So, just to be clear, I can't tell my wife?" Brooks asks. We all chuckle, and Sterling scowls. Brooks holds up his hands and slowly backs away. "Just kidding. I'll see y'all tomorrow at Sunday dinner."

"Kincaid Central!" Ryder calls out.

"Got it!" Brooks calls back as he disappears around the house.

"I should get going too." Orrin stands. "I need to stop by the shop on my way home, and Jade texted saying we're out of milk."

"Me too." Declan also stands. "I don't have a reason other than wanting to see my wife and kids." He grins.

"Let me know when you want to cash in on that babysitting," I tell my brother, holding my fist out for him for a bump as he walks past.

"My wife is all over it. She's planning something. I'll let you know as soon as I know."

"You're supposed to be the one planning and surprising her," Archer tells him.

"Yeah, Dec," Deacon chimes in. "Are you losing your touch now that you're an old married man?" he jokes.

"I mentioned a night out, and she told me she'd handle it. I'm not going to argue with my wife. It's a night out, just the two of us. All night," he says, looking over at me in question, and I nod.

Blakely is a huge help where Beckham is concerned. Besides, it's not like I can't call in reinforcements if I need them. And more than likely, Merrick will be home to help as well. That's the perks of living with my twin, and having a large, close family.

Work hard, and love harder.

We're damn good at both.

"I got you," I tell him.

"See. I don't care what we do. I know how the night ends." Declan wags his eyebrows, and we all laugh. "One tomorrow, right, Dad?" he asks.

"Yes," Dad confirms.

Jordyn and Ryder had a huge building built for our family get-togethers with her inheritance, and everyone is calling it Kincaid Central. It's perfect for our large growing family. The main table is massive, and there are smaller tables for the kids, toys, and huge couches around a big screen. There's a pool table, corn hole, and all kinds of other things, as well as multiple bathrooms. My mom says the kitchen is a dream. I don't know about that, but it is massive. There are a few bedrooms with baby beds and toddler beds for the kids who end up napping while we're there. Jordyn put a ton of thought into the place.

"See ya then." With that, he, too, disappears around the house.

I finish the glass of tea I've been nursing when an idea hits me. "Hey, Ry, I might have a solution for you."

"Solution?" Ryder asks, confused.

"Yeah, with Jordyn working too much."

"I'm all ears, little brother."

"Stella." I can't help the smile on my face thinking about her. I know for a fact she'd refuse if she knew this was my idea. That's why this is perfect. Ryder can tell Jordyn, and she can contact Stella for a job.

"What about your girl?" he asks.

"She's not mine. However, she is looking for a job. I don't know how much she needs to make, and she'd have to figure out childcare, but I'm sure she'd be interested. She's been looking here in Willow River and in Harris."

"You could use Stella needing a job as an excuse to bring up Jordyn hiring some help," Deacon offers.

Ryder points at him. "I knew it would come in handy that Ramsey married a lawyer," he jokes.

"Not a bad idea, son," Dad agrees.

"Give me her number." Ryder pulls his phone out of his pocket, and I do the same as I rattle off her number.

I know it sounds crazy, but I feel a sense of pride knowing that I might have been able to solve another issue for Stella. I couldn't imagine not having a huge support system and having a baby doing it all on my own. I know that she has her grandparents, but George and Harriette are getting up there in age. George has been talking about retirement since I was old enough to understand what the word meant, and possibly, almost certainly, longer than that.

"I'm sure she'd be interested." I don't know Stella well, but Jordyn will be flexible with Ada's childcare hours. This is almost too perfect for what she needs.

"I'm going to go home and talk to my wife, and hand deliver her new employee." Ryder grins.

"Hey, I should get some kind of finder's fee or something."

That causes a chorus of laughter. "How about I don't tell my wife that you're interested in Stella, and we'll call us even?"

"Bro, no deal," Merrick says. "We all know the ladies in the family know you're interested." He's shaking his head, warning me away from Ryder's deal.

"I'm not interested," I remind him. "Can't a guy help a girl out?"

"Sure, but when you're both single and she's hot as fuck." Merrick freezes and flashes a grin at our dad. "Sorry, Pops, but you know it's true. Anyway, not when the lady is sexy," he amends.

Stella is sexy. There's no denying that. Her platinum blonde hair and those baby blue eyes... and her toned legs? Yeah, she's sexy.

"See." Merrick points his index finger at me. "That look. He's thinking about her right now."

"Whatever. I'm thinking about her because we're talking about it."

"Lies."

"So, no deal?" Ryder chuckles.

"Get out of here." I wave him off. His laughter follows him around the house and to his truck.

I stay and talk to the others for a little longer until Mom gets home from the store. Everyone pitches in to help her haul in the groceries before we say our goodbyes and head our separate ways.

In my truck on the way home, I debate about calling Stella and telling her about the job. I really want to, but I know it's better if I don't. If she knew that I was involved in any way, she might not take the job, seeing it as a handout. When in reality, it's something Ryder and Jordyn both need. I might be hard-pressed to get her to believe that.

I fight the urge, knowing it's for the best. When I make it to the house, Merrick pulls in behind me. I'm about to ask him what the plan is for tonight, but he beats me to it.

"Pizza and chill at home tonight?"

I don't know if he's suggesting it because he thinks I'm hung up on Stella, which I'm not. Or because he just wants a quiet night in. In the last year or so, we've calmed down on going out as much as we used to. We stay in more or spend time with our brothers and their wives and kids.

"Sounds like a plan. I'll call it in."

"I picked up a twelve-pack last night on my way home from work. It's chilling in the garage fridge."

"Even better."

The rest of the night, I make it a point to keep my phone in my pocket. I have to constantly think about not checking it. It's stupid, but I don't need to give my brothers any more ammunition to give me shit about Stella when there is nothing going on there.

Am I curious if she'll accept the job? Absolutely. However, I know it's best if I stay out of it. I'm certain Jordyn, and even Ryder can convince her to take the job. That means even if she was planning on leaving Willow River, she's going to stay anyway. This job will get her back on her feet, and she can find her place here.

Chapter 6

Stella

MY EYES ARE HEAVY AS I stare down at my phone at the balance on my bank account. I wish I could blame the low balance on my tired eyes, but that's not the case. Unfortunately, the number is real, and it's decreasing every day. I've only been spending money for diapers, wipes, and things Ada needs, the necessities. Even so, those things are expensive.

I sold everything I owned except for my car, my clothes, and all of Ada's things before moving to Willow River. It wasn't much, but it was enough to get us here, and I've been using it to get by until I find a job. I didn't expect it to take this long. I'm either not qualified because I have no education or because someone with more experience has been chosen over me. It's not looking good, and I'm worried I might have to take my grandparents up on their offer to put me to work at the hardware store, even when I know they don't need the help.

I hate feeling helpless and dependent on other people.

Like Maverick.

That money isn't going to last forever. I really need to find a job soon. Babies are expensive, and I loathe the idea of having to take money or a job that's not really there from my grandparents. I should be looking for a job right now, but Ada was up most of the night last night. She's teething, and she's miserable. We walked the floor for the majority of the night. The only way she was comfortable was if I was holding her. Even then, it was a struggle.

Hoping I can get in a quick fifteen-minute nap before she wakes up screaming in pain again, I lean my head back on the couch and close my eyes. I'm almost there, drifting off to sleep, when my phone rings. I jolt awake because I don't get calls anymore. My friends, or who I thought were my friends, abandoned me when I got pregnant. Apparently, a single pregnant friend hinders their partying ability or something like that. My parents wrote me off, and lord knows Ada's dad never calls to check on his daughter.

Glancing at the screen, I don't recognize the number, and hope swells in my chest. Maybe it's one of the many jobs I've applied for. I clear my throat and then answer. "Hello, this is Stella." I hope I sound professional. If this is a prospective job, I need to impress from the start.

"Hey, Stella, this is Jordyn Kincaid."

Kincaid. "Hi, Jordyn," I answer politely.

"We met briefly when Mav brought you to the soft opening. There are a lot of us." She chuckles. "I'm Ryder's wife."

I can hear the smile in her voice. "There were a lot of you." I laugh nervously.

"You'll learn all of our names in no time. Anyway, my husband mentioned that Mav said you were job hunting."

"I am." I'm not sure where this is going, but hope wells in my chest. Of course, Maverick would have to be involved with that hope. Seems that's been a new common theme since the day he stopped to help me on the side of the road.

"Can you tell me a little about what you're looking for?"

"Anything. I don't have a lot of experience. I worked as a server during my first two years of college. I had to drop out of school when I found out I was pregnant with Ada. My parents... they didn't support me keeping her." I hate talking about my situation, especially with strangers, but if she's a potential employer, I feel that being honest with her is the best policy.

"Oh, so customer service. That's great. I'm looking for help at the boutique. Ry's stressed out that I'm working too much. I don't know if it would be full-time right away, but it would be part-time for sure until things pick up. Do you have time to come in so we can talk more?"

My shoulders relax, and relief washes over me with Jordyn's easy acceptance of my past. The last thing I want to do is sit and discuss the people who were supposed to love me unconditionally but don't. "I can, but my grandma had a doctor's appointment, so I'd need it to be later so she can watch Ada. I promise I'll have reliable childcare," I rush to tell her.

"Oh, just bring her with you." Her tone is nonchalant like it really isn't a big deal that I bring my one-year-old daughter to a job interview.

"Are you sure?"

"Absolutely," she replies without a second of hesitation. "It will be very informal. I just want to go over the job and show you what you'll be doing. We can talk about working hours and all that."

"Okay, well, Ada is napping."

"I'll be here all day. Just come over after she wakes up."

I'm shocked. It's as if the perfect scenario just landed in my lap. "Thank you so much, Jordyn."

"You're welcome. I'll see you and Ada in a little while."

The line goes dead before I can reply. Closing my eyes, I hug my phone to my chest. I'm smiling, and I'm sure if anyone were to see me right now, they'd think I just got a call that I won the lottery.

This feels like I've won the lottery, the job lottery.

Unlocking my phone, I pull up Maverick's name. I know he was behind this. He had to be. I hate that he's still giving, and I'm still taking. Maverick Kincaid has once again made a huge impact on my life. I don't know how, but I will repay him. Before I can chicken out, I type out a text and hit send.

> **Me:**   I'm not sure why you were the one to find us that day on the side of the road, but I'm so thankful that it was you. You've done so much for Ada and me, and we're nothing but strangers to you. Thank you for everything, Maverick. I'll never forget your kindness.

Standing, I rush to my room. As quietly as I can, I pick out an outfit and straighten my hair. I add some mascara and call it good. I'm a mom, and I'm struggling every single day. I don't want to hide that from Jordyn. She needs to know who she's hiring. Chances are this is the best I'll be able to do with a one-year-old underfoot, so I might as well be me. I just hope that's enough.

My phone vibrates, the sound blaring in the silent room, and my belly flips at the possibility that it might be Maverick getting back to me. It's completely ridiculous, and I internally scold myself as I rush for the phone that I left on the bed and check my message. I smile when I see his name.

> **Maverick:**   Strangers? Stel, we've shared two meals together. We're friends.

He follows it up with a string of smiley face emojis.

> **Maverick:** And not that I appreciate the thank-you, but you can stop sending them my way. I know you're appreciative.

> **Maverick:** How's Ada? How are you?

His texts come in rapid fire. I'm holding my phone and can't help but compare Maverick to literally every other man in my life, with the exception of my grandpa. He asked not just about me but my daughter. He knows she's an extension of me, and while I'm certain Maverick isn't interested in me, it's hard for me not to crush on him just a little with how he includes my daughter. Oh, and that big ole heart of his that he so freely gives without expectations.

> **Me:** Friends, I think I like the sound of that.

> **Me:** Thank you.

I send a string of face with tongue emojis.

> **Me:** We're both doing well. And I have a job interview today, so you see, this thank-you is for a new, very nice and incredible thing you've done for me.

Instead of texting me back, my phone rings silently. His name flashes on the screen, and I debate not answering, but after everything he's done for me, taking his call is the least I can do. I step out of my room so I won't wake Ada, and I head toward the living room as I hit Accept.

"Hello."

"What job interview?"

"Like you don't know."

"I don't know."

"Your sister-in-law Jordyn called me today, and she's looking for help at her boutique."

"You'd be perfect for that," he says with conviction.

"You didn't know she was going to call me?"

"No. I truly didn't. I was at my parents' place with all my brothers over the weekend, planning our annual camping trip. I mentioned to Ryder that you were looking when he said that Jordyn was doing too much. He's worried about her since she's pregnant."

"That's close enough," I tell him.

He laughs. "Maybe, but I wasn't sure if Ry was going to be able to convince Jordyn she needed help. She's been through a lot, and she wants this boutique to succeed, and she's beyond determined to make that happen."

"She seems really nice. She even said I could bring Ada with me."

"Told you, Stel, we love babies."

"I'm starting to believe you," I reply, and even I can hear the lightness of my tone. It's the Maverick effect. He just has a way of making you feel calm and relaxed and believe that everything will work out.

"So you're going today?" he asks.

"I am. Ada is sleeping. She said to just come over when she wakes up. I feel bad that I have to take her, but my grandma had a doctor's appointment, and Grandpa is at the store."

"It's fine, trust me. Good luck. Not that you'll need it. Jordyn is a sweetheart, and I have a feeling the two of you are going to hit it off."

"Mav—" I start, and he stops me.

"Nope. No more thank-yous, Stel. Let me know how it goes."

"I'm sure everyone in your family will know," I say, only half joking. They seem to be a very tight-knit group. Not that there is anything wrong with that. It's just not what I'm used to. It's a little overwhelming, if I'm being honest.

"Oh, they will, but I want to hear it from you."

"I can do that." That's a simple ask for all that he's done.

"Talk to you soon," he says. "We'll go out for dinner one night this week to celebrate."

I can't hold back the laugh that sputters out. "You're putting the cart before the horse, buddy." I'm shaking my head, even though he can't see me.

"I'm manifesting," he replies with ease. "Besides, I know Jordyn, and I know you. It's a perfect fit."

"Let's not get ahead of ourselves."

"Be thinking about where you girls want to go to celebrate," he says, ignoring me. "I need to get back to work. Kick ass, Stel."

"Be safe." The words are out before I can stop them. I've heard lots of stories about road construction crews and the dangers of the traffic, and even the equipment. I bite down on my cheek. I hope he doesn't read too much into my request, and I hate that I let my cards show. Maverick isn't a stranger. I've known him for a short amount of time, but dare I say that he's my friend?

"Always, Stella." His tone is serious. "I'll see you soon."

I don't allow myself to obsess over every word of our conversation, and how lucky I am that he stopped to help me that day. Someone was watching over us, or maybe it's just the universe's way of telling me it's time that I caught a small break with the shit life has thrown at me lately.

Two hours later, I'm pulling into the lot of Kincaid's boutique. It took me longer than I thought. Ada woke up from her nap with a diaper explosion, screaming. Not that I blame her. If I had shit smeared up my back, I'd be screaming mad too. I had to give her a bath and change the sheets, tossing them all in the washer before we could leave.

The dark sky that's been looming all afternoon opens up and unleashes huge drops of rain before I have a chance to get us both out of the car and into the building. "Really, universe?" I ask. "You couldn't have given me five more minutes?"

I sit here for close to five minutes, and there's not a break in the downpour. "Ada girl, looks like we're going to have to get creative." Pulling the keys from the ignition, I reach for my purse and phone that's sitting in the cupholder, unbuckle my seat belt, and climb into the back seat.

Ada grins when she sees me, kicking her hands and feet. "We've got this, right?" I ask her. She babbles back, and I smile. This little girl is my entire heart. Unzipping the diaper bag, I shove my purse and phone inside and squeeze to get it zipped shut. The diaper bag is one of those backpack types that has a handle on top to carry it, or you can put it on your back. I'm thankful for that part right now. I slip it on my back and then work on getting Ada out of her seat. She's on board for this, laughing and cooing. Hopefully, that good mood remains once we're out in the pelting downpour of rain.

"Good thing Mommy likes to be prepared," I tell my daughter. I have one of those roll up blankets that's waterproof on the bottom, and soft on the top. I keep it in my car for days when we go to the park. It's not an umbrella, but I actually think it might be better. I can hold it over both of us, and it will offer more protection than an umbrella, anyway.

I tap my pocket where my keys are, making sure that I have them. Adjusting the blanket, I prepare to thrust us out into this mess. "All right, let's do this." I keep a tight grip on Ada and push open the door. Rain hits the blanket, and Ada squirms. "Trust me, kid, I know how you feel."

Slamming the car door shut, I take off running toward the front door. Flinging it open, I step inside the boutique. The wind slams the door behind me, causing Ada to cry out.

"Shh, it's okay. It was the wind shutting the door." I pull the soaked blanket off us and hold it out, but I'm not sure what to do with it.

"Goodness. Let me help you." Jordyn comes rushing over and takes the blanket. She shakes it off and tosses it over a set of plastic chairs by the door. "Those are for the husbands." She grins. "Mine likes to go where I go, but he hates shopping. I assumed there might be others, so I made a place for them to sit and wait," she explains. She offers me her hand. "I'm Jordyn. Nice to meet you again. You too, Miss Ada," she says, dropping my hand, taking my daughter's, and wiggling it around, making her laugh and forget about the rain and the loud slam of the door as we walked inside.

"Thank you for letting me bring her. I know that's not ideal for a job interview."

Jordyn waves me off. "No worries. Family has to come first. Besides, you're going to be my first and only employee. We have to stick together." She offers me a kind smile, and I instantly feel more at ease.

"Wait. Going to be your only employee?" I ask.

She grins. "Yep. This is just a formality. I win in so many ways." She holds up her hand to start counting. "One, I get an awesome employee. Two, my husband is happier. Three, I get to work fewer hours and not have all of this pressure on me. You're welcome, by the way. Four, you get a job with an awesome boss and the perks of being able to bring your daughter to work with you. Five, and this is the best one. Maverick will be thrilled. He's probably going to ask for a finder's fee." She cackles as if that's the funniest thing she's ever heard, which makes Ada do the same. "Come here, cutie." She holds her hands out, and Ada leans into her. "Do you mind if I hold her? I guess I should have asked first."

"Not at all." I transfer my daughter into her arms and watch as she talks to her, carrying on a conversation just as I do. I have a very good feeling about Jordyn and this job.

Thank you, Maverick.

"Right, I guess we should talk about the job." She pulls her attention from my daughter to me.

"Want me to take her?" I ask.

"Nah," she says as the door to the boutique opens. We both turn to see a soggy Maverick walking in. "Maverick." I'm not looking at Jordyn, but I don't have to be to hear the grin in her voice.

"Ladies." He shakes out his wet hair and moves toward us. When he reaches Jordyn, he holds his arms out for Ada, and she goes to him willingly. "Hey there, little lady." He blows a loud raspberry on her cheek, making her laugh.

"What are you doing here?" Jordyn asks him.

"Got rained out and was driving by. I knew Stel was going to be here, and that she had to bring my friend here with her. I decided to stop and keep Ada occupied while you two talk shop."

"Maverick." I let his name hang in the air because "thank you" isn't enough. I'll never be able to say what his kindness has meant to me.

"I'll take this." He steps next to me and, with one hand, helps me remove the diaper bag. "We're going to be in the break room." With that, he walks away, my daughter in his arms, loving every second of his attention.

"You didn't know he was coming?" Jordyn asks me.

"No. I texted him to say thank you for the lead on the job. He called me and told me to stop thanking him. He's already done so much for me, and I mentioned that I had to bring her with me. I never dreamed he'd show up."

"Work hard, love harder." Jordyn grins.

"What's that?"

She places her arm around my shoulders. "The Kincaid family motto."

"Oh." I let that sink in. "Makes a lot of sense." I nod.

"Come on. I'll tell you a story." She pulls me to the register and proceeds to tell me her story and everything she and Ryder went through to be together. We go from her story to mine, where I tell her my past as well.

"You're hired," she says once we're both finished expelling our pasts.

"I don't even know what you need me for." I smile.

"Running the register, which, if you were a server, you'll be fine, stocking shelves, assisting customers. All easy stuff."

"I'll take it. I'll be the best only employee you've ever had," I say before we both fall into a fit of giggles.

"Hey, now, Ada and I want in on this party. Can you believe they didn't invite us?" Maverick asks my daughter. She leans her head on his shoulder, and my heart melts.

"Girls only, little brother."

I expect Maverick to get mad at the little brother comment even if it was said with affection, but he just smiles at her and bends to kiss her cheek. Ada takes that as an invitation to switch hands and reaches out for Jordyn.

"I can take her."

"She's perfectly fine."

I stand here and watch as Jordyn and Maverick play peek-a-boo with my little girl, and relief washes over me. I have a job in a town full of amazing people. Something tells me that life is about to change for the better.

Maverick

I'M ANTSY. IT'S SATURDAY AFTERNOON, and later this evening, I'm picking Stella and Ada up and taking them to dinner to celebrate her new job. I knew Jordyn would hire her—not just because Stella's amazing and needed some good tossed her way, but because my entire family is convinced I'm trying to date her.

Do they think I have no game? Come on. If I were really trying to get her to be mine, everyone would know it. That's the Kincaid way, after all. Well, unless you're Brooks and Palmer. And, well, we all know how that turned out. The man has knocked her up twice already.

Anyway, I'm sitting on the couch, staring at the TV, fighting the urge to check the time on my phone when I know damn well that I still have some time to kill before I'm supposed to be there to pick them up.

Merrick keeps watching me with a smirk on his lips. It's the damn twin thing. I'm not checking my phone, so he won't give me shit, but it's as if he can read my mind, anyway. I love being a twin, but this, it's a pain in my ass at the moment.

"What's going on tonight?" he asks.

"I'm going out."

"Want some company?" he offers.

"I'm picking someone up."

"Does that mean I can't come?"

I glance over at him, and he grins. "Just ask me."

"Fine. Where are you taking her?"

"Who?" I'm being difficult, but he is too.

"Stella."

"What makes you think it's Stella?" I haven't told a single soul that I'm picking Stella up and taking her out to celebrate tonight. I've texted her off and on all week, making sure she knows she can't get out of this. That's what good friends do. We show up for each other, and I know that Stella needs someone to show up for her. Ada too.

"Probably because she told Jordyn, who told Ryder, who told me when I stopped by their place to help him move a shelf."

Ah, the joys of having gossipy brothers. "Fine. It's Stella and her daughter. I'm taking them to dinner to celebrate her getting the job with Jordyn. She's new in town. I'm just being a nice guy."

"That's the story you're going with?" he asks, amusement in his tone.

"It's not a story if it's the truth."

"Just admit that you're into her, Mav."

I shrug. "She's nice. She's been through a lot and doesn't have any friends in town."

"So, you pay for all your friends' cars to be fixed, find them jobs, and then take them out to dinner to celebrate."

"Apparently," I grumble. I know how it looks, but damnit, he's my brother. My twin, the other half of me. Why can't he see I'm just being a good person?

He nods, tapping his index finger against his chin. "I admit it's a nice touch. Reel her in, get her hooked, then really put it on her."

"Put what on her?" I'm pretty sure he's sober right now. I look around to see if I can see evidence of a beer or maybe a shot sitting around.

"The Kincaid charm. I understand she's skittish, being a single mom and all that. You have to be cautious. Good plan to include baby Ada."

"I'm including her because we're friends, and I know she doesn't have a lot of options for childcare at the moment."

"Oh, you know if you wanted her all to yourself, Mom and Dad would watch her. Hell, you could ask any of us, and we'd say yes. Granted, Stella might not be okay with me since I'm a single guy and all that, but the others have wives, and I'm sure she'd be fine with it." He's nodding as he talks as if he needs to convince himself what he's saying is true.

It's all bullshit.

Well, not really. He's right that my parents would gladly watch Ada for an evening, and he's not wrong about my brothers and their wives either. I also know that Merrick would keep her, but he's also not wrong about the single guy thing. At least not until she knows us all better.

I make a mental note to include her in more of our events. I'm sure Jordyn is all over that too. We'll have her used to our clan in no time.

"See." Merrick points at me. "That face tells me you agree with me."

"You're losing it, man." I laugh.

His laughter mingles with my own. "Seriously, bro, if you're into her, let her know."

"I'm just helping her out and taking her for dinner to celebrate her new job. That's it."

"I'm going to be the best man, right?" he asks. "I mean, we're twins."

"Am I going to be your best man?" I ask him. I don't know why I'm even entertaining this conversation. Curiosity, I guess.

"Yeah, I mean, unless you pick one of the others. Then hell no." His grin tells me he's kidding.

"Fine. You can be my best man. When I find the woman I'm going to marry." She's out there. It took some of my brothers years to find their special someone. I'm certain mine will come along eventually, and when she does, yeah, my twin will be my best man.

"Stubborn. You know how this works, Maverick. You've seen it seven times now."

"Friends. Repeat after me. We. Are. Just. Friends."

"For now." He stands and stretches his arms over his head. "I'm headed over to Brooks's place. He's off this weekend, but Palmer is shooting an engagement this evening. I told him I'd come over and help him with the kids. I'd ask you to come, but I know you've got plans with your girls."

"Yeah. No. I mean, yes, I have plans with Stella and Ada. They're not my girls."

"Have fun!" he calls over his shoulder as he makes his way down the hall to his room.

I still have a while before the agreed-upon time that I could pick Stella and Ada up from her grandparents' place. I've thought about calling several times to see if she wanted to move up the time, but I assume when she gave me a time, it was to work around Ada's nap schedule. At least, that's my assumption. I know she didn't have to work today at the boutique. Maybe she was helping out at the hardware store with her grandparents. Regardless, I have three hours, and I can't sit here for a second longer.

Grabbing my phone and keys, I head out to my truck. I'm driving through town when I realize that I forgot a blanket. I plan on taking them to Sunflower Park. The food trucks are going to be there all weekend, and she mentioned she'd like to take Ada there.

Knowing I have lots of time, I head to Harris. It doesn't matter that I'll be driving the twenty minutes back to Willow River, and then another twenty back to Harris. I have three hours to kill and sitting at home is just making me stir-crazy. So, I crank up the radio and get lost in the music as I head toward the Walmart in Harris to buy a blanket.

By the time I pull into the parking lot, my nerves are less frayed, and I'm smiling freely. It's nice not to have to worry about my brother seeing more in my mood than what's truly there. It's a nice summer day. The sun is shining, and there were good tunes on the radio all the way here. That's definitely worth a smile.

There's a cart out in the middle of the parking lot, which makes me roll my eyes. Five more feet and the asshole could have pushed it into the cart corral. Instead, they leave it out in the middle of a parking spot. Not only is it lazy, but that's an open invitation for a door ding. All it takes is a little wind, and the cart could go crashing into someone's car. I'd be pissed if it were my truck.

Inside, I head to the home goods section. I push the cart up and down the aisles, looking for a blanket. I finally find a black and gray quilt. Not very girly, but then again, what am I going to do with a girly blanket? I toss the quilt inside and move to the end of the aisle. I turn left, and on an end cap, there are bubbles.

I wonder if Ada likes bubbles? Who am I kidding? She's a kid; of course she likes bubbles. I grab a green bottle and toss it into the cart. Turning down the aisle, I see all the toys. She's just turned one, so half of these things are a choking hazard for her. Until I reach the end of the aisle and find rubber alphabet blocks, that's something she would play with or chew on while we eat. I toss that into the cart too.

I need some bottled water for work next week, so I might as well get it while I'm here. I head to the other side of the store and stop in the middle. There's a sign for a digital camera on clearance. I take a quick picture and text Palmer and Scarlett.

> **Me:** Is this a good camera?
>
> **Palmer:** It's 20 MP, so yeah, that's a good one.
>
> **Scarlett:** Are you planning on coming to work with us at Captured Moments?
>
> **Me:** I'm at Walmart, and it's on sale.
>
> **Palmer:** And you're in the market for a camera?
>
> **Me:** Yep.
>
> **Me:** What else do I need for this thing?
>
> **Palmer:** A memory card. How many pictures do you plan on taking?
>
> **Me:** Just a few here and there.

Scarlett:	32GB memory card will get you around 1100 images for reference.
Me:	You two are the best sisters ever!
Palmer:	There's more to this story. What do you think, Scar?
Scarlett:	Definitely.
Me:	Can't a guy want to take some pictures?
Palmer:	What's wrong with your phone?
Me:	Nothing, I just wanted something different, and it's on sale.
Palmer:	Sure thing, Mav.
Scarlett:	Tell Stella and baby Ada we said hello.
Palmer:	Let me know when I can add her to the family chat.

Shit. Nosy, gossipy brothers and sisters.

I don't reply. That's not a conversation I want to get into with them. Besides, I bet my savings that they're already texting my other sisters-in-law and talking about me. They have a group text. My brothers and I have the same, and then we have a family one with all of us, minus our parents. There are times when we make a special chat to include Mom and Dad, but for the most part, we keep them out of it so we don't have to worry about cleaning up our mouths for Mom.

Shoving my phone into my pocket, I wave over the clerk and purchase the camera. He upsells me a memory card and a case. Fine, whatever. It's under two hundred bucks for all of it. It will be worth it to see the smile on Stella's face when we get to take some pictures of Ada in the sunflower field.

Camera purchased and the receipt stapled to the bag, I move on to finish my shopping. That is until I pass the baby section. I glance over. One quick glance has me stopping in my tracks. It's a little sundress with a hat that has sunflowers all over them. She has to have that, right? I mean, this is a Sunflower Park photoshoot, after all.

The only problem is that I have no idea what size clothes she wears. I could text my sisters-in-law, they could probably guess, or even my mom, but I've tossed enough fuel at those flames for one day. Instead, I grab my phone and call Stella.

"Hello?"

"Quick question."

"Okay?"

"What size clothes is Ada wearing?"

"What?" she asks. I can hear not only humor but confusion in her tone.

"What size is she? 2T? Wait, no twelve months. She's one, so twelve months, right?" I grab the twelve months and hold it up.

"She's in eighteen months."

"Oh, okay. So, it's not just by age, then?"

"No, not always. Maverick, what are you doing?" she asks.

"Nothing. I'm at Walmart."

"And you needed to know what size clothing my daughter wears?"

"Yes. It's a surprise. You'll see later."

"Should I be worried?" she asks, chuckling softly.

"Nah, it's a good surprise."

"I guess we'll see."

"I'm still picking you ladies up at six, right?"

"Yes. If you still insist that we need to go out to celebrate."

"I insist." I look at the items in my cart and grin. "I'll be there at six, maybe a little before."

"That's fine. She'll be up from her nap, and we'll be ready to go."

"Great. See you soon, Stel." Hitting End, I slide the phone into my pocket and toss the outfit into my cart. Pushing on down the aisles, I grab a case of water and a couple of bags of Cool Ranch Doritos. Merrick and I both love them.

By the time I check out, I still have plenty of time. I head home, unload the few groceries that I tossed in my cart, and unbox the camera. I plug it in to charge. Thankfully, the battery is showing it's 75% charged already. The house is quiet, and I'm thankful Merrick is gone. Without a doubt, he'd be giving me shit over this purchase. Not that he's not going to, anyway. I'm actually shocked word has not made it back to my brothers yet. I guess it's still early. I'm certain by the time I go to bed tonight, they'll have the intel.

An hour later, I packed up my new camera and headed to pick up the girls. When I knock on the door, I step back, not expecting George to answer. I mean, I know this is his house and that Stella is his granddaughter, but I'm still surprised.

"Good to see you, Maverick. Come on in."

"You too, George." I step inside and close the door behind me.

"So, you're taking my girls out tonight?" he asks, smiling.

"Yeah. I thought Stella needed to celebrate her new job at the boutique."

Before he can grill me, Stella walks into the room. "Hey." She smiles, and so does Ada as she lifts her arm and waves. She coos and babbles like she always does when she sees me.

"Ada girl, you know I need snuggles." I walk to where they stand just a few steps away and take Ada from her, rubbing my stubble against her cheek and making her giggle. "You ready?" I ask Stella.

"Yes." She picks up the diaper bag and tosses it over her shoulder.

"I won't have them out late," I tell George.

"You kids have fun." He leans over and kisses Ada's cheek, but she shies away and buries her face in my neck. "I see how it is." George laughs before turning to Stella. "Don't leave an old man hanging, Stella."

"Never, Gramps." She smiles and places a kiss on his cheek. "You and Grams have fun at bingo."

"You know your grams, that's her thing. I just tag along because it makes her happy." He smiles widely.

"Let's get moving." I bounce Ada on my hip. Her laughter fills the room, and it's infectious. What is it about baby giggles?

Once we're on the road, Stella glances over at me. "Where are we going?"

"Well, I thought we would have a picnic of sorts."

"A picnic? You packed us a picnic?" she asks. There's a little awe and surprise in her question, and I wish I would have packed us a damn picnic.

"Not exactly. We're going to a park where there are a ton of food trucks, like fifteen or so. They have anything and everything you could want. I thought we could eat and let Ada play on a blanket."

"That's... very sweet of you, Maverick. You're always thinking about and including her. I appreciate that. I appreciate you. You've made this transition to Willow River so much easier for us, and financially, between my car and the job, you've been our guardian angel."

"I'm no angel; just ask my momma." I laugh. "I'm happy to help out. It's nothing, really. Besides, we both have to eat, and we should do it together to celebrate your new job. How's that going, by the way?"

"Great. Jordyn is so nice, and it's all fairly easy. I've been helping her set up a new display this week."

"That's great. I'm glad it's working out."

"For the first time in a very long time, I feel like things might be looking up for us." I see her out of the corner of my eye and look into the back seat at her daughter. "We have you to thank for that. The day we met you, good things started to happen."

"It was just your time," I tell her.

"You have your theory, and I have mine."

"Fair enough." I pull into the park, and she gasps.

"Sunflower Park? This is where we're going?"

"It is. Is that okay?" From her initial reaction, I'm certain it is, but I could be wrong.

"Yes. Maverick." I can hear the emotion in her voice. "You knew I wanted to bring her here."

"I did, but the food trucks are here tonight too." I nod out the window. "It's like being at the fair, only on a smaller scale. Who doesn't love fair food?"

"Thank you, Maverick." She unfastens her seat belt and leans over to place a kiss on my cheek.

Something happens at that moment. My chest tightens, and I lift my hand to rub it. It's a sensation I've never felt before. "I hope you're hungry."

"Yeah," she agrees.

"I'll grab Ada. Do you want to sit in the back of my truck or find a tree to sit under? I assume a picnic table would be annoying for her being confined." The sun will be setting soon, but for the moment, it's still high in the sky, so that shade will be nice.

"Yeah, I should have brought a blanket."

"I have one. The tree?"

"Yes, the shade is perfect."

"I'll get Ada and the blanket. I have a Walmart bag on the back floorboard. Can you grab that too?"

"I can get her."

"Baby hog," I tease. "Don't deny me snuggles. I get that enough from my family."

"Fine." She rolls her eyes, but she's smiling.

I like her smile.

Chapter 8

Stella

I TAG ALONG BEHIND MAVERICK as he moves through the park. He stops at an enormous tree and drops the quilt that's still in its packaging.

He bought it for today.

I don't know what to do with that information. There are so many layers to this man; I've barely scratched the surface.

"Let me." I place the diaper bag and the Walmart bag on the ground and spread the blanket out on the ground beneath the shade of the tree. "Are you sure you want to use this? It's nice."

He shrugs. "This is what I bought it for. We need some cushion." He smiles down at my daughter, who has her head on his shoulder. "Right, Ada girl?"

At the sound of her name, she lifts her head and places her hands on his cheeks. Maverick smiles at her, and it does something to me. I have to turn away before I ask him to do inappropriate things to me. That's not what this is between us. Besides, even if it was, I have Ada to think about.

When I look away, my eyes scan the area, and I can see that it's not only my attention that he's snagged. There is a group of girls around my age sitting at a picnic table, and they're watching him and smiling. I want to scream for them to look away, but that's ridiculous. Maverick isn't mine. He isn't anyone's, so they can look all they want.

One of them sees me watching them, and with hushed whispers, they all look away. I refuse to think about why that's so satisfying. For all they know, Ada is his, and so am I. They should be ashamed of themselves.

Maverick sits down on the blanket with Ada in his lap. "Guess what I bought?" he asks my daughter. It's as if I'm not even standing here.

I grab the two bags and take a seat next to them. I hold my hands out for Ada, but she shakes her head and clings to Maverick, making him laugh.

"You're good for my ego, kiddo. Can you talk to my nieces and nephews and let them know I'm your favorite?" he teases, tickling her belly. She rewards him with her giggle. "Okay, let me show you what I got." He stretches out his long legs and places Ada on the blanket between them. "Do you like bubbles?" he asks her. He reaches into the bag and pulls out a green bottle of bubbles.

All I can do is sit back and watch this man as he smiles and blows bubbles for my daughter. Discreetly, I pinch the back of my leg to make sure that I'm awake and that all of this isn't a dream. If it is, I hope to never wake up.

"Look, Ada, bubbles." I hold my hand out to catch one. She mimics me and my heart swells for the love I have for this tiny human. No one prepares you for the love you feel for your child.

I don't know how my parents could be so callous writing me off. I'll never do that to Ada. She'll always have an advocate in me, and a home with me. No matter what.

"Mom, Mom," Ada coos as she reaches for the bubbles.

"That was sweet of you, Maverick. Thank you."

He nods. "Look in the bag." He keeps blowing bubbles while Ada claps and tries to catch them. She's crawling all over him, but somehow, he manages to move the bottle out of her reach, hold her steady, and blow bubbles.

"What is this?" I ask, pulling an outfit out of the bag.

"Okay, so hear me out." He glances up at me and smiles before giving his attention back to Ada. "I was shopping. We needed a blanket, and then I walked past that." He nods toward the outfit I'm holding. "You mentioned getting pictures of her here, and what are Sunflower Park pictures without a sunflower outfit? And it has a hat!" he says, with more excitement than a single man should have for someone else's baby that's absolutely no relation to him.

"That was very sweet of you."

He shrugs. "The hat sold me," he confesses. "My sisters-in-law are always making sure the kids' outfits coordinate and fit the theme of that day or event, so I figured you'd want the same."

"How are you still single?" I blurt.

This causes him to laugh. And of course, my daughter has hero worship, and she does the same bouncing on her legs, while Maverick holds her steady with one arm. "I'll find her one day," he tells me.

"Her?" I'm opening a can of worms here. I know him well enough to know the next words out of his mouth are going to have me melting into a puddle on this blanket, but I asked the question anyway.

"The love of my life. The one who constantly makes me smile. The woman who can put up with my silly crazy. My future wife."

And there it is.

A warmth washes over me at his words. I smile at my little girl, who's infatuated, and if I'm being honest, I have a nice little crush on the man as well. How could I not? I make a silent promise at this moment to my little girl that I'll never settle for less than a man who loves like Maverick Kincaid. We're recipients of his kind heart; I can't imagine how life would be being wrapped in his love.

Talk about swooning.

I clear my throat. "Thank you."

"Oh, keep looking." He nods toward the bag. Doing as he asks, I pull out a small black case. "Camera." He winks.

"You even brought your camera?"

He shrugs. "Yeah, I mean, I know cell phones are great these days, but I thought we could use it too."

"Ada, Maverick is spoiling us." Emotion wells in the back of my throat. I have to get myself together. The last thing I need to do is fall for this man. I know without a doubt if I were to let that happen, my heart would be shattered when he finds the woman he just described. More so than when Ada's dad walked away.

"So, what first, Mommy? Are we doing a photo shoot or eating?"

"How long are the food trucks here?"

"For a few more hours. We have time. You tell me what works."

"How about we do pictures first? She's happy right now, so let's try to capitalize on that."

"On it." He hands me the wand for the bubbles and then the container, and I close it up. "Here you go, little lady." He hands Ada over to me and takes the outfit. "I didn't have time to wash it. Is that bad?"

"No, Maverick, it's fine. It was very thoughtful of you. Thank you."

"Stop thanking me, woman." He playfully growls. His smile tells me he's not really upset with me. He quickly tears off all the tags before handing me the outfit. Ada is compliant and doesn't protest when I change her outfit.

"All set?" he asks.

"We're ready."

He stands, grabbing the camera. "Our stuff should be fine here, but just in case, hand me the diaper bag. Everything else can be replaced."

I nod, handing him the diaper bag.

"The baby, too, so you can get up." He reaches for Ada, and once she's in his arms, he tosses her in the air, catching her.

My heart leaps in my throat, and it's on the tip of my tongue to tell him to be careful, but with the gleeful giggle my daughter belts out and the laugh of Maverick's that follows, I don't have it in me. I know he'd never hurt her.

Maverick leads the way to the sunflower field. "They have different spots with benches and stuff all through the field for photo ops," he explains as he steps onto the trail.

"Really?"

"Yep."

"That's good. I was thinking we were just going to have to set her down on the ground and ruin her pretty new outfit."

"Nah, but she can get it dirty. You gotta do what you gotta do to get the shot, right?" He chuckles, bouncing Ada in his arms. "How about we start here?" He stops next to the first photo op we reach.

I smile because it's perfect. It's an old wooden barrel surrounded by sunflowers that we can place her in.

"We're going to have to be quick," I tell him.

"On it. Do you want to run the camera, or do you want me to?"

"I don't know how to work it," I confess.

"That makes two of us," he replies.

"You don't know how to work your own camera?" I ask him.

"Nope. I just bought it today. It was on sale."

"Wait. You bought this today?" I knew it sounded like that earlier, but I thought that I was hearing things. Now that it's confirmed, I don't know what to think or what to say for that matter.

"Yeah, I was shopping, and it was on clearance."

"Do you need a camera?"

"We needed one for this." He waves the hand that's not holding my daughter toward the sunflower field.

"Maverick!"

His head falls back in laughter, which my daughter imitates. "Hush. Can you figure it out, or do I need to call for help?"

I pull the camera out of the case and turn it on. It says *point and shoot*, and I place it on the automatic setting. "I can do it."

"You sure? I have two photographers in the family."

"I'm sure."

"Perfect. Okay. Get where you need to be, and I'll put her in the barrel. You're about to play dress up," he tells Ada. "It's going to be so much fun. Mommy is going to take lots of pictures to show you when you're older. When you're thirty and start to date, or maybe forty, she can show your boyfriend." A frown mars his face as if he hates the idea of her dating.

That feeling is back. The melting sensation that reaches my entire body, even between my thighs. It only happens with him.

Shaking out of my thoughts, I aim the camera and take a few test shots. "Ready."

"All right, Miss Thang, let's do this." He places Ada in the barrel and her bottom lip puckers. She reaches for him. I open my mouth to tell him to switch places with me but stop when he drops to his knees and makes a silly face at her. He moves his head around, and Ada grins. He looks back at me and moves a little to the left so that she's looking at me. He stands, and her eyes follow. "On three, Stel, you ready? I'm going to jump out of the way."

"I'm ready."

"One. Two. Three." He falls to the ground, and Ada laughs. I catch her at the perfect time when her eyes are bright, and she's still looking in my direction.

"How is it?" Maverick asks.

"Good. So good." I can't stop smiling. It's better than I could have hoped.

"How about another?" He stands back up and dances around. Ada's eyes follow. She reaches out to him, her little arms in the air, and the smile on her face could light up the night sky.

"On three, Mommy," he says again. "One. Two. Three."

This time, he jumps in the air, and she follows the movement. I'm able to take a few shots. When I pull the camera away to look at them, tears well in my eyes. In one pose, her head is tilted back. The setting sun is in the background, along with the sunflowers, and she's smiling up at the cloudless sky.

It's the perfect picture.

"Maverick." I smile. "These are so great."

"I can't wait to see them." He scoops Ada up into his arms and starts walking. "On to the next stop."

I rush to catch up with them. "Want me to take her?" I offer. I don't know why, but I always feel guilty when someone else helps out with her. I guess because I'm used to doing it all on my own, and she's my daughter.

"Nah, we're good."

We walk a few more feet and come to a bench with a pot of fake sunflowers.

"Wow, they've really thought of everything, huh?" I ask.

"They have. Okay. How about we set her on the bench, and I hide behind it, holding onto her so she doesn't fall? Just try not to get me in the picture."

"Sure, I can try." I laugh. "You know I'm not a professional, right?"

"You've got this. Right, Ada? Mommy's got this in the bag." He places her on the bench and steps behind her. She tries to stand, and I can see how this is going to be an issue. Maverick must, as well. His head pops over the back of the bench, and she bounces and laughs.

I snap the shot.

"Call out for her. When she looks away, I'll duck," Maverick suggests.

"We can try. She's pretty fond of you," I tell him. "Ada. Look at Mommy. Adddaaa," I sing her name. Just as Maverick had suggested, she glances over her shoulder at me. He falls to the ground, and I catch my girl smiling, staring at me over her shoulder.

It's gold.

Maverick lifts her into the air, holding her over his head. They're both smiling, and again, I snap the shot.

"Time to switch it up." Maverick hands Ada off to me and takes the camera. "You ladies, take a seat on the bench."

"No, we don't have to."

"Yes, we do." He nods, and I know I'm not getting out of this. I take a seat on the bench and hold Ada. He makes faces, and her arms go up for him, and he snaps a few pictures.

"Now, a selfie." He moves to sit next to me, sliding in close. One arm goes around my shoulders, while the other flips the camera around, and he snaps a few pictures. When he looks at the screen, he nods. "Not bad, considering I couldn't see where I was aiming."

Ada fusses, so I stand with her. "I think she's had enough. She lasted longer than I thought she would."

"Because she's a natural, right, Ada?" She reaches for him, and he takes her without delay. "You hungry?" he asks her.

"She's probably getting there."

"What about you? Hungry?" he asks me.

"Yeah, I could eat."

"Come on, then." He starts walking back to our spot under the tree. "Okay, this is what we'll do. You can see most of the trucks from here. Tell me what you want, and I'll make a few trips to get what we need. I'm thinking fries for short fry here." He taps Ada on the nose.

"Oh, I can get ours."

"Stella." His tone is full of warning. "Since when do you pay for your own celebration dinner?"

"Since you bought my daughter a dress, and you bought a camera, and bubbles, and a blanket. Since you do so much for us."

"Nah, still not happening." He hands Ada over. "Tell me what you want, or I'll get one of everything."

I know he's not joking. "I can split some fries with Ada."

"And?"

"Maybe a pulled pork sandwich."

"Got it and to drink?"

"Lemonade or sweet tea."

"Got it. We'll start with that and go back for seconds and dessert."

I don't bother to tell him that's too much. I know I'd just be wasting my breath. Instead, I sit on the blanket and pull a sippy cup of milk out of the small cooler bag I filled with ice packs before we left. Ada takes it and drinks greedily.

"He's one of the good ones. When you get older and you're ready to settle down, I hope you find a man like Maverick to spend your life with."

She drinks, staring up at me. She does not understand what I'm saying, but that's okay. One day, she will. One day, I'll be able to tell her about this amazing man who came into our lives when we were down on our luck. I'll be able to tell her all the wonderful things he did out of the kindness of his heart. I'll be able to show her the pictures from today and tell her the story.

Maybe, if we're lucky, I'll find us a Maverick of our own before that day gets here.

"Here's the first round." He places two sandwiches and a massive bucket of fries on the blanket. "I thought we could let her get started. One of those is yours. I'm going to go grab our drinks." He walks off, and Ada sits up, reaching for a fry.

Ten minutes later, Maverick is back with two lemonades and cheese sticks. "We can split these too." He settles himself on the blanket. He spreads out his legs, locking in an area for Ada to crawl between us.

"Thank you for this."

"Congratulations on the new job."

"Thank you. It feels good to be employed and not in a job that was created for me by my grandparents."

We grow quiet as we eat our food. Ada feeds us each a french fry as she crawls back and forth between us, staying within the barrier that Maverick has made for her with his legs.

"She almost took a step last night. Grandma was sitting in the chair holding her hands and I was on the floor. She stood there for a few seconds after Grandma let go. She lifted her foot, but she started to fall, so Grandma caught her."

"Caden, Brynlee, and Beckham are her age, and they are doing the same. It won't be long."

"How many nieces and nephews do you have?"

"Let's see. I'll start with the oldest brother and move on to the youngest. Orrin has one—Orion is two. Declan has two. Blakely, who just turned eight, and Beckham, who's one. Then we have Brooks. He has Remi, who is two, and Leo, who is just a few months old. Rushton has Caden, who is one as well. Jordyn and Alyssa are both expecting. Then we have my cousin, Ramsey. Her little girl, Brynlee, is also one."

"So many. I don't know that I'll ever remember all the names."

"Nah, we're easy to remember. You'll get the hang of it. Especially working with Jordyn. You'll have the family tree memorized in no time."

"Maybe." We finish eating, talking about anything and everything. I tell him more about Ada's dad, and he tells me stories of him and his brothers. It's the best night I've had in longer than I can remember.

When he pulls back into the driveway a couple of hours later, I tell him so. "This night has been wonderful, Maverick. Thank you for dinner, the outfit, the photos, and the company." I can feel my face flush. I'm glad the car is dark.

"It was my pleasure. I'll grab Ada."

"I can get her."

"I know you can, but you can also let me help."

I don't argue. Instead, I pick up the diaper bag and rush to open the door for him.

"Where do you want her?"

"Just in the Pack 'N Play. I need to change her and put her jammies on her."

"I hope her sleep schedule isn't thrown off too much."

"It was worth it." The admission comes freely, and I find I don't want to take it back. It was worth it. I wish I could have a thousand, no, a million more nights just like this one. I know he has to go. This wasn't a date, and we're in my grandparents' house, but I almost ask him to stay anyway.

"I'll see you girls soon." He leans in and kisses my cheek, and then he's gone.

The house is quiet, so I assume my grandparents are already in bed. I'm thankful for the chance to soundlessly get Ada ready for bed and get lost in my thoughts.

Thoughts of Maverick.

Chapter 9

Maverick

TODAY WAS LONG AND HOT, but it's over and is finally the weekend. We worked twelve-hour days all week to be able to take the weekend off. I'm sitting in my truck with the air conditioning on full blast when my phone rings. I hit the button on the dash to answer. "Yo," I greet Ryder.

"What's going on?"

"Just getting off work."

"Yeah? Can I ask a big favor?"

"Sure. What's up?"

"I'm at the boutique, and Jordyn needs some shelving moved around the stockroom."

"I take it I'm your last resort?" I laugh. My brothers know I work long, crazy hours in the summer, so that's usually the case.

"No, actually, you were my first choice."

"Aw, you love me."

"I thought I might need a bargaining chip because you're probably drained after working in this heat all week."

"Nah, you know I don't mind helping out." I pause. "But out of curiosity, what's your bargaining chip?" It's probably dinner. My stomach grumbles just at the mere thought of food.

"Stella."

I sit up straighter in my seat. "What about Stella?"

"She's here. Helping Jordyn after hours."

"Got it." I pull my seat belt on and back out of the parking spot.

"Drive safe, little brother." He's laughing as he ends the call.

I don't even have it in me to be pissed off about it. It's been two weeks since I took Stella out for her celebration dinner. We've texted a few times, but I haven't seen her since that night.

Twenty minutes later, I'm pulling up outside the boutique. I grab my phone and keys and make my way to the door. It's locked, so I have to knock. Jordyn comes rushing over and smiles at me in greeting.

"Hey, Mav. Thanks for coming. My husband won't let us help." She rolls her big brown eyes.

"You know I don't mind." She leans in for a hug, but I hold my hands up to stop her. "I'm a mess from working, J. I probably smell like ass," I joke.

"I'll take my chances." My sister-in-law wraps her arms around me in a brief hug. She steps back and smiles up at me. "Ry's in the back." She starts walking, and I follow her. My eyes scan the room, looking for Stella. I assume she's in the stockroom with Ryder.

Sure enough, as we get closer, I hear the laughter of a baby, and I quicken my step. Stepping into the room, I see Stella holding Ada, and Ryder playing peek-a-boo with her. "Ada girl," I say, and she turns toward my voice. When she sees me, she grins and reaches her arms out.

I walk to them and take her into my arms. "I'm dirty," I tell her.

"It's fine," Stella tells me. "When we get home, she'll be in dire need of a bath. She looks like she's been rolling around with pigs. She's had a long, tiring day." A soft smile graces her lips as she watches her daughter in my arms.

"You got to come to work with Mommy, huh?" I ask Ada. She places her hands on my cheeks and grins. On instinct, I kiss her nose, making her giggle.

"Yeah, my grandparents are out of town until Sunday. They're going with some friends to a winery and Airbnb."

"That's great that they do that," Jordyn speaks up.

"Are you on call for the hardware store?" Ryder asks her.

"No. They have a great team. I guess if something comes up, I'll handle it, but Gramps didn't seem concerned."

"Yeah, they take these trips a few times a year, right?" I ask. "I've heard George talking about them a time or two when I've been in the store."

"They do," Stella confirms.

"Have you been helping Ryder today, Ada?" I ask her.

Her reply is to lay her head on my shoulder and snuggle close. I rub her back gently.

"Aw." Jordyn sighs.

"She's ready for a nap, but there's been too much excitement," Stella tells me.

"She likes you." Jordyn smiles at me.

"Of course she does. We're best buds, right, Ada?" I hold her a few more minutes before handing her back to her momma. She cries and reaches for me.

"I'm so sorry. She's exhausted."

"Hey, hey." I pull her back into my arms and rub her back. She rests her head on my shoulder and whimpers.

"Mav, why don't you try to get her down for a nap? The Pack 'N Play is up in my office," Jordyn tells me.

I look over at Stella. "You good with that?"

Stella bites down on her bottom lip and nods. Her face is sad. I don't like her face to be sad. I step closer and wrap an arm around her shoulders. I have both of them in my arms, and when she smiles up at me, I know I did the right thing. "I don't mind putting her down."

"I'm sorry. She's never done this."

"It's okay to let others help you, Stel." I look down, and Ada's eyes are already closed. "I'll walk her around for a few minutes. She's already out."

"Okay." She steps out of my hold, and I nod to Ryder. "Give me a few to get her down."

"No worries. We'll head back to the office so it's quiet." He laces his fingers with his wife's and leads her out of the room.

"You keep saving us," Stella says so softly I almost don't hear her.

"She's just tired, and I've got strong shoulders." I wink at her.

"Must be the arm porn," she mutters.

I bite down on my cheek to keep from smiling.

It's a good thing my niece Blakely isn't here. I'm sure they'd have a full-on conversation about said arm porn. I stroll around the boutique, gently rubbing Ada's back. Her breathing is deep and even, but I give it a few more minutes before I try to put her down. Uncle Maverick has been burned by thinking my nieces and nephews were sound asleep, only to find out their little eyes pop wide open when I lay them down. I've learned a thing or two over the years.

After I'm pretty certain she's sound asleep, I walk back to the counter where Stella is folding scarves. I feel her eyes on me the entire time. She's a momma bear, and that's such an endearing trait.

"I think she's ready," I whisper.

"Okay." She drops the scarf she was folding and leads the way to Jordyn's office, where she nods toward the Pack 'N Play. Gently, I lean over and lay Ada down. She stretches but stays asleep.

"Jordyn has a baby monitor," I whisper. Turning toward the bookshelf, I grab it, turn it on, and then take the receiver and nod toward the door. "We're all set up to babysit," I explain. "You never know when someone is going to need help, so we like to be prepared. Especially at the rate my brothers and their wives are popping out babies." I smirk, and she smiles.

With the baby monitor in one hand and the other pressed lightly against the small of her back, we walk the short distance down the hall to the stockroom.

"All right, what do we need?" I ask my brother and his wife.

"Baby?" Ryder addresses Jordyn.

"I want to move that row of shelves over here against the other two. Make this one long wall of shelving. That leaves the other shorter wall for the table to open and unpack boxes. Then I'll order more shelves and make another row to give us more storage space."

"On it." Ryder kisses her cheek, and he and I get to work, bringing her vision to life by moving the shelving where she instructed.

It doesn't take us long to get everything where she wants it. "What else you got for us, J?" I ask her.

"That's it. I wasn't very prepared, or I would have had the other shelves here to put together."

I nod. "Ryder, let me know when you're ready to start assembling."

"Definitely. I'll call in the cavalry, and we'll have them put together in no time."

"I'm going to order dinner," Jordyn says. "Is everyone okay with Mexican?"

"Yeah, but they take forever to deliver on Friday nights. I'll go pick it up. Just call it in."

"I should get home," Stella speaks up.

"Nope. You're letting me feed you for all of your help today. It was your day off."

"I wasn't much help with Ada being here."

"You were a tremendous help. Besides, you still haven't given me an answer about tomorrow."

"I did." Stella sighs. "I told you that I can't go. My grandparents are out of town, and I don't have anyone to watch Ada."

"What's going on tomorrow night?" I ask, inserting myself into the conversation.

"Girls' night. We're all going to the Willow Tavern, and I've been trying to convince Stella to go with us."

"You should go," I tell Stella, leaning my shoulder into hers.

"No sitter." She shrugs.

"I'll watch her."

"What?" She whips her head around to look at me.

"Ada loves me. I can watch her."

"That's—no. I can't ask you to do that."

"I thought I just heard him volunteer." Jordyn grins.

"I'll even go over to his place to help," Ryder offers. "We've watched our nieces and nephews lots of times. Besides"—he slides his hand over Jordyn's still flat belly—"I need all the practice I can get."

"I don't need the help, but if it makes you feel better, sure." I shrug. "Ryder can help me."

"Maverick," she sighs my name.

"Stel...." I drag out the word with a smile. "Go have a good time. You deserve it. You know Ada loves me, and she'll be fine. You can call and check on her whenever you want, however many times you want."

She opens her mouth to, I'm sure, turn down my offer, but Ryder speaking up stops her. "I promise you that your baby girl will be in good hands," he assures her. "I can't imagine how hard it is raising her on your own. Declan was a single dad to Blakely before Kennedy came along. He had eight brothers, our cousin Ramsey, and our parents to rally around him. You can't do it all, Stella. You know, they say it takes a village." He smiles kindly, and I turn to her.

I watch her closely, and I can see the minute she gives in. Her shoulders fall as if she has no more fight in her.

"Okay," she agrees.

"Yes!" Jordyn whisper-shouts. "I'm so excited. Now, what does everyone want to eat?"

Stella reluctantly gives Jordyn her order, and they say ten minutes.

"I'll be back. Do we need anything else?" I ask them.

"No. I have drinks in the break room."

"Got it. I'll be back."

I rush out to my truck and head across town to the Mexican restaurant. The food is ready as soon as I get there, and as I'm climbing into my truck, I see the diner across the street. Changing course, I cross the street with our bag of Mexican food in hand and walk up to the counter. I order Ada some mashed potatoes and gravy. I'm not sure she eats Mexican, but I know she loves her mashed potatoes.

"Can I have a large glass of milk as well?" I ask. I'm sure Stella has that covered, but maybe she's stayed longer than she intended. If she's got milk, she can just put it in the fridge and take it home with her for later.

Bags in hand, I step up to the door of the boutique, and Ryder is there, pushing it open for me. "Damn, that smells good." He pulls the door shut and makes sure it's locked back up since it's after hours.

"Right? My stomach has been growling since I stepped into the restaurant to pick it up."

He leads the way back to the break room, and I place the bags and the cup on the small table.

"That's a Dorothy's cup." Jordyn points at it. "Don't tell me you stopped to get one of her sweet teas and didn't bring one for the rest of us."

"No, and even if I did, you said you didn't need anything else."

"But I didn't know sweet tea from Dorothy's Diner was on the table," she says with a pout.

"It's a Dorothy's cup, but it's not sweet tea. I got Ada some mashed potatoes. I wasn't sure about her eating our Mexican, and I grabbed a glass of milk in case she was almost out. I know you all have been at it all day." A choking sound has me turning to look at Stella. She has her hand over her mouth, and her eyes are wet with emotion.

"Maverick Kincaid? How are you real?" she murmurs.

Jordyn moves to stand beside her, placing her arm around her shoulders. "It's not just him. They're all like that. Raymond and Carol raised nine amazing men."

"It wasn't a big deal," I tell them. I feel as though I've been saying that a lot lately. Having to defend my actions. It's not my fault Ada is too damn cute for her own good, and I want her little belly to be full.

They both ignore me. "They're all like this? All nine of them?" Stella asks, shocked.

"Pretty much. You could ask any of my sisters-in-law, and they will agree with me."

"Maverick and Merrick aren't married." Ryder smirks.

Jordyn shrugs. "Stella can speak for him."

I grin because Stella is beautiful, and if a woman has to speak on my behalf, I could do worse. So. Much. Worse.

"Let's eat." I pass out everyone's food, leaving Ada's in the bag for now. I scarf mine down, as does Ryder.

"Did you two even chew?" Jordyn asks with a laugh.

"I'm a growing boy."

"Boy?" Stella scoffs.

"What?" I turn to her, flashing her the grin my momma says could get me out of anything. My brothers, they say it drops panties. I will neither confirm nor deny if the latter is true.

"Nothing." She shakes her head and takes another bite of her burrito.

Gathering my trash, I stand to toss it away as Ada's cries sound over the baby monitor. "I'm up. I'll go get her. Finish eating."

"I can—" she starts, but I'm already out of the room, headed toward Ada.

"Hey, sweetheart." I move to lift her up. She has big tears on her cheeks, and she shudders a breath. "It's scary waking up in a new place, huh?" I ask her. I wipe her tears with my thumbs, and she rests her head on my shoulder. "You're a little snuggle bug, aren't you?" I rub her back, soothing her until her whimpers quiet down. Reaching into the Pack 'N Play, I grab her blanket. At least, I think it's hers. Either way, I grab it and offer it to her. She takes it, holding it close to her chest.

"Guess what?" I ask. Not that I expect her to reply. "You're having mashed potatoes for dinner."

I walk into the small break room and take my seat with Stella on one side, Ryder on the other, and Jordyn directly across from me. Ada lifts her head from my shoulder when she sees her mom but makes no move to go to her.

"Hey, sweetie. Did you have a good nap?" Stella asks her daughter softly.

Ada lays her head back on my shoulder.

"Hey, kiddo." Ryder reaches over and grabs her foot, which makes her giggle. He holds his hands out for her, and she goes to him easily.

"You hungry, bug?" I ask Ada.

Reaching for the bag that has her food, I open the small container of mashed potatoes and gravy. I hand Ryder the spoon, and he starts to feed her.

"I can do that," Stella tells him.

"Eat." Ryder doesn't pull his eyes away from Ada as he flies the spoon of mashed potatoes toward her mouth. She laughs and opens wide.

"I feel bad," Stella announces.

"Don't feel bad. You'll get used to it," Jordyn tells her. "They're all baby hogs." Ryder clears his throat. "Fine, we're all baby hogs. Just relax and enjoy the break."

"But I'm getting a break tomorrow when they'll have her."

"Relax, Stel." Reaching over, I place my hand on her thigh. I give it a gentle squeeze. "We offered to do this. Today and tomorrow. Eat your dinner without having to worry about feeding Bug and relax."

She sits very still, her eyes downcast. When she looks up, her blue eyes are glowing with an emotion I can't name. "Thank you, Maverick. Ryder, Jordyn, thank you. Moving to Willow River was scary. I only had my grandparents and Ada, and I was worried about a job, and so many things. This job, everything Maverick has done for me. It means so much."

Ada grunts and Ryder laughs. "Sorry, little one, Mommy was distracting me." He goes back to feeding her, and out of the corner of my eye, I see Stella relax. Realizing my hand is still on her thigh under the table, I remove it before standing. "Is her diaper bag in the office? I'll get her cup," I offer.

"Her cup is in the fridge. There is a reusable water bottle of milk next to it."

"We'll just use what I brought, and you can take that back home with you." I fill up the cup and hand it to Ada. She drinks greedily before opening her mouth like a little bird for another bite. We all laugh at the cuteness overload.

We chat while all three ladies finish their dinner. With plans for Ryder, Jordyn, and Stella to meet at my place tomorrow night, I walk Stella and Ada to her car. "Drive safe," I tell her as I step away.

"You too, Mav."

I grin at her using my nickname and wave as she pulls out. I watch until I can no longer see her taillights before climbing into my truck and heading home. I need a shower, and my bed is calling my name.

Chapter 10

Stella

"MOMMY'S NERVOUS," I TELL ADA. She's sitting on my bedroom floor, playing with her blocks. "It's been too long." The last time I went out was the night before I found out I was pregnant with Ada. From the moment I knew of her existence, I started living my life for her. I know I need to allow time for myself, but when you're a single mom, when you have to love your child for both parents, it's tough. I never want her to feel unwanted. Sure, she's too young to have those feelings, but loving her and being there for her is who I am now.

I'm her mom.

"I have nothing to wear," I mutter. Ada babbles, and I smile. Flipping through my closet, I settle on a pair of jeans with rips on the knee. Tired of overthinking my slim options, I pick a black flowy tank top. It's been a long time since I've worn it. Now for shoes. I drop to my knees and dig into the back of my closet. I find a pair of black heels, and my feet ache just thinking about wearing them. Quickly, I dismiss them and grab the black ballet flats.

Ada crawls over to me and pulls herself up. I kiss her cheek, and she returns the gesture with a sloppy kiss of her own. "It's not like I'm trying to impress anyone," I tell her. Images of Maverick fill my mind. But let's be honest—he's out of my league. Not only that but he's never made me think he's interested in more than friendship. Other than the super sweet things he does for me and Ada, but I've learned that's who he is. According to Jordyn, all of his brothers are the same.

Mr. and Mrs. Kincaid sure know how to raise them. I wonder if it's something in the water in Georgia?

Standing, I strip out of my robe and slide into the jeans. They fit me like a glove. It's been so long since I've worn them. I forgot that they make me feel sexy. It's been ages since I've felt that way.

Slipping into the black, flowy tank, I snatch Ada into my arms and grab some toys before going across the hall to the bathroom. Pulling open the shower curtain, I place Ada in the tub and drop her toys in with her. She laughs. She immediately crawls toward the faucet, but with the design of the shower, she's still too short to reach the handle. Pretty soon, I won't be able to use this method. She's going to be walking and running all over the place. She's really close. It will be any day now.

Tearing the towel off my head, I comb out my hair and blow it dry. Hitting the button for a cold shot of air, I point the dryer at Ada, and she giggles. It doesn't take long to run the straightener over my locks. My hair is straight already, but the straightener helps smooth it out. I don't do it every day, but tonight is a special occasion. I'm going out for the first time in almost two years.

After I apply mascara and sheer lip gloss, I'm ready. I've never worn a lot of makeup, and I don't see that changing anytime soon. Besides, even if I wanted to, I wouldn't have the time to devote to it. I've seen those videos on social media. Those ladies have a million steps to go through each day. I'm not about that life.

Scooping Ada up into my arms, I kiss her cheek. "All right, kiddo, it's time to get you packed up. You're going to spend some time with your buddy Maverick and his brother Ryder tonight while Mommy has some mommy time."

I'm nervous about leaving her with Maverick. I've only known him for a short amount of time, but I can't deny how good he is with her, and she adores him. It's obvious anytime the two of them are together.

It's only a few hours. We're also staying in Willow River, so it's a short five-minute drive to get to his place. I won't be far, and my gut tells me I can trust Maverick. In fact, I think he might be the most trustworthy person I've ever met. He's solid and dependable and sexy as hell, but I'm not going to think about that last part. I can't. With how sweet he is to us, if I allow myself to think about that, I'll fall down into a rabbit hole that will only end in pain. Been there, done that, got my daughter to prove it.

Derrick was a charmer. We were only casually dating, but he was good to me and apparently told me what I wanted to hear. Lesson learned? Before you sleep with someone, you need to know their life goals. Do they want kids? How do they feel about kids in general? Sure, they could lie, but I have a feeling Derrick wouldn't have. Would his confession have changed my mind about sleeping with him? I doubt it. I was pretty wasted the night our daughter was conceived. The one and only time we slept together. The one and only time I'd ever slept with anyone.

The lesson of a lifetime. Birth control is not one-hundred-percent effective; I knew that, but I still thought with a condom, we were protected. The universe said, "Hold my beer," and gave me the best thing to ever happen to me. Sure, there were bumps along the way, and her father is an asshole, but she's my best friend. I wouldn't change a single thing if it meant she wasn't mine.

Back in my room, I place Ada on the floor to play, making sure the bedroom door is shut. I pack the diaper bag with extra diapers and wipes. I add in a couple of pairs of pajamas in case she has a diaper blowout or some messy eating. I make sure there are some teething tablets, baby Orajel, and some Tylenol. I don't think they'll need it, but you never know. You can never be too prepared. I've learned that since becoming a mom. I grab another small tote and toss in her favorite blanket and her favorite toys.

Ada crawls over to me and holds onto my legs to stand. She bounces up and down and giggles.

"Don't worry, sweetie, we're not moving out." I laugh. "Mommy is just making sure you have what you need tonight." I zip up both bags and toss them over one shoulder before bending and lifting her into my arms, settling her on my hip. We make our way to the kitchen, where I put Ada in her high chair and pour out some puffs for her to snack on.

Does Maverick have a high chair? Do I need to bring mine? I better make sure. Grabbing my phone from my back pocket, I dial his number.

"You're not canceling," he answers.

"I'm not. But do you have a high chair?"

"Yeah. I've got one of those that straps to the kitchen chair and folds up."

"Okay. Good. Okay," I say again.

"Stel, she's going to be fine. You'll be five minutes away."

"No. I know." I blow out a heavy breath. "I'm nervous," I admit.

"Why are you nervous?"

"This is the first time I've been out since finding out I was pregnant."

"What?"

"My friends, they wanted to party. We were in college. I didn't want to tag along and watch them get wasted, and Derrick, Ada's sperm donor, he wrote me off when I told him." I've told him this, but I'm spewing the words to him again in my nervousness.

"My sisters-in-law are all amazing women. I promise you there are no expectations or judgments from them. You're going to go. Have a couple of drinks, and relax. Tonight, you're not in charge of everything. You let me handle all of that. I promise I'll keep your baby girl safe."

"I believe you," I tell him. "Ada's my best friend, Maverick, but you—you're giving her some competition."

"Yeah?" He sounds pleased by my confession. "I'll share that title with her," he tells me.

"She's always going to be my number one." My daughter is my heart and my entire world. She will always be.

"As she should be."

"Okay. I'm packing some snacks, and I'll bring milk." I rattle off all the extras I shoved into the diaper bag and the extra bag.

"That all sounds perfect, Stel." He doesn't berate me for being overly prepared. He just accepts it.

"So, I guess I'll see you soon?"

"Yeah, Stel. I'll see you girls soon."

I pack snacks into the extra bag before zipping it up and going over my mental checklist before loading Ada up in the car and heading toward Maverick's place.

"She's usually asleep by eight, but it's a new place, so she might not. She likes to snuggle with her blanket, and I usually rock her." I explain our normal routine. Boring but structured. That's important for babies.

"Got it." Maverick smiles at me.

"I'll call to check on her," I tell him.

"That's fine too." He reaches into his pocket and pulls his cell phone out, holding it up for me to see. "Fully charged, and the ringer is on high."

I nod. "Thank you. Are you sure?"

"Stella." Ryder says my name, and I turn to look at him. "She's safe. We'll protect her as if she were ours. Let's go. I'm dropping you ladies off so you can drink."

"Oh, I can't. I have Ada."

"You can," Ryder insists. "Just a couple. I'll drive you girls home later, and we can make sure your car gets to your place."

"I don't want to be too much trouble."

"Stella. Give your girl a kiss and get your ass in the car." Ryder's tone is serious.

I look over at Jordyn. "You heard the man." She leans over and kisses Ada's cheek, who is in Maverick's arms and loops her arm through mine.

"Love you," I tell my daughter, also kissing her cheek. I step back and squeeze Maverick's arm. "Thank you for this."

"Go. Have fun. We're having our own little party as soon as Uncle Ryder gets back, right, Ada?" he asks my daughter. She babbles back to him like she always does, placing her hands on his face and running her fingers through his stubble.

Something happens when he refers to Ryder as her uncle. My belly twists, not with dread, but with longing. I wish these amazing men—hell, this amazing family—was ours. It's people like me and Ada, who have very few people in our lives that we can count on, that know what it means to have this kind of support system.

"I'll be back, bro. You two party animals don't start without me."

"If you need me—"

"I'll call, Stella. I promise. If we need you, I'll call," Maverick assures me.

I wave and allow Jordyn to lead me out to their car.

An hour in, and I'm glad I let them talk me into this. All the ladies are easygoing and friendly. They've included me in their conversations and recalled stories of their husbands and kids, especially Blakely, making me laugh endlessly.

"Wait. It was a condom wrapper?" I ask, sputtering with laughter.

"Yep." Kennedy places her palm on her forehead. "She asked Maverick if it was a golden ticket."

Something a lot like jealousy swarms inside my chest, but I ignore it, choosing to let the laughter take over. I know Maverick has been with women. Hell, he's not even mine. However, a couple of drinks in, I've accepted that I'm developing a crush. Okay, maybe the crush is already developed.

"That's great," I say, finishing the rest of my margarita.

The night is one of the best I've had in—maybe ever. I feel welcomed, and we all get along so well it's as if we've all been thick as thieves our entire lives. I'm so relaxed that I drink more than I should have. I'm still able to take care of Ada. I know my limits, but I'm also feeling really good. Definitely past where I had intended to let myself go, but I've been having such a good time I didn't even notice.

I've only called to check on Ada once and sent off just two text messages. I'm proud of myself for that. Maverick even sent back pictures and a short video of Ryder making Ada giggle so hard that her entire body was shaking. It helped me to relax further. Not only that, but I opened up to them. They were asking questions about life before Willow River, and I ended up telling them everything about getting pregnant, Derrick refusing us, and my parents kicking me out. I'm surprised how good it felt to talk about it. Why, I'm not sure. I've already told both Maverick and Jordyn about all of this. Something about opening up when I'm used to holding everything in is therapeutic.

"You ladies ready to head home?" a masculine voice asks.

I look up to see one of Maverick's brothers. When he leans down and kisses Alyssa, I figure he must be Sterling. The ladies helped me remember their spouses tonight.

"We're ready."

"We are too." He nods to a table in the back.

I gasp when I see it's all the brothers, and the other must be Ramsey's husband. Ryder and Maverick are missing. "Have you been here the entire time?" I blurt.

"We have."

"No. I feel terrible that Ryder and Maverick missed a brothers' night." I reach for my phone to call and apologize when a hand lands over mine. I turn to look at the man standing behind Jade. This must be Orrin.

"This is what we do, Stella." He gives me a kind smile. "When the wives go out, so do we. We stay out of the way, and a few of us stay sober to make sure we get everyone home safely."

"Really?" I ask in awe.

"Really," Jade assures me.

"It's fine, Stella," Jordyn says sweetly from her seat next to me.

"That's... really sweet. Now I see where Maverick gets it." I slap my hand over my mouth, not meaning to say that out loud. Everyone just laughs but doesn't mention it. Instead, they discuss who is driving who home, and then we're ushered out of the bar.

"Why isn't Merrick with us?" I ask, once in the back seat of Orrin's car.

"He's sticking around a little longer. We have to drive back by the Tavern on the way home, so I told him I'd swing back by and pick him up."

"Then you'll have to come all the way back here. I could have waited."

"Nah, he's going to stay at our place. Orrin and I are having a day date tomorrow, and Merrick is going to watch Orion for us. We do this every so often. We have breakfast, run errands, do grocery shopping, and sometimes we go see a movie. It's not overly romantic, but it's our time," Jade explains.

"Oh. That's nice. And important." I'm not just saying that. It really is nice how they all show up for each other. It's a little intimidating, if I'm being honest, the way they love. "Thank you for taking me back. Wait, you're going to have to take me home, too, after picking up Ada. I'm so sorry."

Jade reaches back and places her hand on my knee. "Relax, Stella. It's just across town. It's not like it's way out of our way. We'll get you and Ada home safely."

"Thank you," I whisper as I sit back in my seat and send up a silent thank-you for bringing these people into my life.

When we reach the house, the lights are low. Orrin, Jade, Jordyn, and I make our way to the door. I get there first, so I knock softly.

HOME OF THE KINCAID BROTHERS

"Just go on in," Orrin tells me.

"I can't do that."

"Sure you can. Mav doesn't care. Besides, he has your baby girl in there." Jordyn turns the handle and pushes open the door.

Orrin motions for me to follow her, so I do. I don't look back when I hear the soft click of the door closing behind him. I know that Orrin and Jade are right behind us. I follow Jordyn into the living room and stop frozen. Ryder is asleep on the couch, a remote in his hand. Then there's Maverick. He's in the recliner; it's reclined back. His eyes are closed, his breaths deep and even, matching my daughter's, who is asleep on his chest. His big hand is resting against her back as if he needs to protect her.

Tears spring to my eyes.

I hear commotion beside me and turn to see Jordyn with her cell phone pointed at them, taking a picture. "What are you doing?" I ask her quietly.

"You're going to want to remember this."

I don't argue with her. She's right. I do want to remember this moment. However, what Jordyn doesn't realize is that the image before me will forever be ingrained in my mind. How could I ever forget this kind, loving man, treating my daughter as if she's special to him?

Jordyn slides her phone back into her pocket and practically skips over to Ryder. She touches his hand, and his eyes flutter open.

"I missed you," he tells her.

I place my hand over my chest to ward off the ache that's forming there. What I wouldn't give for a man to love me like that.

"Take me home, husband."

"You got it."

They say their goodbyes and head out the door. "I hate to wake them," I tell Jade and Orrin.

"Then don't. Merrick is staying with us. Just take his room or take Maverick's, and he can take Merrick's."

"I can't just spend the night," I say too loudly.

"You can, Stel," Maverick's groggy voice greets me. "She's peaceful, and I'm too damn comfortable to move."

"Come on." Orrin places his hand on my shoulder. "I'll show you to Maverick's room. He can take Merrick's if he decides to come to bed."

"I can take her," I tell Maverick.

"Nah. We're comfortable. If she wakes, I'll bring her in to you."

"Are you sure?"

"Stella, go to bed. I'll be right here." He closes his eyes, ending the discussion.

My eyes find Jade's. "This is crazy."

"No, it's not. It's late, and it makes sense she's sleeping, so it's good not to move her. Just get some sleep. You can leave in the morning. Come on, I'll take you." She gives her husband a soft smile letting him know she's taking over.

I nod. Truth be told, I like the idea of being here with him. I'm sure if I was completely sober, I'd argue, but then again, I'd be sober enough to drive myself. I guess at least this way, I won't have to worry about Orrin and Jade going out of their way to take me back to my grandparents' place. Besides, it's not like my grandparents are there to worry about why I didn't come home.

Jade takes me to Maverick's room and promises to call me tomorrow. I kick off my shoes and slide beneath the covers that smell like him.

Chapter 11

Maverick

ADA SQUIRMS AND MY EYES snap open. I run my hand up and down her back to soothe her. The room is dimly lit by a small lamp in the corner of the room.

"I can take her," a sweet voice whispers.

I look over at the couch to see Stella curled under a blanket, watching us. "I thought you went to bed?"

She nods. "I did, but I couldn't sleep." Slowly, she slides out from beneath the blanket and stands, making her way toward me. "I'll put her down."

I don't argue with her because I have to piss, and my little bug throws off the heat. My shirt is soaked in sweat. I move my arms to the sides and allow her to lift Ada from my chest. She snuggles her baby girl and moves down the hall to my room, where the Pack 'N Play is. Stiffly, I climb out of the chair and head toward the bathroom.

After taking care of business, I strip off my damp shirt and toss it into the hamper before making my way to the kitchen. I pull three bottles of water from the fridge. One for her, and the other two are for me. I down the first one and toss the bottle into the recycling bin before taking a long pull from the second.

"Thirsty?" Stella asks.

"Yeah." I slide the other bottle over to her.

"Thanks."

I study her as she twists off the cap and takes a small sip. "Something on your mind?"

"What?" Her brow furrows in confusion.

"You said you couldn't sleep. I thought maybe something was bothering you, and you might want to talk about it."

"Strange bed. Strange house."

"Right." I nod. "Did you have fun tonight?" I walk around the small island and make my way to the living room. I don't ask her to follow me, but I know she is. I sit down on the couch and pat the cushion next to me, offering her a seat.

"I did. It was really nice. Everyone was welcoming and easy to talk to."

"My brothers all hit the jackpot with their wives," I agree.

"They're all great," she says, her eyes trailing over my bare stomach.

I flex just a little, and she licks her lips. I have to focus on not smiling. It's always a good time having the attention of a beautiful woman. "Stel?" I ask after several long heartbeats of her biting on her bottom lip, staring at my abs.

She looks up. Even in the dim lighting, I can see the blush on her cheeks. "What happened to your shirt?"

My laugh has her shaking out of her stupor and slapping her hand over her mouth. She closes her eyes, and I'm tempted to grab her hand and let her trace my abs. I work hard for them; they may as well be enjoyed.

"I'm sorry," she says. "You're just... distracting. It's been a long time for me." She curses under her breath. "I should go back to bed." She starts to move, but I'm faster, clamping my hand gently over her wrist, preventing her from doing so.

"How long?" I'm asking for trouble, and we both know it.

"Too long."

"Come on, Stella. We're friends, right? You can tell me."

"The night Ada was conceived."

I whistle. "Damn. I bet your pussy is mad at you." I laugh.

"Maverick!" she scolds, but she's laughing and relaxes back into the couch.

"What? You can't tell me I'm wrong."

"We shouldn't be talking about this."

"Why not? We're friends. Pretend I'm one of the girls."

Her eyes rake over my bare chest again. "Yeah, that's not happening."

"You can touch them."

Her mouth falls open in shock. I expect her to refuse. Instead, her eyes regard me hungrily. Reaching out, I take her hand and pull it to my chest. She presses her palm flat against my abs, and a garbled sound falls from her lips.

I move my hand, letting her take the lead. I'm still frozen, and my abs are slightly flexed as she starts to explore.

"How many hours a week are you in the gym?"

"Not many, to be honest. I used to go three or four times a week, and I still do when I'm laid off, but in the summer months, this is all the day job."

She nods but doesn't give me her eyes. Well, that's not true. Her eyes are on me, just not on my face. "Are there eight of them?"

I chuckle lightly. "Yeah, babe, there are eight." She starts to move her hand, and I stop her. "Your hands are soft."

"I moisturize," she mutters, tugging on her hand, and I let her this time.

"You should get some sleep." My cock is way too interested in Stella and her soft hands. I should most definitely put some distance between us.

"I'm not tired."

Well, damn. "Movie?" I offer. Surely, she'll crash once we get a movie started, right?

"Are you sure? I don't want to keep you up."

"Yeah, I'm not going to sleep anytime soon. Bug and I fell asleep early."

"Why do you call her bug?"

"Does it bother you?"

"No. Not at all. I'm just curious."

"She's a little snuggle bug. She's always resting her head on my shoulder."

Her smile is soft.

She's fucking gorgeous.

"I like that," she says softly.

"Here." I hand her the remote. "You pick."

"Really?"

I shrug. "Sure, do your worst." I watch her as she scrolls through the channels and lands on the Lifetime channel.

"Is this okay?"

"Fine by me. We grew up watching romance with my mom, and now my sisters-in-law and my cousin, Ramsey."

"The Kincaid men keep their ladies happy." She's nodding thoughtfully.

"We do. That's what you do when you love someone."

"I wouldn't know," she mutters.

My chest grows tight at her words. I hate that she's never known that kind of love. She's too sweet and far too beautiful to have never experienced it. Not that I would know. I've never experienced it, either, but I've watched it happen. I grew up watching the way my dad loved my mom, and I've been lucky enough to witness seven of my eight brothers fall in love, and Ramsey too. I know what it's supposed to look like. And one day, when I find it, I'll grab hold of it with both hands and never let go.

Pulling the blanket off the back of the couch, I cover her with it. She smiles and settles back against the couch. We're not even to the second commercial break when her head hits my shoulder. I wait for a good ten minutes before I adjust my position to lie down and move her with me. By some miracle, she doesn't wake up. I know she had a few drinks, and she has to be tired. Babies wake up early, at least all the ones I've ever been around do, so I know it's been a long day for her. She settles onto my chest, and I pull the cover over her.

Snagging the remote without moving us—thanks to my long arms—I turn the volume down low, hoping she'll be able to sleep through it while I watch the rest of the rom-com she chose.

My eyes are growing heavy, and just as I feel sleep closing in, I feel a soft press of her lips against my bare chest. At first, I freeze, but then I decide to show her that I'm awake. She might be asleep. I can't tell by her breathing. Lifting my hand, I run my fingers through her hair. It's soft like silk.

She kisses me again, and I shift on instinct because my cock is responding to her lips against my skin. I'm a man, and there is a sexy-as-fuck woman lying on my bare chest, kissing me. It's impossible to hide my reaction to that. I'm hoping I can adjust myself so my hard cock doesn't wake her up.

However, when I move, she moves. Her legs fall to either side of mine, and my hard cock is nestled between her thighs. If she moves or sits up, her pussy is going to be in direct contact. I don't know what I should do. Normally, if a woman is this close to me, it's because we're about to get to know each other better in the most intimate of ways, or we already have.

We're not there.

Stella is a friend who is going through a lot. The last thing she needs is me and my cock altering the friendship we've started, but damn, she also takes my breath away. Her tight little body using me as a bed is hard to resist.

Knowing that I need to change this situation before I'm no longer in control, I grip her hips with the intention of sliding off the couch and leaving her to rest. That was before she lifts her head and those mesmerizing blue eyes of hers find mine. She's breathing heavily, so I know she's been awake.

My hand has a mind of its own as I reach out and tuck her wayward hair behind her ear. "Hey," I whisper.

"Hey."

We stare at each other, neither of us willing to make a move. I need to do the responsible thing and slide out from under her, but that's a tough choice to make when she feels perfect lying on top of me. I'm trying to talk myself into following through with my plan. When she lifts up, her palms press against my bare chest.

Fuck. Me.

Her pussy is covering my cock. I'm as hard as steel, and there is nothing between us but a few scraps of clothing.

Her nails dig into my bare skin, and I lift my hips in response, causing her to moan. I should stop. I know I should, but her blonde hair is glowing in the dim lighting of the room, and she looks like an angel perched on my cock.

An angel with a pussy that's been untouched by a man for almost two years. I really wish she had never told me that, but I only have myself to blame. I asked.

"Maverick."

The way she says my name, it's half moan and half question, and my cock twitches. That sets off her next reaction, which is to rock her hips into mine.

"How much did you have to drink tonight?" I ask.

"A few," she answers as she closes her eyes, tilts her head back, and rocks against me. Again.

"How many is a few, angel?"

"Enough to have the nerve to do this, but not too many that I don't know what I'm doing."

Fuck. "I'm going to need you to break this down for me. Tell me what you want."

"I want to come. It's been so long."

Son of a bitch. "Do you make yourself come, Stel?"

"Sometimes, when I'm not too exhausted, but it's not the same, Maverick."

Sitting up, I take her with me. She's still straddling my hips, and we're both sitting up so that we're face-to-face. I push her hair back over her shoulders and place my index finger beneath her chin, lifting her eyes to mine.

"You're not allowed to ghost me after this. We're friends, and it stays that way." I don't know why, but it's important to me that things do not change between us. She's new in town and is starting to become friends with my family. The last thing we need is awkwardness.

I don't bring women around my family. None of us ever have unless we knew in our hearts that she was the one. This is a little too close to home for me, but I want to give this to her. I want her to know she can come to me. If she needs a sitter or if she needs a release, I'm more than happy to provide both.

"I know what this is." Another shift of her hips has me lifting mine.

Damn it all to hell, she's sexy.

"This is me giving you what you asked for. But tomorrow, we pretend like it never happened. No running from me."

"Yes. Okay. Yes," she says, grinding a little harder.

I still don't know how intoxicated she is. She seems as though she knows what she's asking for, but I still can't let things go too far. I can give her what she needs. Can I give her what she's asking of me without crossing the point of no return? Sure, I'll be fisting my cock in the shower as soon as she falls back asleep, but I'm okay with that.

"Stand up, angel. I need these jeans off." The words are barely out of my mouth before she scrambles off the couch and quickly shimmies out of her painted-on jeans. "Panties too." She doesn't say a word while doing as I ask. "Lose it all." I'm pretty certain this is a onetime thing. No way in hell am I passing up the chance to see all of her. I'm a gentleman, but I'm also a man in front of every man's fantasy. I'm cashing in on seeing all of her.

Doing as I ask, she strips down to nothing and stands before me, her chest rapidly rising and falling with each breath she pulls into her lungs. Her hands hang at her sides.

"Come back to me."

"What about you?" she asks.

"Tonight is all about you, Stel."

She accepts my answer and straddles my hips. I'm in a pair of thin basketball shorts that do nothing to conceal how turned on I am. My hands land on her hips, and I tug her down so she can feel what she does to me.

"Mav," she moans.

"Can I touch you?"

"Yes. Yes." Her head bounces up and down with her words, both showing and telling me she's on board.

Lifting my hands, I test the weight of her breasts in each palm while tracing the pad of my thumb over her nipples.

"W-What are you doing?"

"Enjoying the hell out of this moment." Leaning forward, I suck a hard nipple into my mouth, and she groans, arching her back, giving me better access. I don't know how long I play with her tits. Long enough to give them both equal attention and long enough to feel her pussy soaking my shorts.

She runs her finger through my hair, gripping the strands, holding my body close to hers. "Your skin is so soft," I murmur as I trail my index finger from the valley of her breasts and over her quivering belly. I don't stop until I'm running that long digit through her folds, witnessing how turned on she is.

For me.

"All for me?" I ask. I know it is. We both do, but I ask the question anyway.

"For you," she answers.

"What do you want, angel? My hands or my mouth?"

She rocks against my cock. "This."

"Not tonight." I can't believe those words are leaving my mouth, but I know it's the right choice. If we ever make it to a moment like this again sometime in the future, and she's completely sober, I'll give her anything she wants. Right now, tonight, she only has two options. Leaning in, I trail kisses down her neck while my index finger still explores her wet pussy. "Choose, Stella."

"Hands. I need... a part of you inside me."

I don't bother to tell her my tongue would be inside her had she chosen my mouth. I'm too worked up to be rational. I want her to come apart for me, just as badly as she wants to fall apart.

I tap her ass. "Lift for me. Up on your knees."

She does as I ask, and I immediately slide one finger inside her. She moans and falls forward, gripping my shoulders. "That—never had that."

I don't stop moving my hand as I question her. "What do you mean?"

"Never felt this good."

My brain spirals. "Stella, how many men have you been with?"

"One—one time. Ada—" she says, her voice breaking on a moan.

This is not a conversation we need to have right now, but I file this information away for another time. Should I be in this position again, we will talk about that little nugget of information she just dropped on me.

"Tell me if this is too much." I pull my hand out and add another digit.

"No. Not too much."

"Good." I slowly work my fingers in and out of her. She's tight as fuck. My cock aches to be inside her, but I push my needs down, far, far down, as I focus on giving this beauty what she needs.

"Fuck my hand, angel. Ride it. Take what you need."

"I—I can't do that."

"You can. Roll your hips." I help guide her with my free hand, and it only takes a few seconds before she takes over. I curl my fingers, and she moans. It's a deep, throaty sound that fills the room.

It's going to be hard to sit on this couch and not think about this moment with her.

We don't bring women here. This is our safe place. Where our family is always welcome. I'm breaking a lot of my own rules for her, to give her what she needs, but I have no regrets.

Her pussy squeezes my fingers like a vise, and I know she's close. "Come for me, Stel. I want my hand dripping with you. Take what you need, and come for me."

"Maverick!" she calls out as her body shakes. She falls into me, resting her head on my shoulder, and I work her over until she goes still.

When I pull my hand away, she groans in protest. A few seconds later, she lifts her head and smiles shyly. I bring my hand to my mouth and lick my fingers clean. Her eyes widen as if she can't fathom me wanting to taste her.

"You want a taste?" I offer her my fingers. I expect her to say no, but she shocks me when she leans in and takes both digits into her mouth. She does this thing with her tongue, where she's tracing my fingers in her mouth, and I can feel cum leaking from the end of my cock.

It's time to shut this down.

"You go get cleaned up first. You can grab a T-shirt out of my room to sleep in. The dresser is by the window. Second drawer down."

She nods and slowly climbs off my lap. When she bends down to pick up her clothes, I second-guess my decision to send her to bed alone, but I know it's the right choice.

"Thank you, Maverick."

"Stop thanking me, Stella. If you think for one minute that tonight wasn't as much for me as it was for you, we've got some talking to do."

She nods and rushes off down the hall.

I wait until I hear the bathroom door close, then pull my cock out and fist it. It's not going to take much to take me there. I'm stroking myself when I hear the door open. I should stop, but I don't give a fuck if she finds me. Luckily, a few seconds later, I hear my bedroom door close. Closing my eyes, I tilt my head back and replay what just happened in my mind. When the memory of her calling out for me presents itself, I make a mess of my hand and my chest.

I'm breathing heavily, and even though I should be sated, I'm not. I still want her. That's a problem. Stella and I are friends. I let things get carried away, something I won't do again. That's not what this was about, so I shove those feelings down deep and stand to strip out of my shorts; I clean up and make my way to the shower.

Tonight definitely took a turn in events that I wasn't expecting, and I know no matter what happens in the light of day, I won't regret it. I also know I won't let her push me away. Stella will continue to be a part of my life. I'll make sure of it.

Chapter 12

Stella

H E TOLD ME NOT TO run, and that's exactly what I did. Ada woke up early, just as she always does. I quickly changed her diaper, filled her sippy cup with milk from the fridge, gathered our things and rushed out of the house, quiet as a mouse. The entire time, I was certain that Maverick would wake up. That he would catch me rushing from his house with my face red and my tail between my legs.

It's been an entire week, and I still feel embarrassed. I begged him to let me come.

Begged him.

I don't regret it. How can I when it was the hottest night of my life? With only one sexual experience to compare it to, I know I don't have much to go off, but I can say with certainty that Maverick knows what he's doing.

"Earth to Stella." Jordyn waves her hand in front of my face.

"Sorry," I mutter.

"Where were you just now?"

"Lost in thought." I shrug, hoping that she buys my excuse.

"Care to share with the class?" she asks.

"Nope."

Jordyn grins and points at my face. "What's that about?" She waves her finger around.

"What's what about?"

"The blush. Girl, you better spill."

"Nothing to spill."

"Fine. I'll start, and you can fill in the blanks."

"It's nothing. I'm just distracted."

"I'll be the judge of that." She claps her hands together in glee, and I know before I leave today, Jordyn Kincaid is going to know my secret. She's going to know what I begged her brother-in-law to do to me.

"Okay, so here's my theory. We dropped you off at Maverick's place on Saturday night. He was sound asleep holding your baby girl to his chest, protecting her as they both slept as if she was the most precious thing in the world to him."

"That's not new information," I remind her.

"No," she agrees. "It's not. However, I think something happened after we left you there."

"Yes. I went to sleep. Woke up way too early when Ada woke and headed home."

"And in between.... *That's* the part I need you to fill in for me. I know that it's something." She pauses, reaches over, and places her hand on mine. "You can talk to me, Stella. Yes, he's my family, but we're friends and coworkers. I'm not just your boss."

"I know." I sigh, defeated. I need to talk to someone about this. I can't stop thinking about Maverick, and the fact that he's my friend. He said so himself. I shouldn't want my friend to do wicked things to me. It's wrong, and I hate that I can't shake this. That I can't shake him.

He's called a few times this week. He was mad that I left without saying goodbye, but I told him I needed to get home to do laundry and needed to run to get diapers and essentials for the week. He bought it, or at least he let me believe that he bought it.

We've texted off and on. You know, just like friends are supposed to. He's sweet and always asks about Ada, but just as he promised, he hasn't mentioned our night together on his couch. I don't know if he's keeping a promise or if he really is that detached. Did that night mean nothing to him?

And that brings me to my next problem. I can't separate what happened from the man. He's gone above and beyond since the moment I met him to help me out. He went out of his way to give me what I asked for on Saturday night, but now, he seems like it's nothing to him. Like I'm just a friend. He warned me, and I was so worked up that I thought it was just words. I know it's how things need to be. I'm a single mom. Maverick doesn't need that kind of baggage in his life.

"Stella?" Jordyn prompts.

"We... did things." Why do I feel like a teenager recalling my first sexual experience? I guess because it's not far off. Doesn't matter that I'm an adult and a mother. It doesn't change my sexual history.

She grins. I roll my eyes at her, and she schools her features, standing to her full height from where she's been leaning against the counter where we were unboxing jewelry to put into the display case. "Tell me more," she says, biting her cheek to hide her smile.

"I went to bed. I tried to fall asleep and couldn't. I felt bad he was taking care of Ada, so I moved to the couch in the living room. I thought I could be close in case she woke up and not disturb him."

"And?"

"I couldn't sleep there either. Instead, I curled up under the blanket and stared at the two of them. His big hand never moved from her back, holding her. Protecting her." I don't even need to close my eyes to draw up the image in my mind. It will be there, living rent free forever.

"Okay. Then what happened? I don't like cliffhangers," she mutters, making me smile.

"Ada stirred, and he woke up."

"And?"

I blurt it all out. Every last desperate plea that fell from my lips, I divulge to my new friend, my boss, his sister-in-law about the man we're discussing. "So, yeah, I'm a little distracted," I mumble after spilling the details.

"He's into you."

"What? No, he's not. He felt bad for me. He stopped us. He wouldn't even sleep with me. I'm a charity case to that man. I have been since the moment we met. Don't get me wrong, I appreciate every single thing he's done for Ada and me, but that's all we are to him. A charity case, friends at best."

"That's not true. Friends, yes, he even told you that himself. He doesn't see you as a charity case. It's not who he is."

I cover my face with my hands. "Fine, but still, I begged him, Jordyn. I threw myself at him. How can I ever face him again?"

"Easy, you just do."

Before I can respond with my rebuttal, the chime over the door alerts us to a customer. My breath hitches when I see him walking toward us. I'm holding my breath until he leans in for a hug.

"Hey, Stel." He hugs me before moving to do the same to Jordyn.

"Merrick," I breathe.

He whips his head toward me. "How did you know? I thought for sure I could convince you I was Mav."

I shrug. "I just knew."

"What's up?" Jordyn asks him, taking the heat off me.

"Ryder mentioned you had some shelves that need to be put together. We finished up a job and aren't starting another until Monday, so I'm off early. Thought I'd stop by and get a start on them."

"You're the best. Thank you, Merrick."

He nods. "Just point the way." The phone rings, and Jordyn lifts a finger at him before answering it.

"So, how could you tell? It's the smile, right? My smile is better than Mav's?" He graces me with said smile, prompting one of my own.

"I could just tell." I shrug, not wanting to admit that whenever Maverick is near, I can feel him. It's as if there is a tether of electricity that zaps between us, holding me captive.

Merrick tilts his head to the side. "You like my brother."

"Which one?"

He laughs. "Come on, Stella."

"He's a good friend. He's done a lot for Ada and me. I guess just from being around him, I could tell." It's the best answer I can come up with without giving myself away.

"It was the hug." He nods as if he's proud of himself. "My touch. You knew it wasn't him by my touch."

"Maybe." I give him another shrug as if I'm not sure when he's hit the nail on the head.

"He likes you, too, you know."

I scoff. "Come on, Merrick. You and I both know Maverick is way out of my league."

His mouth falls open in shock. "Do you really believe that?"

"Yeah, I mean, he's one of the good ones. He's the kind of man who won't get you pregnant and walk away. He's a man of his word, and I know from experience both are extremely hard to find."

"You're wrong. Not about him being a man of his word or the kind of man who owns up to his responsibilities. You're wrong about you not being good enough for him. You are enough, Stella. I have a feeling my brother will make sure you understand that."

With that cryptic message, he walks off toward the storage room.

"Thank you," Jordyn says, ending the call. "That was the supplier for those cute boat shoes. They're sending over the contract." She grins widely. Her boutique is a huge success, and Jordyn works her ass off to bring new products in every week. "I'm going to go get Merrick set up." She bounces away, and I smile.

I feel lighter having told her about my night with Maverick, and maybe a little because I missed having friends and someone I could confide in. My move to Willow River is turning out to be the best decision I have ever made.

It's Saturday night, and I'm out in the yard with Ada. We're sitting on a blanket, playing with some of her toys. The sun is setting, and soon it will be dark and time for us to go back inside. It's late August, and I know soon we won't have these warm evenings to sit outside and play.

I'm stacking blocks up for my girl to knock over. They're these rubber blocks with all different types of animals on each one. I love them because they're soft, so she can chew on them, and if she happens to fall on one, she won't get hurt. They don't tell you how much you worry once you become a parent.

Ada squeals and claps her hands, and I smile. It doesn't take much to make her happy. The sound of a vehicle stopping has me lifting my head. We're not expecting company that I know of. My heart races when I see who it is. He climbs out of his truck and heads our way with a grin on his lips.

"Ladies," he says as he settles on the blanket next to me. Ada giggles, and she pulls herself up, holding onto my shoulder. She reaches her free hand out for him. "Hey, Bug," he says fondly. "Are you playing outside with Mommy?"

Ada bounces on her legs, laughing.

"Yeah, we've been out here for a while. Just soaking up the fresh air." I don't tell him I've been thinking about him all day. All week. I also don't tell him I told his sister-in-law what happened between us.

Ada reaches out for him again. He smiles. "Come here, Bug." He holds out his hands just out of her reach. She giggles but takes a step while holding onto my shoulder. "You can do it, sweet girl. Come see me." He pulls his hands back a little, and she takes another step. I hold my breath as I wait for her to take another.

She does.

Another and another until she can no longer hold on to me. Maverick scoots back, just out of her reach, to the very edge of the quilt that we're sitting on. Ada pauses and then lets go of me. She wobbles a little but then takes a step. She's taken three so far up to this point but then falls. Maybe today she'll take one more. My girl is so close to walking.

I'm still holding my breath as she takes an unsteady step toward him. "There you go, Bug," Maverick praises. "You can do it. Come see me." He's smiling like he just witnessed the best magic trick the world has ever seen. His eyes are glued to my daughter. I look away and focus on counting her steps.

"Three," I whisper.

With each step she takes, Maverick moves a little further away.

"You got this, Bug." He pulls his hands close to his chest, and Ada toddles to him. He catches her, wrapping her in his arms, raining kisses all over her face. "You did it!" he says excitedly. Ada claps her hands, content to be in his arms.

Maverick's eyes find mine, and they're alight with pride. "How many, Momma?"

"Eight," I say, wiping the tears from my cheeks. "That's her most yet." And she did it for him. For the man who has shown us so much kindness and friendship. The man I can't seem to get out of my head.

"Eight!" Maverick cheers. He hugs her again, and she grabs a fist full of his hair and tugs. He doesn't seem to mind.

I watch them for far longer than I should until I find my voice. "What are you doing here, Maverick?"

"I was bored sitting at home, so I decided to take a drive. When I saw the two of you out here, I thought I'd stop and say hi."

"No plans tonight?"

"Nah. Merrick is with Orrin, working on a dent in the door of his truck. The house was quiet. I was actually going to grab some dinner. Have you ladies eaten?" he asks.

"We have."

"Then how about some ice cream? It's the perfect night for some ice cream, right?"

"Ada's bedtime is soon."

"We can go to Dorothy's. Just across town." He's not begging, but I can hear the hope in his tone. "What do you think, Bug? You want some ice cream?"

Ada snuggles into him, and he smiles, rubbing her back. "Okay, bedtime is close. How about this? I'll go grab me some food, and both of us dessert while you put her down?"

"You really don't have to do that, Maverick."

"I know, but I want to."

Shit. I can't be alone with him. Sure, my grandparents are inside, and Ada will be as well, but still, that's too close. It's still too soon. I need more space to process what happened last weekend.

"We can all go. She can stay up a little later."

He smiles. "You sure?"

"Yeah. I just need to grab my purse and the diaper bag."

"I'll get Bug loaded in the truck." He stands effortlessly with Ada in his arms, and bounces her on his hip, making her laugh all the way to his truck.

Quickly, I gather the blanket with the toys wrapped inside and carry it into the house.

"Is that Maverick Kincaid?" my grandpa asks.

I swallow thickly. "Yeah." I'm not ready for the questions that are sure to follow.

"I thought that was him."

I wait, but no questions follow that statement. "We're, um, we're going to take Ada for some ice cream."

Gramps nods. "Be safe. You have your phone and key, right? Do you need money?"

My heart swells in my chest at his easy acceptance of me and my life decisions. "I have both, and no, I don't need money. Thank you for the offer." I start to walk away when his words stop me.

"The Kincaids are a good family, Stella. You can trust him."

I don't know why he thought he needed to tell me that, but his words deserve an answer. I turn to glance at him over my shoulder. "Outside of you, he's the best man I've ever met. Love you, Gramps." With that, I turn back toward my room to grab what we'll need. I probably gave too much away. I probably let him see too much, but my grandparents have been my solid foundation through all of this. He deserves my honesty.

A few minutes later, I walk out to the truck with the diaper bag that holds everything Ada and I need. Maverick is waiting at the passenger side door, pulling it open for me. "You didn't have to do that," I tell him as I climb into his truck.

"Get in the truck, Stel."

Instead of going to the diner, we hit the only drive-thru in town and make our way to the picnic tables that line the edge of town right along Willow River. Maverick grabs Ada and his bag of food while I gather the diaper bag and our two milkshakes. Ada is going to share with me. She doesn't really need the sugar this close to bed, but this is a treat for her. For both of us.

"Wow. It's really serene out here this time of night." There are about half a dozen picnic tables and several benches for visitors to sit and look at the river.

"Yeah. On the other side of the river, it's not this nice, but it's great fishing."

"Do you fish a lot?" I ask him.

"Not really. We used to go a lot when we were younger. Now that we're all older, have jobs, and most of us have families, we don't get to go as much. We'll fish next weekend."

"What's next weekend?"

"The annual Kincaid men's camping trip."

"Ah, that's right. Jordyn mentioned that. They're having a girls' weekend, I guess."

"They usually do. Last year, we also started a Kincaid family camping trip. Everyone goes, and it's a blast. It's actually more fun than when it's just us guys if I'm being honest. My sisters-in-law are all amazing, and the nieces and nephews are always a great time. It's fun to watch them get to learn and experience the same things we did as kids growing up."

"That sounds nice."

"You ever been camping?"

I laugh. "No. My parents are more... stuck-up assholes, honestly. They look at something like camping as being beneath them. And I know damn good and well, my mom went when she was younger. I mean, come on, you know my grandparents. She married up—her words, not mine—and yeah, no camping for me."

"I'll have to take you some time. Ada would love it."

"I'm sure she would, especially if you're there. She's really taken with you."

"That's because we're best buds, right, Ada?" he asks.

She reaches for him. He shoves the rest of his burger into his mouth and pushes the wrapper into the bag before taking her from me across the picnic table. "You don't have to give in to her every time, Maverick."

"What?" He raises his voice as if he's offended. "How rude," he says, barely holding his laughter. He lifts his shake for a drink and takes a long pull while Ada leans in, wanting some as well.

"No, sweetie. You can have some of Mommy's." I lift my cup to offer it to her, but she's having no part of it. It doesn't matter that they're both vanilla. She wants his.

"She's fine." He offers her the straw, and she takes what I'm sure is a slobbery drink. She's not been drinking out of straws for long.

"You're spoiling her."

He shrugs. "That's what we do. Just ask my brothers. It's like our superpower."

"You might not think that way when you have one of your own."

"Like I'll have a choice. I have eight brothers, and Ramsey, my cousin, who, as you know, is like a sister to us. I've spoiled their kids and bought them the loudest toys I could find. Payback is coming my way, and I'm good with it. When I have kids of my own, I'll take it like a man." He chuckles.

"At least you're prepared." I laugh. Ada thinks she's missing out on the fun, and she reaches for me. Maverick hands her over across the table before gathering his trash and taking it to a nearby can. When he comes back to the table, he sits next to me, his back to the table so that he's facing the lake.

Ada smacks at his shoulder, and he leans in, kissing her cheek. "I see you, Bug," he says affectionately. She pulls on his shirt until he's leaning in close. So close I can feel his hot breath fan across my cheek. "What's up, cutie?" he asks her.

Ada kisses my cheek, then looks at Maverick like it's his turn. A wicked smirk tugs at his lips. "You want me to kiss Mommy too?" he asks her.

She just tugs on his shirt harder. "She's just playing," I say, feeling my heart thunder in my chest. I can't help but wonder if his lips are as soft as I remember.

"I don't know, Stel. I can't leave my girl hanging."

My belly flips. I know he's not calling me his girl. He's calling Ada his girl, and that, too, makes my heart melt like hot butter, but the way his eyes held mine when he said it, my heart doesn't seem to be able to separate my desire for him and reality.

He leans in close and presses his lips to Ada's cheek, and then just as quickly, his lips are pressed to mine. His tongue softly traces my lips before he pulls away. Ada laughs, loving this game they're playing. She doesn't have a clue that my heart is about to pound right out of my chest.

"It's getting late," I say, my voice gruff with desire. I have to shut this down.

"Yeah, I've kept you ladies out long enough." He stands and holds his arms out for Ada. She goes to him without a care in the world. Somehow, I manage to stand on wobbly knees and follow him to the truck.

This is bad. This is really bad. I'm falling for Maverick Kincaid, and I don't know how to stop it.

Chapter 13

Maverick

THERE IS NOTHING LIKE SITTING around a campfire drinking a cold beer. I look forward to these annual trips with my brothers. Now that we're all older and have jobs and families, it's harder to sit and just chill. Sure, we see each other every week, but it's with the hustle and bustle of life surrounding us. This is our time, and I hope we never stop doing it.

"We're thinking September for the families," Orrin tells the group. "Toward the middle of the month, probably. Dec, we'll defer to you on that because Blakely is the only one in school."

Declan nods. "Yeah, if we do three or four days, she can miss a Thursday and a Friday. Not a big deal. Kid's smart as a whip."

"Oh, we know." Brooks laughs. "She's too smart for her own good sometimes."

"I'm thinking she needs a little help with her spelling," Ryder jokes.

"And you." Sterling points at me. "Get a handle on those golden tickets, will you?" he says, barely containing his laughter.

"At least I used a golden ticket," I mumble under my breath. What I don't tell them is that it's been far too long since I've needed to use a golden ticket. That was the second week of October, and it's late August. Hooking up just doesn't have the same appeal that it used to. The gold ticket fiasco put things into perspective. I don't need to bring that shit around my family. If I'm being honest, I don't want to bring it around me either.

"You okay, Mav?" Archer asks. "You look like you're thinking awfully hard."

"I'm good. Just realized you fuckers are rubbing off on me," I confess. These are my brothers, my best friends. I can tell them anything.

"How so?" Rushton asks.

I shrug. "Hooking up is losing its appeal. Blakely and her golden ticket put a lot of things into perspective for me. I don't want to bring that around the family. The kids especially."

"That's one reason. Maybe it's also because of a cute little blonde who's new in town." Merrick smirks, tipping his beer to his lips.

"That's right," Deacon chimes in. "I hear you've been seeing a lot of her."

"Nope. Not seeing a lot of her." Not really. I mean, it's been a week since I've laid eyes on her. That's not a lot.

"Really?" Ryder jumps in. "Jordyn says you're Stella's savior."

I roll my eyes. "I helped her out. That's not recent news. Hell, I brought her to Kincaid Central and let her meet all of you. I was running late, and I thought it would be good to introduce her since she was new in town. There are a lot of us; I thought that might make her feel like she wasn't so much of an outsider."

"You were awful attentive," Sterling teases.

"I was being a nice guy. Dad, help me out here. You raised us to help those in need." I give my father a pleading look, hoping that he'll jump in with some of his words of wisdom and bail me out.

"Your mother and I tried to instill that in each of you. I think we did a pretty damn fine job, if I do say so myself."

"Told you," I sass my brothers.

"You've taken her to dinner, right?" Sterling asks.

"I did. Her and her daughter. I thought it would be nice to celebrate her job with Jordyn. I know she'd been stressing about it, and like I said, she's new in town."

"She stayed at our place after girls' night," Merrick reminds everyone. Not that they needed the reminder.

"Yeah, Ada was sound asleep, and she was exhausted too." Instantly, my mind takes me back to that night. Not that it's ever far from my thoughts. For the rest of my life, I'll never forget the image of Stella straddling me while I made her come.

I expected things to be strained between us, and I think she was pulling away a little, but I refused to let her. She promised me that things wouldn't change, and I made damn sure of that. I smile when I think about last weekend and our trip to get ice cream. Ada taking so many steps. It was cool to get to be there for that.

"Maverick, brother, it's okay to admit you like her," Brooks says gently. "Trust me, man. I've been there. Hiding it is so much work and puts a strain on your relationship."

"I hear what you're saying, but that's not where we are. We're friends. Her kid is cute as hell. That's it. That's all there is." It doesn't matter that I know what her pussy tastes like or that, with the help of her daughter, I tasted her lips again. Both were onetime incidents that I know I'll never have the privilege of again. There is no point in mentioning it. Stella and I are friends. We've crossed a line or two, but friends are what we are. I've never had a female friend, and I'm digging it. I like spending time with her and Ada. I'm not screwing that up for a piece of ass.

"Leave him be," Dad tells them. "He'll tell us when he's ready."

"There's nothing to tell."

Thankfully, Ryder's phone rings, breaking up the conversation and giving me a break.

"Hey, babe," he answers, holding his phone up to his face. "What are you doing?"

"Uncle Ry! Is my daddy there?" Blakely asks.

Ryder chuckles. "Yeah, munchkin, your daddy is here. We're all here." He turns his phone and pans it around the fire, and we all wave at our niece.

"You know that fire's hot. You better be careful," she warns.

That earns her a laugh from all of us. "We know, Blakely. We're being careful," Ryder tells her patiently. "What are you doing?"

"We're having girls' weekend. We're doing our makeup, and our hair, and our nails, and baking, and watching girl movies. The baby boys are here, but Mommy says that's okay. Because they're not men yet. When they're older, they'll go with you and Daddy and Grampa and all my uncles. I got lots of uncles."

I'm smiling so big. This damn kid, she's the absolute best and never fails to put a smile on my face.

"Sounds like you're having a great time."

"The best. Oh, and baby Ada and her mommy, Stella, are here too. They're not Kincaids, but they're girls, so that makes it okay," she rambles on.

My ears perk up at the mention of Stella and Ada. I texted her a few times during the week. She knew I was going camping this weekend, but she didn't mention joining girls' night with my family. It must have taken Jordyn all week to convince her to go.

"That's cool," Ryder says with all the enthusiasm our eight-year-old niece expects from her uncles. We have most definitely spoiled her rotten, and not a single one of us has regrets. I feel confident that I can speak for my brothers on that topic.

"Can you give the phone to Aunt Jordyn?" Ryder asks her.

"Okay, Uncle Ry. Love you. I need to call my daddy." She hands the phone off to Jordyn, and Declan grins as his phone rings. He pulls it out of his pocket to talk to his family.

It's as if a domino effect has taken place. All of my brothers, hell, even my dad, are on their phones, checking on their significant others.

"I gotta piss," Merrick says, standing and ambling off to do just that.

I debate for a hot second before pulling my phone out and texting Stella.

> **Me:** What are you ladies into tonight?
>
> **Stella:** You know it's girls' night.
>
> **Me:** Didn't know you were there though.
>
> **Me:** Not until Blakely told us.
>
> **Stella:** It was last minute. Jordyn was refusing to take no for an answer.
>
> **Me:** Having fun?
>
> **Stella:** I am actually—lots of fun. You have a great family, Maverick.
>
> **Me:** I won't debate this.

Me:	How's Ada? Any more steps?
Stella:	She's perfect. No, just a few here and there. Not as many as last weekend when she was trying to get to you. I think she might be crushing on you.
Me:	Tell her I'm single.
Stella:	Robbing the cradle, Kincaid?

I laugh out loud, unable to hide it, gaining the eyes of my brothers, who quickly dismiss me and go back to talking to their wives and kids.

Me:	Nah, Bug and I are best buds.
Stella:	I'm watching you, Kincaid.
Me:	Good thing we're friends then. You can keep an extra close eye on me.
Stella:	Why are you blowing up my phone? Aren't you supposed to be doing manly camping things?
Me:	My brothers and my dad are all checking on their wives and kids.
Stella:	Merrick?
Me:	You got a thing for my brother, Stel?
Stella:	Nope. But last I heard, you two were still single and had no kids that you're aware of. Something you need to tell me, Kincaid?
Me:	Kid free.
Me:	Merrick is taking a piss.
Stella:	So eloquent.

Me:	Fine. Merrick is using the restroom. By restroom, I mean he's finding a tree to hide behind to offer some relief to his full bladder.
Me:	Better?
Stella:	Wise ass.
Me:	Aw, Stel, you like my ass?

She sends back a string of laughing emoji. I bite down on my cheek to hide my smile. The last thing I need is more commentary from my brothers. I already had one outburst of laughter. Another will send them on high alert. I need to school my features and wrap this up before they notice.

Stella:	Behave, Mav. Have fun, but behave.
Me:	Yes, ma'am.
Me:	Tell Ada we have another ice cream date as soon as I get home.
Stella:	When do you get home?
Me:	We're leaving tomorrow morning, so we should be home by noon. Pick you girls up at six? Dinner and ice cream?
Stella:	You don't have to keep taking us out. What's your excuse this time?
Me:	Can a guy not want to hang out with his best friends?
Stella:	Best friends?
Me:	Yep. See you at six.
Stella:	Maverick!
Me:	Spotty service, Stel. I gotta go.

I hide my grin as I slide my phone into my pocket. Who says spotty service with text messages? Oh, well, she'll know why I said it. I know she's not going to text me again. She knows that regardless of what she says or how she tries to talk me out of it, I'll be at her grandparents' place tomorrow at six to pick them up. She knows that I'm lying about spotty service. Serves her right. I told her I wasn't going to let her run from this friendship. That's a promise I intend to keep.

It's one minute until six when I pull into her grandparents' driveway. We got home around noon, unpacked, took a long hot shower, and then went to the store and started laundry. Merrick was still at the house when I left. I invited him to come with us. That's the issue with living not only with a brother who's also your twin. He just smirked and said he didn't want to be the third wheel on our date. I made the mistake of telling him he wouldn't be because Ada would be there. The fucker just laughed at my mishap.

This is not a date.

Just two friends hanging out.

I'll never hear the end of this, but Stella and I are friends, and I can't hide that. I don't need to hide that. Eventually, they'll realize that their assumptions are wrong and let it go. Until then, I need to suck it up and take their teasing. I've done my fair share of teasing where each of them is concerned. I've earned it, that's for sure.

I'm climbing out of the truck when the front door opens. Stella walks out to the driveway and sets Ada on her feet. She holds her hands for a few seconds, and then Ada lets go. I kneel and open my arms. I'm about twenty feet away from her. She takes one step and then another. With each step, she becomes more confident, and the smile on her little face brightens.

"Look at you, Bug." My smile matches hers, I'm certain. My heart races with each step she takes. When she's within reaching distance, I pick her up and swing her around, raining kisses on her cheeks. "You did it! Look at you, big girl, taking so many steps." She returns my affection with a sloppy kiss on my cheek.

"She started that today," Stella says, joining us.

"That definitely deserves a celebration dinner and some ice cream."

"You don't have to keep making up reasons to celebrate, Maverick. Ada and I are good. I promise."

"I'm not making it up. This is a big deal. I mean, we were eating and grabbing ice cream anyway, but this makes it even more important. Right, Bug?" I gently rub my beard against her cheek, making her squirm and giggle.

"Are you ladies ready?"

"About that," Stella says, chewing on her bottom lip. "I thought we could eat here," she rushes to say. "My grandparents went to dinner and a show in Atlanta. They'll be back late, and I thought I could make dinner for you. You do so much for us, and you never let me pay." She shrugs.

"You want to make me dinner?" I'm smiling because her words cause a fluttering feeling in my chest. Has a woman I'm not related to ever wanted to feed me? Not that I can ever remember.

"Fine. But I'm going to run out and grab dessert."

"I can make something," she counters.

"Nope. That's my offer."

"Fine." She reaches for Ada.

"I can take her with me. I'm just running uptown. That way, you can focus on cooking."

"You don't have to do that, Maverick."

"I know I don't, but she wants to go bye-bye with me, right, Ada?" I ask her. Her answer is to rest her head on my shoulder.

"She really likes you." Stella's eyes are soft as she watches her daughter in my arms.

"Do you need anything while we're out?"

"No—actually, yes. If you don't mind, I need a gallon of Vitamin D milk for her. We're almost out. Let me run and get you some money."

I wave her off. "It's fine, Stel. What are we having for dinner?"

"Grilled chicken, baked potatoes, and mac and cheese, Ada's favorite."

"Sounds good. We'll be back soon." I turn, make my way to my truck, and work on getting Ada settled into her seat.

"Here." Stella appears beside me, a little winded. She hands me a small diaper bag. "You probably won't need this, but better safe than sorry."

"Thanks." I smile at her and place the bag on the floorboard of the back seat. I step back, letting Stella have room to say goodbye. "We'll be right back." I don't know why I do it, but I lean down and press my lips to her forehead. To reassure her that I'm not a monster because I have her daughter? Honestly, I don't know, and I'm not going to think about it. It happened. Friends can give chaste kisses on the forehead. Sterling used to do it to Alyssa all the time.

Waving to Stella, I back out of the driveway and head to the small grocery store in town. I plan just to pick up some ice cream and, of course, the milk Stella asked for.

"All right, Bug," I say to Ada once I have her seated in a cart. "What kind of ice cream do we want?"

She kicks her feet and grips the handle of the cart, cooing back at me. This kid is cute as hell.

"I'm thinking of some cookies and cream, and I know your momma likes chocolate, so we'll grab her some of that, and maybe they have those little individual cups of vanilla for you. We'll check and see," I tell her, pushing the cart down the aisle.

"Maverick?"

I stop and turn to look over my shoulder. "Hey, Scarlett," I greet my sister-in-law.

"Ada, right?" she asks, nodding toward my companion.

"Yeah, this is Ada." I don't explain why she's with me. I can already see Scarlett's wheels spinning.

"Fancy seeing the two of you here." She grins.

"Her mom was busy, so Ada and I came to get some ice cream."

Scarlett nods. "We really like her. All of us," she tells me.

"Stella's a nice woman."

"And this little cutie, she was taking some steps last night."

"Today, she took about forty. It had to be. I was about twenty feet from her, and she walked to me the entire way." Even I can hear pride in my voice. I'm still jazzed that I was the one giving her that motivation.

"Really?" Scarlett's eyes widen. "Look at you, Miss Ada. Great job." She offers Ada her hand, and she takes it, gripping Scarlett's finger, then looking up at me as if she needs my approval.

"You remember Scarlett, Bug? She's my sister."

"Bug?" Scarlett asks.

"Yeah, this little cutie likes to snuggle."

Scarlett's eyes brighten.

"The night I watched her, she was a little snuggle bug," I add to alleviate her trying to play matchmaker. Not that it's going to do any good. I have a feeling my sisters and my brothers are already scheming.

Can't a guy just be friends with a woman and her kid?

"Aw," Scarlett says.

"Well, we better get moving. I told Stella I would have her right back."

"I'll see you both soon." Scarlett grins again and pushes on down the aisle.

"Ice cream, milk, and then home." I rush through our trip, grabbing all three flavors and a gallon of Vitamin D milk. As we make our way to the register, I see a small stuffed ladybug. I stop and pick it up, checking it out. Ada reaches for it, and I know that she's going home with it. I hand it to her, and she smiles, hugging it to her chest.

We expertly make our way through self-checkout, and Ada doesn't cry when I have to scan her bug before giving it back to her. "Okay, Bug, here's the deal." I glance into the rearview mirror. She's holding her new stuffed toy and watching me. "We tell Mommy that the bug insisted on coming home with us, deal?"

Ada giggles, and I take that as her agreement. I know Stella is going to tell me I'm spoiling her, but come on. It's a bug, and she's my bug. She needed it. That's my story, and I'm sticking to it.

"Okay, remember what we talked about?" I ask Ada as I lift her out of her seat. I grab the bag and her diaper bag and make my way to the front door. Ada is lifting her bug to show me, and I give it a kiss. She does the same, mimicking me.

"What's that?" Stella asks, opening the door for us.

"Funny story. This ladybug here insisted on coming home with us. Right, Bug?" I ask Ada. She offers the bug to her mom. When Stella tries to take it, she pulls it back into her arms, holds it tight, and rests her head on my shoulder.

"Mav, you're spoiling her."

"Told you," I whisper to Ada under my breath, knowing Stella can hear me.

"You're impossible." She takes the grocery bag and the diaper bag from me. "Come on in. We eat in fifteen," she tells me.

"We did it," I tell Ada. I carry her to the living room, and we play until Stella calls for us to come and eat. We're not doing anything special, and it's the best night I've had since the evening I took them to the park.

Who knew these ladies would be better companions than my brothers?

Stella

I GO OVER MY MENTAL checklist one more time. The diaper bag is stuffed so full it barely zips, but I want to be prepared for whatever might happen. The mini cheesecakes that I made are in a container on the kitchen counter, and the two packages of shortbread cookies for the kids sit next to them.

"Okay, kiddo. I think we're all set," I tell Ada. She's sitting in her high chair, playing with her stuffed ladybug. She loves that thing. She sleeps with it and drags it around the house with her. She's walking all over the place, and it's tiresome to keep up with her, but I love watching her grow and learn.

"You're only going to be gone a few hours." Grams laughs when she eyes the overstuffed diaper bag.

"I know." I huff out a laugh. "I just want to be prepared. This is our first playdate."

"Stella, sweetheart, playdates are just as much for the moms as the kids. The ladies want to get together and chat while the kids play. They invited you because they want you there. Just relax."

It's hard to relax when it's the family of the man you've fallen for. The same man who likes to give forehead kisses and has placed me in the friend zone. *Firmly* in the friend zone. I want them to like me. I know that my crush on Maverick is on me, but still, his family is great, and I want Ada to be a part of that any way that she can be. They're amazing people. I want her to see that's how life can be.

If I'm being honest, I want that for me as well. I'm seeing how the other side lives. The side that likes to joke and laugh, and not take themselves too seriously. I'm seeing how family shows up for each other, and it's endearing, and I can admit that I yearn for that for me and for my baby girl.

"I know," I finally admit.

"Go and enjoy yourself. You have too much on your shoulders. Live a little. Yes, you're a mother, but mothers can be happy too. When you're happy, she's happy." She nods toward Ada.

"I just... don't want them to be right. They said I would never amount to anything, and neither would she," I confess.

My grandma's face grows red. "You listen to me, Stella. Your parents, they don't have a loving gene in their body. Your mother, she hated this small town and always claimed she was worth more. This town and the people in it, they would do anything for their neighbors. Everyone knows everyone, and it feels safe and secure."

"I love it here," I tell her. "I wish I could have visited more growing up."

"Me too, sweetheart, but my girls are here now. That's what matters. Live your life for you and that little girl. Push everything they've ever said out of your mind. You're an adult, a damn good mother, and you have a good head on your shoulders."

"They told me I would hate this place. That I would never want to stay."

Grandma scoffs. "Their noses are too far up their asses to see what's right in front of them. Willow River has embraced you and Ada. This is your home now. I know they told you not to, but stay anyway. Prove to them that you can make it on your own."

"But I'm not on my own. I'm mooching off you and Gramps."

She waves her hand in the air while rolling her eyes. "You're our family, and you're getting back on your feet. You have a great job and friends, and that little girl is thriving. You are making it, Stella. I see good things for you here in Willow River."

"Thank you. You and Gramps. You saved us. We didn't have anywhere to go." I think about Derrick and how he hasn't reached out even once since the day he stood us up. The day my car broke down, and we met Maverick.

"That's what we do. Now, you two go and enjoy yourselves. If you forgot something, I'm sure one of the ladies has it, or you can come home to get it or pick it up in town. Don't stress. This is your home now."

"I love that," I say, tears burning the back of my eyes.

"Love you, sweetheart." She kisses my cheek, does the same to Ada, and walks out the door.

"Okay, toots, let's get this loaded in the car." It takes me three trips. One for the food, one for the overstuffed bag, and then another to make sure we didn't miss anything. I took Ada with me each trip. I could have asked Grams to watch her for me, but it's my job. I'm her mother. I can do this.

I place Ada in her seat, and she cries as I pull her ladybug out of her hands to strap her seat belt. "I'll give it right back." I try to soothe her. She's, of course, pissed, so I hope that she settles once we get on the road.

Ten minutes later, I'm pulling into Brooks and Palmer's driveway. It's full of vehicles. Taking a deep breath, I climb out of the car and have to take the ladybug from Ada again to get her out, and she's not impressed.

I bounce her in my arms, giving her the beloved toy back, but she's still unhappy. "Come on, sweetie. It's okay. I'm sorry, but we had to get you out of your seat."

"Need some help?" a male voice asks.

I turn to see Merrick. Ada lifts her head, looks at him, and reaches for him. "I'm sorry. She thinks you're Maverick."

"Close enough." He takes her from my arms. She looks at him and starts to wail with tears. "Hey, cutie, don't cry. What do you have here?" he asks her, but she's not having any of it.

"Bug?" I hear. Ada and I both turn to watch as Maverick approaches. Ada cries. Her bottom lip wobbles as she reaches for him. Maverick takes her easily and holds her against his chest. She snuggles up to him like she always does. "What's going on?" he asks, rubbing her back.

"She's not impressed that I'm not you. Smart kid." Merrick nods.

"She was mad before we left the house. I had to take her ladybug to strap her into her seat. She'd just gotten calmed down when I had to take it again to get her out. Merrick offered to help, and she reached for him. She was instantly pissed, and now, here we are." I motion to where she's in his arms, tears on her cheeks, but she's quietly cuddling with her ladybug.

"Mommy was right, Bug," he tells her as if she understands, and maybe she does. "And look, you have your ladybug back."

She sniffs, and my heart breaks. Stepping toward them, I wipe her tears. "I'm sorry, baby, but I had to." I know I shouldn't be apologizing. I'm not supposed to be her friend. I'm her mother, but maybe Maverick has the right idea, and she really does understand.

"Back to my original question. You need some help?" Merrick asks.

"Um, yeah, sure. Wait... I thought this was a playdate?"

"It is. For all of us. The kids, the moms, and the dads, well, that includes Mav and me, because where one brother goes, we all go," Merrick explains.

"Oh. I thought it would just be the ladies and the kids."

"Nah, we like to help. Give you ladies time to chat, and the same for us. Think of it as a shared playdate time." Merrick laughs.

I can't help but laugh with him. "Makes sense. Okay, um, some food. I can get the rest." Reaching into my car, I grab the container of cheesecake bites. Here, I thought I made too many. The cookies are in a grocery store bag, and I hand them both to Merrick. "Thank you."

He winks. "You're welcome. I'll see you three inside." He grabs Ada's foot and she grins. Her earlier mood forgotten.

"Hey, Stel." Maverick bends and presses his lips to my forehead.

"Hi. I wasn't expecting to see you."

He slides his arm around my waist and pulls me close. "I knew my girls were going to be here."

His words, they make my heart gallop. Oh, how I wish we were his. I offer him a smile, one that I hope hides that I want him. I have to get over this thing I have for my friend. It can only end with my heart broken, and I've had enough heartbreak.

"We should head inside." I step out of his hold, instantly missing the heat of our bodies pressed together. It's on the tip of my tongue to offer to take her, but we both know he won't let me. Hell, at this point, at this moment, I don't think she would let me either.

Grabbing the overstuffed diaper bag, I close the door and follow Maverick into the house.

The playdate that I thought would be a girls' night in turned into everyone in the basement hanging out. When I say everyone, I mean everyone. All the men, the wives, and the kids. We're all down here, and it's loud and happy, and I'm loving every minute of it.

"I've been looking at property," Merrick announces.

"What?" Maverick seems shocked.

"Yeah, it's not on the market yet. You know Brad Mayfield, right?" he asks the room. Most everyone nods. "Well, his wife got transferred to Nashville for her job. They can't afford to buy there until they unload here. He's offering it to me for a steal."

"Damn, bro, talk about pulling up the big boy pants." Maverick leans over from where he's sitting and offers Merrick his fist.

Merrick smiles. It's a shy smile, one I've not seen on him before. "I'm excited. I'm going to the bank on Monday. Brad called me on the way here to tell me it's mine for that price if I want it."

"You need help?" Ramsey and Jordyn ask at the same time. Everyone in the room laughs but me. I know they both came into some money—apparently, more than I assumed, but it's not my place to ask.

"Thank you both, but I got it. I have good savings, and the house is really a steal. It's three acres, three bedrooms, two and a half bathrooms."

"You let me know if that changes," Ramsey tells him.

"And me," Jordyn adds. "We got you."

"I know you do," Merrick says softly. "I can handle the money and the finances. I was more worried about Mav."

"Me?" Maverick asks.

"Yeah, I'm leaving you on your own."

Maverick laughs. "Mer, come on, man. We both knew it was temporary. One day, we're both going to have one of these—" He points to Palmer and then nods to Ada, who is sleeping on his chest. "—and one of these. I'm stoked for you. Maybe it's time I start looking as well. Move out of the rental."

"Not a bad idea," Deacon, Ramsey's husband, chimes in. "You're better off putting your money into something you own, than blowing it on rent."

"Agreed. If you all see anything, let me know."

Everyone agrees, and the heavy moment that Merrick anticipated doesn't exist.

"Daddy, I'm hungry," Blakely whines. She comes over to sit on Declan's lap.

"We're going to eat soon," he tells her. "You should have eaten all of your lunch."

"I was full of Mommy's crusty-ass pancakes."

"Blakely!" Kennedy scolds.

"What? That's what they were."

"Blake," Declan says in warning.

"Daddy, I read the box."

Kennedy stills then bursts into laughter. "Oh, my—Blake—" She's laughing so hard she can't even form a sentence.

"Care to share with the class, babe?" Declan asks.

She's wiping tears from her eyes as the rest of us try our hardest not to laugh at what Blakely said. She grabs her phone from the table and pulls up a picture, showing it to Declan, and he starts laughing too.

"Blake, sweetheart. The pancakes that Mommy made were Krusteaz."

"Let me see." She pulls the phone from her dad's hand. "Daddy, that says crusty ass. Are you sure you went to school?"

Sterling grabs the phone and checks the screen before he, too, is rolling with laughter. Kennedy is still snickering as her phone is passed around to all of us. "Gotta give it to ya, kid. You never fail to disappoint," Sterling says as the phone makes its way back to him. He takes another look at the screen, grinning from ear to ear before passing it back to Kennedy.

"I guess we better get the food ready," Alyssa says with a huff of laughter.

"What can I do to help?" I ask.

"We just need to set out the cold stuff. All the Crock-Pots are already plugged in." Palmer explains.

"I'll help." I stand and make eye contact with Maverick. "I can put her down."

"Nah, we're all set, Stel." He gives me a lazy smile that has heat pooling between my thighs. I nod and follow Palmer and the rest of the ladies to the kitchen area of the basement.

"I saw that look he gave you," Jordyn says, leaning her shoulder into mine.

I huff out a breath. "You're seeing things that aren't there."

"We can see the way you look at him too," Ramsey says gently. "You should go for it."

"He's made it clear we're just friends, and I'm okay with that. I respect his choices."

"But if he were to change his mind?"

My face heats, and they all laugh.

"No words needed." Crosby grins. "Nothing to be shy about. If anyone knows the power of these Kincaid men, it's us."

"She's not wrong," Jade chimes in. "We all fell pretty hard. They make it hard not to."

"There's nothing going on."

"But something has happened. It's written all over your face." Crosby winks.

"Fine. We might have kissed and done some... other things, but it was a onetime thing. I offered more. He turned me down. End of story."

"Stella, come on, you were drinking."

"I think you should try again," Scarlett tells me.

"Oh, yeah," they all agree.

"What's going on over there?" Orrin calls over.

"Nothing, dear," Jade calls back, and we all laugh, not even trying to hide it.

"Come and eat!" Ramsey calls out to the rowdy crew.

"I'm going to go grab Ada so Maverick can eat," I tell the ladies.

"Stay. He'll bring her here, and I doubt he's going to let you eat after him." Alyssa gives me a pointed look, challenging me.

"He's not going to care."

I feel a hand on the small of my back. "Go ahead and make yourself a plate. I've got Bug."

"Uh, no, that's okay. I can take her." I reach for her, and he turns sideways.

I'm shocked, frozen still when he reaches up with the hand that's not holding my daughter and tucks my hair behind my ear. "Take care of you for once, Stel. I got our girl."

My heart stops.

Our girl.

Oh, how I wish on everything I can think to wish on that was the case. I wish Maverick were her father. He never would have abandoned us. Even if he and I never became more, he would still be there for his daughter and me by association. He's given me that support when it's not his responsibility. That's just the kind of man he is.

Doing as he says, not wanting to make a scene or draw attention to us, I make a plate for both of us. I take a seat next to him and slide him the plate I made for him. He leans over and kisses my cheek. "Thanks, Stel." He scarfs down his food, holding my slumbering daughter, without issue.

"Did you chew?" I ask him.

Merrick chuckles from across the room. "We all eat fast, Stel. It's our superpower."

"Sheesh." I take my last bite and stand and gather our plates. I take Merrick's, Sterling's, and Alyssa's with me as well. "Anyone need anything from the kitchen?"

They all shake their heads, so I toss our trash and take my seat next to Maverick as my phone rings. No one ever calls me. At first, I think it might finally be Derrick calling to check on his daughter, but I see my grandmother's name and my heart stops.

"Grams? Is everything okay?"

"Oh, yes, dear, everything is fine. Henry, down the road, was doing some digging, and he hit some underground electricity.

The entire road is out of power. They're saying several hours. Your grandfather and I are going to stay at a hotel in Harris. We were going to get you a room as well."

"Oh, no, you don't have to do that. I can get my own room."

"What's going on?" Maverick leans in close, putting his hand on the small of my back.

"Grams, give me a few, and I'll call you right back." She agrees, and I end the call. "Henry, my grandparents' neighbor, was doing some digging and hit some underground electricity, and the power is out on the entire road."

"Damn, he must have hit a mainline or something," Kennedy speaks up.

"Anyway, my grandparents are getting a room in Harris and wanted to know if they should get me one as well." I stand and reach for Ada. "I should go so that I can get a room."

"Stay at our place," Merrick speaks up.

"What? No, I can't put you all out."

"You won't be. I've had a few of these." He holds up the beer he's drinking. "Besides, Brooks conned us all into helping him build shelves out in the garage tomorrow. I'll just stay right here, and you can take my room at the house."

"No, Merrick, I can't let you do that."

"You're right. You're not letting me do it. I'm offering. Besides, you've sat here. You know how damn comfy this couch is."

"He has a perfectly good spare room he can sleep in upstairs too," Palmer chimes in. "It's better than paying for a hotel."

"Stel, come on. You've stayed there before. Don't waste money on a hotel when you can stay at our place."

I make eye contact with each of the ladies, waiting for them to offer me a room. By the grins and smirks on their faces, that's not going to happen. I sigh, wanting to stay with him. I know what happened last time won't happen again, but I just like being around him. Today has been a great day, and I'm not ready for it to end.

"If you're sure...?"

"We're sure," everyone in the room speaks up, and I laugh.

"Thank you." I stand and move to the back of the room to call my grandmother back. She seems thrilled that I'm staying with Maverick. With the promise to call her tomorrow, I end the call.

When I get back to the couch that I was sitting on, Ada is awake and drinking greedily from a sippy cup.

"Hey, sweetie. Come see Mommy." She does without complaint. I'm surprised; she's been glued to Maverick most of the day. If she wasn't on his hip, she was chasing after and playing with her new friends.

This is what it's supposed to feel like to have a partner.

I shut that thought down immediately. I can't let my mind go there. The attraction I feel is bad enough. My heart is already invested. I can't make it worse.

Chapter 15

Maverick

"YOU CAN HAVE MY ROOM," I tell Stella as we walk into the house. I have a sleeping Ada in my arms. She slept all the way home. She really wore herself out chasing after the other kids today.

"No. No, that's okay," she blurts. "I can just take the couch, or Merrick said I could sleep in his bed."

That's not happening. "You can sleep in my bed."

"Really. I don't want to put you out."

"Stel, you're not sleeping in my brother's bed." No way. I can't say why, but the thought of her in Merrick's bed pisses me off.

"Why? He offered, and that's why he stayed there, right?"

"No."

She gives me a perplexed look. "Well, I'm not forcing you out of your own bed when there's another in the house that's not being used that I can sleep in." She places her hands on her hips and stares up at me. All I want to do is kiss the scowl off her lips. Closing my eyes, I take a slow, deep breath and exhale. I have to stop thinking about kissing her.

"The Pack 'N Play is in my room. You should be with Ada." It's a stretch, and we both know it. She knows damn good and well that I'm happy to help with Bug if she wakes up tonight. However, I'm not above playing dirty. I don't want her sleeping in my brother's bed. She'll be in mine. That's how this is going to go.

"Fine." She huffs. "It's a big bed. We'll both sleep there." Her eyes widen at her own words.

I stand still, waiting for her to take them back, but she doesn't. Instead, she turns on her heel and makes her way to my room. "Your momma, she's something else," I whisper to the sleeping baby girl in my arms. I walk back to the front door, making sure that it's locked before turning off the lamp I switched on when we walked in. Slowly, I make my way down the hall to my bedroom door. I push it open to find Stella already in bed under the covers.

My cock stirs.

Fuck me. She's my friend, dammit. I need to forget about how tight her pussy gripped my fingers and how sweet her lips taste pressed against mine.

I. Need. To. Forget.

"Did you find something to sleep in?" I ask her.

"Yeah. I stole a T-shirt from the basket of folded laundry."

Walking to the side of the bed she's lying on, the side where the Pack 'N Play is, I sit on the edge of the bed. "Thought you might want to say goodnight," I tell her.

She sits up and leans in to kiss Ada's cheek. "Night, sweet girl," she whispers. Her eyes meet mine, and it takes all I have not to lean in and kiss her. "Thank you, Maverick."

"I got you, Stel." I glance down at Ada. "Both of you." Standing, I lay Ada down, making sure her ladybug is within reach. "I'm going to go change." I grab some basketball shorts. I usually sleep in just my boxer briefs, but I can't do that sleeping in the same bed with her. Hell, I'm tempted to just sleep in Merrick's room, anyway. I'll wait until she's asleep and slip out of the room.

My friend is sexy and alluring. I know she's off limits, but my body still responds to her. I'm a man, and she's dream girl material. Of course I'm going to respond to her. If she were anyone else, I'd have already turned on the charm.

When I step back into the room, I toss my dirty clothes into the hamper and slide under the covers. Before I can think better of it, I lean over and kiss her shoulder. "Night, Stel."

"Night, Mav."

Moving back to my side, I stare up at the dark ceiling. This is a king-sized bed, but it might as well be a twin. I'll never be able to fall asleep knowing she's lying next to me. I've never let a woman in my bed. Stella is the first. That's because she's different. We're friends. She's not just some girl. She's so much more.

I don't know how much time passes. I'm certain Stella is asleep. I need to get up and go to Merrick's room, but for some reason, I can't seem to make myself leave. The bed moves, and the next thing I know, Stella is snuggled up to me. Her head is resting on my chest, and her palm on my abs.

Lifting my hand, I run my fingers through her hair. "Stel?" I whisper. She doesn't reply, which means she's asleep. I should have left when I had the chance. I could still, but I won't. Show me a man who has a beautiful woman snuggled up to him and wants to get away from her. Not me. Not when the woman is Stella, my sweet, sexy angel.

Now, I'm certain I'll not be getting any sleep. I close my eyes and try to will myself to slip off into a slumber. My body relaxes into the mattress, and I think maybe I can fall asleep. That is until Stella's hand starts to roam. My eyes pop open. My body is frozen still as her hand trails down to my cock.

"Stel," I croak out her name.

She tosses her leg over mine. Her knee brushes against my cock. My cock that's rock hard for my best friend. I'm probably going to hell for this, but fuck me, I only have so much willpower.

"Stella," I repeat, this time a little louder. I don't want to wake Ada, but her momma, on the other hand, needs to open her eyes. She needs to stop this before we can't.

I tap her shoulder, and her body jolts. Her hand freezes. I'm sure she's embarrassed. Not that she needs to be. If our situation were different, I'd be pinning her to the mattress. "I can't help it," I say in regard to my hard cock. "You're beautiful, Stel."

She lifts her head just slightly to look my way. There's just enough light flowing through the blinds of the bedroom window to see she's wide awake, staring at me, with her hand on my hard cock.

"We could pretend again," she whispers.

"Pretend what, angel?" I know damn well what she's talking about, but I need to hear the words flow from those soft, delicious lips of hers.

"We could pretend that tonight never happened. You know, like before."

"What's not going to happen, Stella?"

"I'm sober."

I should make her say it. I should make her spell it out, but those two words tell me everything I need to know. We're adults. We have needs. It's been so damn long since I've been inside a woman, and Stella, well, it's been since the night she conceived Ada.

"You have to promise me, Stel."

"I promise. I know we're just friends, but it's been so long, and I—need this, Mav."

"Nothing changes. You can't run from me. You can't avoid me."

"Yes, all of that," she says, bending to kiss my abs. Her touch sends a spark shooting throughout my body.

"This is your show, angel. You take as little or as much as you need from me. Tonight, I'm yours."

"I—I don't know how to do this."

"What do you mean?"

"Gah." She drops her head so that her forehead is pressing against my abs. She mumbles something that I don't quite understand.

"You need to tell me, angel."

"Don't want to," she grumbles.

"Then this stops here."

She lifts her head and expels a heavy breath that brushes against my abs. My cock twitches. "One time. I've had sex one time."

Hearing it again still baffles me. She's a fucking smoke show. "One time?" I ask for clarification, worried, I heard her wrong.

"Yeah, and guess what? I'm that cliché that got pregnant. We used protection, but...." Her words trail off.

"Sit up for me." She does as I ask. Kind of. Instead of sitting so that I can see her, she straddles my hips, resting her hands on my chest. So, I sit up, bringing us face-to-face. "I know we're friends, and this isn't going to change that. However, I need to make sure you know that if that were to happen. If our protection fails, and you end up pregnant, I'm going to be there. In fact, I'll be so there that you're going to get sick of me. You can be my friend who's also the mother of my child. I want to be there for every step, every milestone. I promise you, Stella. I'm not him."

I feel anger like a fire roaring with flames at the way her ex has treated her and Ada. How could a man turn his back on his kid? Sure, you're young and not ready, but guess what? You enjoyed the sex, and you knew the chances, asshole. One day, I'll meet him, and I'll be able to tell him exactly what kind of coward he is. Hell, I'm sure he already knows it. He's yet to show his face in Willow River, which is where his baby girl has been for months.

"I know that. I'm on the pill. I was then, too, and we used a condom, but it was just one of those freak things."

"I'm not him." I have to calm myself down. She's not accusing me. Hell, I'm the one who brought it up, but damn that fuckstick for abandoning them. Did he not understand the two treasures he had? They were his, and he let them go.

"You don't need to tell me that, Mav. You've been there for me since the day we met. I was no one to you, but you still helped me. You stuck around, and that means more to me than you will ever know. I just—I've been busy being a mom, trying to keep my head above water. You make me feel safe. Secure."

Warmth fills my chest, and I want to beat against it like a caveman so that I can make her feel that way. My hands cup her cheeks. "This is your night, Stella. You know you're safe with me. Take what you need, with the confidence that I want you to do it, and if that same freak occurrence happens, I'll be there."

Nothing could keep me away from my kid.

"Kiss me."

"My pleasure, angel." I angle her head slightly as I press my lips to hers. She opens for me, giving me her trust. I slide my tongue past those sweet lips and explore her mouth. My hands move to her ass, where I grip her, rocking her against my cock.

"No. Mav, no." I stop immediately. "I want you inside me."

"I'm just getting you ready for me."

"I'm ready for you. Believe me, I'm ready." She moves off my lap and stands next to the bed. I watch with the glow of the moonlight as she tugs my shirt over her head and slides her panties down her creamy thighs. "Ada. We'll have to be quiet."

"Do you want to move?" I don't want to. If this is my only chance to be inside this woman, I want it to be in my bed. A place where no other has been before her. Stella deserves that privilege.

"No. I can be quiet."

An image of her screaming out my name flashes through my head, but that's not where we are. That's not this moment. Not with her daughter sleeping in the same room. It feels a little creepy, but I know it's what parents do. Hell, my brothers have talked about this—being quiet while their kids are sleeping. It's not like Ada is old enough to know what's going on. She will be soon, but right now, tonight, she's not. This is Stella's decision since she's her mom, and she says it's fine, so yeah, this is happening.

"You're wearing too many clothes, Kincaid." She gives me a shy smile.

I raise my hips. "I think I need your help." It's bullshit, and we both know it, but she doesn't call me out on it. Instead, she climbs onto the bed, kneeling next to me. She grabs the waistband of my shorts on either side of my hips and tugs. She tosses them to the floor and then goes back, repeating the process for my boxer briefs.

"Oh," she says when she lays eyes on my bare cock for the first time.

"Still think you're ready?" I ask her. I know what I'm working with, and it's been so long for her. I don't want to hurt her. "Nightstand, top drawer." She again climbs off the bed and opens the drawer, pulling out the unopened box of condoms. "Check the date," I tell her. They've been in there for a while. I'm sure we're okay, but better safe than sorry.

"I can't see." She laughs. "How long ago did you buy these?"

"A while ago. We should be fine, but I'm not risking you, Stel. Use my cell phone for a light."

She uses my cell phone and nods. Dropping the phone back to the nightstand, she pulls out a small foil packet and climbs back on the bed. She hands it to me, but I shake my head. "You can do the honors."

"I've... never done that."

"That's fine. Just try. We have an entire box." Something about being the man she gets to experience this with does something to me. I can't explain what this feeling is. My chest is tight and warm, and I almost feel... possessive of her. She's not mine, but for tonight, she is, and I want her to have this. To take what she needs from a man she knows will stand by her side should something happen.

With shaking hands, she tears open the wrapper and gets to work sheathing my cock. She tosses her leg over mine so that she's straddling my hips. My cock is nestled against her pussy.

"You sure you're ready for me?"

"Stop asking."

I chuckle, holding my hands up in the air. I'm lying back on the pillow while she stares down at me. "This is your show, Stel."

"Then I think it's time we start it." Lifting up on her knees, she palms me and guides me inside her heat.

I grit my teeth at the feel of her tight, wet, warm pussy strangling my cock. This—being inside her—is like nothing I've ever experienced. It's different from every other time. So much so that no other time exists for me except for this one.

"You feel so good," I say, rubbing my hands over her bare thighs.

Her eyes are closed, and her head is tilted back. I watch her in the moonlight; her blonde hair shines. The silky strands almost glow in the dim lighting. "Tell me what you need, Stella."

"I'm so full." Lifting her head, she peers down at me. "I don't know what I need."

"Rock against me." I place my hands on her hips and help her move back and forth. She moans. It's a deep sound that makes me want to lose control. She gains a rocking rhythm, so I move my hands back to her thighs. She lifts and then slowly sinks back down, repeating the process before rocking her hips and then lifting. It's delicious torture.

"You keep fucking me like that, Stel, and I'm gonna come," I warn her.

"Isn't that the point?"

I sit up and wrap my arms around her, capturing her lips with mine. She slows her movements but doesn't stop. When I pull away, I'm out of breath. "I don't come before you do."

"I don't know if I can," she admits shyly.

"Oh, angel, you can. I promise you that." I trail kisses from her jaw down her neck, working my way to her tits. When I capture a hard nipple between my teeth, she squirms, her nails digging into my shoulders.

"Don't stop—that."

I smile as I continue to nip and suck before moving to the other side. Her chest is rising at a rapid pace with each breath she pulls into her lungs. Releasing her tit, I move my lips to hers. She tastes so damn sweet. I could easily become addicted if I allowed myself to do so. My cock throbs. I'm close.

With one hand cupping the back of her neck, controlling the kiss, I slide the other between us. My thumb gently grazes her clit.

"M—Maverick," she pants, pulling out of the kiss. She rests her forehead against mine.

"What's up, angel?" I know exactly what's up. She's about to detonate, and I'm here for it. Her pussy is going crazy. I know she's close.

"I—Th—That. Yes, that." Her hot breath fans against my face, and I want to inhale every inch of her and what she's willing to give me.

"You ready to come for me, Stel? Can you be quiet?"

"I—I don't know if I can," she admits.

"You need my hand?"

She nods, and I place my hand over her mouth. "Rock, baby. Whatever feels good to you, do it. Chase the fire."

She bucks her hips. It's an uncoordinated mess, but it's doing it for her, because her pussy feels like a vise around my cock.

"There you go," I praise. "Good girl." I press my thumb a little harder, and she stills. Her scream is muffled by my hand. She pulls my hand from her mouth as she tries to catch her breath.

"You."

"I'll get mine. That was for you."

"Now, Mav. I need it. I need to feel you. I—I need you to come."

"Put your hand over your mouth," I tell her.

"What? Why?"

"Just trust me." She does as I say and covers her mouth with one hand while bracing the other on my shoulder. Gripping her hips, I flip us over to where I'm hovering over her. I brace my hands on either side of her head. "Ready?"

She nods, her hands still covering her mouth. I don't hold back. I thrust in and out of her like my life depends on it. Over and over, my hips fall into hers as the friction builds between us with each thrust.

I'm close.

So. Fucking. Close.

"Touch yourself," I tell her.

"What?"

"Rub on your clit, Stel. You're going to come again. This time, we're going to do it together."

"Mav—"

"Come on, angel," I coax. She does as I ask, and her back arches off the bed at the first touch. "Good fucking girl," I grit. I keep fucking her, and I feel it the minute she detonates for the second time. I let go, losing myself inside her.

Once we've both caught our breath, I pull out, careful of the condom. "I'll be right back. Don't move." I drop a kiss to her lips, because I need to, before climbing off the bed and rushing toward the bathroom. I take care of the condom and clean up before wetting a warm washcloth to help her do the same.

Back in the room, I climb back into bed. "Spread your legs, angel."

"What? What are you doing?"

"Taking care of you." She does as I ask, and I clean her up before tossing the cloth to the hamper. Reaching for the covers, I pull them around us.

"I should go to Merrick's room," she whispers. "I shouldn't sleep here."

"Stay anyway." I hold her in my arms. "We're just sleeping, Stel."

"Naked."

"What? Can friends not sleep naked?" I tease. She swats at my hand. "It's fine, Stella. We'll get dressed when Ada wakes up, and I'll make you girls breakfast before you go home." I expect her to argue, but to my surprise, she drops it. Good. I'm not ready to let her go just yet. Tonight was out of this world and unexpected. It's a onetime thing. We can't keep letting this happen, so I'm soaking up every ounce of her I can get. That includes holding her naked in my arms while we catch a few hours of sleep.

Stella

"WE'LL BE BACK SUNDAY EVENING," my grandma reminds me.

It's only the tenth time—no exaggeration—she's reminded me of when they'll be home. I smile and nod every time. I love this woman. "I know, Grams. I hope you have a great time."

They're headed off to one of their weekend trips. This time, just two nights. I aspire to be them when I'm their age. So in love with the person you chose to spend your life with, and still taking weekend getaways. Taking the time to escape the hustle and bustle of life and owning their own business.

"Thank you, sweetie." She leans in and kisses my cheek.

"Call us if you need us," my grandpa says, pulling me into a hug.

I wrap my arms around him, hugging him back. "I'll be fine, but I promise." I step out of his embrace. "I'm taking Ada back to Sunflower Park for a picnic. I'll send pictures." I know that will make them feel better about leaving me here alone. Not that I mind. I'm saving as much money as I can to get a place on my own. Not that I don't love living with them, but I want my own space. I want Ada to have her own room too. I've already decided that Willow River is our home. This place and the people who live here have embraced us, and I can't imagine living anywhere else. I can't imagine raising Ada and her growing up anywhere but here.

"Oh, is Maverick going?" Grandpa asks. There's a twinkle in his eye that I ignore.

"No. This weekend is the Kincaid family camping weekend. I guess the entire family goes." I say it almost as if I'm not sure, but I know for a fact that if your last name is Kincaid, you're on that camping trip.

"And you're not going?" Grandma asks.

"I'm not family, Grams. Maverick and I are friends. The ladies and I have become close friends as well, but this is a family-only event." What I don't tell her is that Maverick invited me. He insisted that Ada and I were as close as family as we could get, but I declined. He once told me they never bring anyone to any Kincaid camping trip unless it's a fiancée, wife, or someone they know for sure could be either.

I'm not that person.

Not in Maverick's eyes, no matter how insistent my heart is that I could be that person for him. We're just not there. We've shared some amazing moments. Moments that I will cherish in my heart for the rest of my life, but that's all this is. That's all we are.

Ada and I stand on the front porch, waving goodbye to my grandparents before heading back into the house.

"Well, it's just you and me, kid," I tell my daughter. She wiggles for me to let her down, so I do, watching as she toddles to the basket of toys that sits in the corner of the living room. She dumps that basket out every chance she gets. I feel like I pick it up a hundred times a day. "We're going to work on learning to pick up our toys," I tell her, pointing my finger at her. She shakes her hand at me and babbles. I bite down on my cheek to keep from laughing. I'm trying to be the authority figure, and this kid makes me laugh.

"You light up my life, Ada," I tell her, blowing her a kiss. She smacks her hand against her lips and tosses her hand out, sending the love right back to me.

My heart is full.

I take a seat on the couch while she plays. Jordyn and the other Kincaid ladies have gotten me into reading. I'm reading a new release from Rebel Shaw, and I can't seem to get out of it. I even woke up before Ada today. Instead of going back to sleep, soaking up the extra time, I read instead.

I'm addicted.

I'm just getting into a spicy scene when my phone rings. Carefully marking my page, I set the book down before I pick up my phone. I smile when I see Maverick's name. "Aren't you supposed to be doing family things?" I tease, answering his call.

"We're doing all the family things." He laughs. "What are my girls doing?"

He's been doing that a lot since *that* night—the one where we took things to the highest level, only to get up the next day and act as if the entire night was just a dream. We woke up naked, curled in each other's arms. Maverick acted as though it was no big deal, slipped into some shorts, and grabbed a fussing Ada, telling me to take my time.

"Nothing much. Ada is playing with her toys, and I was reading."

"Anything good?"

"Yeah, it's one that Alyssa and Jordyn suggested."

"So, it's one of those spicy books."

I can feel my face heat. "Yep." I am not ashamed of what I read, but that doesn't mean that I want to discuss it with him. *My friend.* The same friend that I keep crossing all kinds of boundaries with.

"Read me some of it." I can hear the teasing tone of his voice.

"What? No. You should be spending time with your family."

"I'm here. We're getting ready to go on a hike. I still wish you would have come with us."

"Family only, Kincaid. No breaking the rules."

"Whatever," he grumbles. I can clearly see him rolling his eyes in my mind. "Can I talk to Bug?"

"I can try. She's pretty enthralled with her ladybug and the tool set my grandpa bought her."

"Hang up. I'll call back and video chat. If she can see me, she'll be more interested." He sounds excited at the idea.

"You do know she's a one-year-old, right?" I tease.

"Me and Bug are tight. Besides, I know my girls. They want to see me, and I want to see both of them."

Insert racing heart here. "Okay. Call me back." I end the call quickly and blow out a heavy breath. "He's a lot, Ada," I tell my daughter, not that she's listening. Just talking to him has me yearning for what I know we will never be. I need to distance myself from him, but I'm at the point where I'll take Maverick in my life however I can get him. Pathetic, I know, but that's what happens when you feel for someone the way I feel for him.

Before I have a chance to compose myself, my phone rings again, this time with a video call. I answer as I stand from the couch. "Hey, hold on," I tell him.

"Wait."

I stop walking and look at the screen for the first time. "What?"

"There she is." He grins. "I said I wanted to see both of my girls." His eyes are soft as he studies my features.

What do I say to that? That I'd do anything to be his? "Here I am." I smile lamely.

"I see you, angel," he replies, his voice low and gravelly. It's sexy and has my belly quivering.

I ignore him, because what else can I do? Beg him to be mine? I can't do that. "Ada!" I say excitedly. "Do you want to talk to Maverick?" I move to where she's playing and lower to the floor next to her. "Look." I turn the phone so that she can see Maverick.

She giggles and shimmies with excitement as she reaches for the phone. I pull it back out of her reach. "Ma, Ma," she says. She claps her hands and tries again to grab the phone.

"That's right, Bug. It's Mav. How's my girl?" he asks her.

She takes the phone from my hand and kisses the screen. "Ma," she says again.

I laugh. "Are you giving Mav kisses?" I ask her.

"Ma." She pokes her finger at the screen.

"I love your kisses, Bug." Maverick laughs.

I take my phone back, ready for a fight, but she doesn't protest as she stands and leans close to the screen. "I can see your nose hairs, kid," he teases. Not that she understands that. "When I get home, we need to go out for some ice cream," he tells her.

Ada nods. He's taken us out enough for the cold, sweet treat. She knows exactly what ice cream means.

"You're spoiling her, Mav."

"That's my job. To spoil my girls. Right, Bug?"

I hate when he does this. No, that's not entirely true. I don't hate it; I love it just as much as I love him. Yeah, I've gone and fallen in love with my best friend. We met in the most unconventional of ways, but since the very first moment we met, he's been in my corner no matter what the situation. He dotes on my daughter and treats her like she's his own flesh and blood. He made it impossible for me not to fall in love with him. I've known for a while now that this man owns my heart. I tried to fight it, but he made it impossible.

"We should let you go." I pull the phone away, and Ada cries. I lift her into my arms. "Sweetie, Maverick needs to go."

"Ma," she cries.

"Hey, Bug. I promise I'll come and see you as soon as I get home, okay?"

"Ma." Her bottom lip trembles, and her eyes well with tears.

"Aw, you're breaking my heart, Bug. I love you, kiddo. I promise as soon as I get home, I'll come and see you."

"Ma." She continues to cry for him.

"I should let you go so I can calm her down." I'm slightly bouncing her on my hip while holding the phone away so that he can see us.

"Let me know how she is." His voice is sad, and his face shows the same.

"She'll be fine, Mav. Go enjoy your weekend with your family."

He opens his mouth to argue, but I stop him. "Say bye-bye, Ada."

"Bye bye, Ma." She waves, but there are still tears in her eyes. She blows him a kiss. I watch as this incredible man catches it and blows her one right back.

"Bye bye." Maverick waves, and I end the call, cutting them off there. If not, this would go on all day and night.

"Ma, Ma, Ma," Ada cries.

"Hey, it's okay. Maverick will be back tomorrow." They only did a short two-day trip this time because they didn't want to take Blakely out of school for too long. They were considering longer, but Declan and Kennedy decided against taking her out of school for two days. "Do you want to go to the park? We can see the sunflowers," I say with the most enthusiasm I can muster. You'd think I was just told I won a million dollars, but I need her to cheer up.

She whimpers, and I'm at a loss. I eye her ladybug on the floor. Bending down carefully, I grab it and hand it to her. She immediately holds it to her chest and snuggles as she sniffles.

"Want Mommy to rock you?" I ask, already making my way toward the recliner that also rocks. Best and most comfortable rocking chair invention ever.

"Mom, Mom, Ma."

"I know, baby. Maverick misses you so much. He'll be home tomorrow, and he's going to come and see you." Her body shudders as she catches her breath from her tears. Her breaths are shaky, and her chest rises rapidly as she comes down from her tears. My heart is cracked wide open seeing her like this. I'm not the only one who has fallen in love with Maverick Kincaid. I rock her for about fifteen minutes before she's sound asleep. I carry her to our room and place her in her bed just as my phone beeps from the living room. I pick up the baby monitor before pulling the door almost fully closed.

Back in the living room, I grab my phone and see a text from Maverick. Which is exactly who I was expecting it to be.

Maverick: How is she?

Me: Just got her down for a nap

I snap a picture of the baby monitor showing her sleeping in her crib and send it to him.

Maverick:	She broke my heart, Stel. I was ready to come home.
Me:	You can't do that. She's just missing you.
Maverick:	I miss you both so much. You should have come with me.
Me:	What part of family-only weekend are you not grasping? That's breaking the rules, and you know it.
Maverick:	You're family, Stella. You work for Jordyn, you're friends with all of my brothers' wives, and you're my best friend.
Me:	My last name isn't Kincaid.
Maverick:	Neither is Deacon nor Ramsey's.
Me:	Come on now, that's a stretch, and you know it. That's your cousin and her husband.

I send him a string of eye roll emoji. He's being ridiculous.

Maverick:	But she's sad.
Me:	There are a lot of things in life that are going to make her sad. I can't coddle her, and neither can you.
Maverick:	Did you see the tears? You must have missed them.

I can't help but smile. He really does love my little girl.

Me:	I saw the tears. I was the one who dried them. You're there, and we're here. That's the end of it.

Maverick:	Fine. We're heading out in the morning. I should be home around noon. I'm coming straight there.
Me:	Go home, unpack, and get ready for the week.
Maverick:	I'll be there. I'll text you when I'm close. We're going to grab some food and get Ada some ice cream.

I don't want to argue with him because I want to see him. I miss him, and he's only been gone since yesterday morning. He's not mine to miss, but I miss him all the same.

Me:	Fine. I know there's no point in arguing with you.
Maverick:	Nope. Not when it comes to the two of you.
Me:	Go on your hike. Be safe and have fun.
Maverick:	What are you doing tonight?
Me:	Thinking about Sunflower Park. Not certain.
Maverick:	Be safe. Text me when you get home.
Me:	No. You don't need to be worrying about me. You're with your family this weekend. Enjoy this time.
Maverick:	I can still be here and enjoy my family and worry about my girls.
Maverick:	Text me when you get home.
Maverick:	Please.

I smile. Sweet, affectionate, loves kids, and is not afraid to say please. He's going to make some woman very happy one day. Some woman that's not me. I'll be pushed to the side when he finally meets someone, and that thought alone has me easily agreeing. Not that I was going to outright refuse.

Me: Okay.

Maverick: Thank you.

Me: You're welcome. Now. Go. Hike.

Maverick: So bossy.

I don't reply because I know if I do, he'll keep going. He'd sit there all day on his phone with me, and that's defeating the purpose of taking a family trip. Picking up my book, I dive back into the story while Ada sleeps.

I end up falling asleep too. The house was quiet, and I was having a hard time getting lost in the story when my thoughts kept straying to Maverick. By the time Ada and I both wake up, it's pretty close to sunset. We both must have been exhausted. It's too late to go to the park, so I make us some dinner. I make some chicken salad with canned chicken for me, and some mac and cheese for Ada.

We eat together, and I work with Ada on her words. She's talking more and more each day. And by talking, I mean words we can actually understand. "Noodle," I say, pointing to a cheesy noodle on the tray of her high chair. She ignores me and grabs it, shoving it into her mouth.

"That's good stuff, huh?" I ask her.

"Yum."

"That's right. Yum."

When she finishes, I leave the mess for later and take her to the bathroom for her bath. I let her play for close to an hour. She's pruned, and my hands are as well from playing with her. I cherish these moments. Derrick has no idea what he's missing out on.

Once she's changed into her jammies, I carry her back to the living room for a movie to wind down for the night. Realizing I haven't checked my phone, I leave her on the living room floor and go in search of it. I find it in the kitchen. Glancing at the screen, I see seven missed calls from Maverick. My heart falls. Something must have happened. My hands shake as I return his call.

"Stel?" he answers, his voice laced with panic.

"Yeah, it's me. What's wrong?"

"What's wrong? You were supposed to text me when you got home. The sun set an hour ago. I texted you, and no reply. I called, no reply. Are you okay? Ada?"

"I'm sorry. Yes, we're both fine. I didn't mean to scare you. We both fell asleep, and it was too late to go, so we stayed in. I gave her a bath and left my phone in the kitchen. I didn't hear it over the giggles and the splashing water."

"You're okay. You're both okay." It's not a question; it's more of him trying to reassure himself.

"I'm sorry, Maverick. I didn't mean to worry you." My heart squeezes at the fear I hear in his voice.

"She's fine. They're both fine," he tells someone.

"I'm so sorry."

"I just— You didn't call, and when you didn't answer, I panicked. You always answer or get back to me right away."

"We're home. Everything is all good. I promise."

"I need to see. I'm calling you back." He ends the call, and before I have a chance to take a deep breath, it's ringing with a video call.

"Hey, Mav." I smile softly.

"Where's Ada?"

I walk into the living room, where she's crawled onto her beanbag and is watching her movie. "She's okay," I say softly. I turn the phone so that he can see her, but quickly step away. I don't need a repeat of earlier.

I move back far enough I can see her, but hopefully she won't notice I'm on the phone and want to know who it is.

"Fuck. I never want to go through that again."

"I'm sorry," I say again. I don't know what else to say. I didn't do anything wrong, but I still feel like I should apologize.

"You have nothing to be sorry for. It's all on me. I just worry."

"I know you do." This man and his heart.... I swear I don't know how it fits inside his chest. "We're still going to see you tomorrow when you get home, right?"

"Yeah, baby. I'm coming straight to you."

"Okay. Enjoy your last night. We're going to watch a princess movie and go to bed."

"Right. Okay. Stel—" He hesitates. "I'll see you tomorrow."

"See you tomorrow." I end the call and move back to the couch, taking a seat. This time, it's me that's blowing up his phone. I send him a picture every fifteen minutes or so of Ada doing something cute, or of the movie. Just reminding him we're okay. It's all that I know to do to ease his fears.

When I put Ada to bed, I send him a picture of the monitor with a goodnight message.

Me: Night, Mav.

Maverick: Night, angel.

I don't know why he calls me that, but I don't hate it. Climbing into bed, I close my eyes and dream of the man who holds my heart. Not just mine, but my daughter's too.

Maverick

THE WEATHER THIS WEEK HAS been complete shit. I've been rained out three of the five days, today being the third. It worked out, though. Since Merrick was rained out, too, we've been moving him into his new place. He closed on the loan last night, so he and I have spent the day taking everything to his new place.

It's a bittersweet day, but we knew we wouldn't be living together forever. Besides, his place is really nice, and the previous owners had the house professionally cleaned so it was move-in ready. It worked out in his favor that we were both off today. We borrowed an enclosed trailer from Orrin that he uses to haul parts when he needs them. We got everything in one load. He bought new living room furniture, since everything we have was handed down.

"What about the kitchen? You can't eat off nothing but paper plates, bro," I tell him.

"I'll just order what I need online. I hate shopping for that shit. Hell, I hate shopping. Period."

"I'm sure any of our brothers' wives would help you. I could ask Stella too."

"Nah, I'll figure it out. How is Stella?"

I shrug. "Good. She's working today, or I would have roped her into helping us." I laugh.

"I love you, Mav, but you're lying to yourself, brother."

"What are you talking about?"

"Stella. She's not just your friend."

"Yes, she is. Why is that so hard to believe?"

"Do I really need to dumb this down for you?" he asks, as if the mere thought of having to explain himself is exhausting.

"Yeah, I guess you do. Why do you and everyone else keep insisting we're not just friends? Sterling and Alyssa were best friends for years."

Merrick tosses his head back in laughter. "They're married now and having a baby."

"So, that doesn't mean all male and female friendships turn out that way." I truly don't know why they don't get it.

"You smile when you hear her name. When she walks into a room, your eyes light up like they did when we were kids and Santa brought you that BB gun you'd been asking for. You love on her daughter as if she's your own, and when you thought something had happened to her, you freaked the fuck out. That was just last weekend, brother. Have you forgotten already?"

"First of all, of course I'm excited to see my friend. I'm happy that she's settling into Willow River, and I love that she's making friends. As far as her daughter, she's the cutest kid. Bug and I are tight. She's my friend, too, just ask her." I chuckle. "And last weekend, of course I freaked out. She was home alone. We were all away, as were her grandparents. Anyone who could have helped her was out of town. She was supposed to text and didn't. I would worry the same way if it were one of our brothers' wives, or hell, you or one of our brothers. That's what you do for family."

"You're insistent that she's your family."

"Friends can be family, Merrick. You don't have to have the same blood flowing through your veins."

"I agree with you, but this goes beyond that. You're wasting time pretending like she's not the one, Maverick."

"I'm not pretending anything."

"Okay." He raises his hands to ward off my defense. "I'm just trying to help you out. One of these days, it might be too late. I don't want to see that happen to you."

"It's all good, Mer."

He nods. "All right. I'm going to take this trailer back to Orrin's shop."

"I'm going to head on home. I need a shower."

"Yeah, I'm going to stop and grab some essentials from the store. I can't live here without food."

"It's going to be weird, knowing your room is empty, and that you'll never be sleeping there again."

"You can stay here tonight," he offers.

"Nah, this is your new pad. Enjoy it. It's a great place, man. I've been looking too," I confess.

"Yeah? Find anything?"

"No, but I'm not in a rush, but like you, I think it's time."

"It's gotten old, right? The constantly going out and chasing women?"

"Yeah, it really has. I guess our brothers were right. They said we'd grow out of it."

"Let's not go crazy. If we start telling them they were right, we're never going to hear the end of it." He laughs.

"Bet." I nod. "Bring it in, brother." I pull him into a hug, slapping his back. "Proud of you, man."

"Thanks, Mav." He reaches into his pocket and pulls out a handful of keys. "You get yours first. You're always welcome here. No matter what."

"Love harder." I recite half our family motto. We all have keys to each other's places with an open invitation. Even after my brothers were married, their wives were on board with this. Sure, we knock if we think there might be a chance for funny business, but regardless, we know we are always welcome.

Shoving the key into my pocket with a mental note to add it to the keyring in my nightstand that has the keys to my other brothers' houses, I head back toward home. Thankfully, the rain has stopped. It's still a dreary day, and the chances for rain to start again are high, but at the moment, it's just cloudy skies.

As I'm driving through town, I spot Stella's car sitting outside Dorothy's Diner. I forgot she told me she was off work at noon today. She must be getting a late lunch. I find a parking spot down the street, maneuver my truck into it, and head inside to see if she wants some company.

As I'm passing by the window and heading toward the door, I see Stella sitting at a table in the back. I freeze because she's not alone. There's a man, probably around my age, sitting across from her. He reaches across the table and places his hand over hers.

My heart stalls before it begins to beat to the tune of a jackhammer in my chest.

Why is he touching her?

My feet are frozen to the floor. My eyes are locked on the two of them, three of them. Ada is there as well. She's in Stella's arms, holding onto her momma. She doesn't like this man, or maybe it's just that she doesn't know him.

How does Stella know him?

My mind is racing with questions, while my heart feels as if it could explode. I don't understand what's happening inside my body. Seeing her with someone else... it's not sitting well with me. She's sitting across from a man I don't know. He's familiar with her. I can tell from their body language. The only one who's not sure is Ada.

Stella hands Ada to the man over the table, but he shakes his head. Refusing to take her. Ada reaches for Stella, clearly not on board with this man holding her.

My hands ball into fists at my sides.

That's my family.

My chest heaves with each breath I pull into my lungs. My lungs are burning. It physically hurts to breathe, watching the scene before me unfold. The guy reaches for something on the seat next to him. He hands Stella an envelope. They exchange a few words, and Stella shakes her head. I can see the anguish on her face. I don't give a fuck who this guy is to her. He's hurting her. He's hurting my girls.

That has my feet moving.

With each step, I come out of my stupor. As I reach for the door, the guy in question comes rushing out. His shoulder bumps into mine. He doesn't stop or apologize, he just keeps on walking. I turn and watch him as he gets into a black sedan. I think about chasing after him, but he's not important. My girls are what matter right now.

Turning back around, I step into the diner. Stella sits with Ada standing in the booth next to her. Ada is clinging to her momma while Stella's head is bowed. Whatever was in that envelope is opened in front of her, and there are tears rolling down her face.

I slide into the booth, taking the seat he vacated. "Just leave, Derrick," Stella says, not bothering to look up at me.

Derrick.

Ada's sperm donor. Now it's all making sense.

"It's me, angel," I say, keeping my voice low.

At the sound of my voice, both girls look up. Ada reaches for me immediately. "Da Da," she cries, wiggling her arms, wanting me to take her.

Da Da.

If I thought my heart was thundering before, I was wrong. Only this time, it's not worry or anger or jealousy. It's love. Love for this tiny human.

"Stel, can I hold her?" I ask, my voice cracking with emotion. I want to just scoop her up in my arms, but something tells me that I need her momma's permission this time.

"You know you can," Stella replies, wiping at her cheeks. She helps Ada up to the table, and I scoop my girl into my arms, holding her to my chest. She immediately places her head on my shoulder, and I rub her back.

"I got you, Bug."

She whimpers, tucking her body tight into my chest.

"What's going on, Stella?" I can't hide the worry or the emotion in my voice. Ada calling me Da Da, and seeing Stella so upset breaks my heart. I never want my girls to know pain.

My girls.

As I rub Ada's back and wait for an explanation from Stella, it hits me.

Merrick was right. They were all right.

Stella isn't just my friend. She's my fucking heart. The love of my life.

I've placed her in the friend box because the thought of not having her in my life is soul-destroying. I was keeping her at arm's length when I should have been holding her as close as I could. Both of them belong in my arms, with their hands gripping my heart inside my chest. It belongs to them.

"Not here." She's barely holding on to her emotions. Her voice is gritty, and her eyes are welling with more tears.

"Do you have a tab?"

"No. We didn't get that far." She wipes at her cheeks, but more tears continue to fall silently.

I nod, pulling my wallet out and dropping a twenty on the table. "Let's go, baby." I stand with Ada in one arm. I offer my free hand to Stella. She takes my hand and allows me to pull her from the booth. She grabs the papers and shoves them back into the envelope before pushing them into the diaper bag.

I lead them out of the diner and down the street to my truck. This time, I open the passenger door for Stella and wait for her to climb inside. Once she's settled, I lean in and kiss her lips. "I've got you, baby."

Her sad tear-filled eyes find mine, and I vow to give this woman the world.

"Ready to go bye-bye, Bug?" I ask my daughter. That's what she is. She's mine. No one can tell me any different. She chose me, and I chose her back. From this day forward, I'm her father. That's just how it is.

"Da Da, bye-bye."

"That's right, sweetie." I put her in her seat and kiss her cheek before closing the door.

"My car," Stella says.

"It's fine where it is. We can come and get it later, or I'll have my brothers bring it to my place. Right now, we're getting out of here."

She doesn't object.

Reaching over, I lace her fingers with mine. She grips my hand tightly, as if I'm her lifeline, and I want to be. I am her lifeline, and she's mine.

"I'm going to lay her down." I nod toward a sleeping Ada in my arms. I was able to get her out of her car seat without waking her up.

"Okay."

"Get comfortable." I nod toward the couch. "I'll be right back." In my room, I put Ada in her Pack 'N Play. Well, it's not hers, but it might as well be. She's the only one who's used it in recent months. I make sure her ladybug is close. I turn on the monitor and grab the handheld unit, taking it with me to the living room.

"She go down okay?" Stella asks.

"She did." I place the monitor on the coffee table. "You want something to drink? Have you eaten?"

"No, thank you, and yeah, I ate lunch."

"What's going on, Stella?"

"Derrick texted me this morning that he was coming to Willow River to see me. He said he wanted to talk. I thought maybe he was finally coming around, you know? He's her father. He's missing so much. She's this amazing, smart little girl with so much love to give and he's missing all of it. Every day I think about the things he's missing out on. I thought he finally had his shit together." She huffs out a humorless laugh. "I guess he does, just not in the way I had hoped. I really wanted my little girl to have a daddy who loves her."

"She has that."

"What?" She tilts her head to the side in confusion.

"Me, Stella. She has me. You heard her earlier."

"I'm sorry about that."

"I'm not."

"Maverick, my head is a jumbled mess, and I can't process this."

"Then let me help you. I'm her father. The two of you are mine. My girls. She'll never know what it's like to grow up without a male role model in her life. She has nine uncles, because we have to count Deacon." I smile. "And me."

Her bottom lip trembles and it reminds me so much of Ada. "Help me understand."

"I'm fucking this up." I stand and drop to my knees in front of her on the couch. I take her hands in mine, tracing her knuckles with my thumbs while I try to gather my thoughts.

"I'm going to screw this up, but I'm just going to be me for a minute. Bear with me, okay?"

She nods. "Okay."

"I learned something today." She smiles at that. "I saw you with him. Let me back up. I saw your car as I was driving through town, and you know me. I take every opportunity to be with the two of you. So I stopped. As I was walking inside, I saw you with him. I didn't like it."

"What do you mean?"

"I mean, I'm pretty sure I know what a heart attack feels like. I was angry, jealous, envious, confused. I didn't want another man anywhere near my family. Not a man I didn't know. I didn't want another man holding my little girl or putting his hand over my woman's."

I stare down at our joined hands, trying to find the right way to say what I need to say.

How do I make her understand? How do I make this incredible woman fall in love with me? There is no such thing as life without the two of them being mine. It sounds crazy and possessive, but I don't care.

"Maverick?" I can hear the confusion and hope in her voice.

Peering up at her, her big blue eyes are swimming with tears, but inside them I see faith. I latch on to that and tell her exactly what's inside my heart. "I'm in love with you. Not because you're my best friend, but because you live here." I pull one hand away and place it against my chest, over my heart. "You and Ada, this is where you'll stay."

"M—Maverick."

"All this time, I was determined to keep you in this box, as just friends, because the thought of not having you and that little girl in my life hurt too much. So, I did what I thought I needed to do. I kept you close yet still so far away. I should have been gripping you as tightly as I could. I should have held you both close. Without me realizing it, you both slipped over the walls around my heart and made it your own."

"You love us?"

"I do." My admission has her lips pulling up in the corner. "I love both of you with everything that I am."

"I love you too." Her grin is now a full-blown smile.

"Yeah?"

She nods.

"That's good, angel, because I want to build a life with you. I want to be Ada's daddy and give her brothers and sisters to play with."

Her breath hitches. "I want that too. I've loved you for so long. I hid it because I knew that's not how you felt."

"I was too stupid to see it. My brothers tried to tell me. I refused to listen. I wasted so much time."

"No. It gave us time to fall in love. To get to know each other without the pressure of a relationship. I wouldn't change it, Maverick."

There is nothing left to say, so I slide my hand behind her neck and guide her lips to mine. I kiss her with all the love that's been bottled up in my heart. I kiss her until we're both breathless.

I move to the couch and pull her onto my lap. "Now, tell me about Derrick. What did he want?" She tries to move off my lap, but I hold her tight.

"I need to get something. I'll be right back."

Reluctantly, I let her go. She digs around in the diaper bag and pulls out the envelope. I'd forgotten about it. She comes back to the couch, takes her rightful seat on my lap, and hands it to me.

I kiss her shoulder, wrapping an arm around her waist, holding her tightly as I open the letter with my free hand and start to read. With each word, I feel both anger and happiness. Anger that this man could toss that sweet little girl away so easily, but happiness that he's out of our lives. Ada will only ever know me as her father.

"He doesn't know what he's missing," I say, dropping the legal document to the couch that outlines how Derrick is signing away all of his rights to Ada.

"Yeah," Stella whispers.

My mind is all over the place as I process what I just read, but it keeps coming back to one thing. Ada is mine. "Stella?" I wait for her to turn to look at me over her shoulder. "I want to be her daddy."

She stares at me slack-jawed and in shock. When I don't say anything else, a sob falls from her lips. "I love her, Stella. I love you both with an intensity I didn't know I was capable of. It hit me like a ton of bricks when I saw the two of you in that diner today."

"She loves you." Stella turns so that she's straddling my lap. Her arms wrap around my neck, her face burying there as she cries. I hold her tightly, giving her time to let go. I'm here to pick her up when she's ready. "She called you Da Da."

"She did," I say as she lifts her head to look at me. Her face is red and blotchy, and her eyes are red as well.

"That's a big deal, Maverick. I can't just let her call you that or encourage it. Not until I know this is forever."

"Oh, baby, this is forever."

I can see the worry in her eyes. I get it. She's a mom first, and taking care of her little girl and protecting her and her heart are her number one priorities, and I wouldn't have it any other way.

"Marry me."

Her entire body stills. "What?" she murmurs.

"This isn't your official proposal. I know better than that, but consider it a pre-proposal."

She laughs. "That's not a thing."

"This is our life, angel. We make it what we want it. What I want is for you to know that I love you and your daughter. I want you to be my wife and her my daughter. One day in the very near future, I'll ask you the right way. I'll drop to one knee and present you with a ring, but until then, I need you to know that's where this is going for me."

"Maverick." My name is a whisper on her lips.

"I love you. Marry me."

"My pre-proposal answer is yes." Tears swim in her eyes, but her smile tells me another story. Not one of sadness, but one with tears of happiness and love, and our future growing old together.

I whoop out a yell and grip her in a fierce hug. Ada cries over the monitor and I wince. My yell must have woken her up.

"I'll get her." Stella climbs off my lap and heads down the hall to my room to grab her.

"Mom, Mom," Ada sniffles.

"Hey, sweetheart. Did we wake you up?" Stella asks softly. Her voice trails off, so I know they're on the way back to the living room.

"Hey, Bug," I say when they get close.

"Da Da," Ada says. She doesn't reach for me, but that's okay. Her tiny hands are already gripping my heart.

"I'm sorry I woke you up. Mommy made me very happy," I explain.

Stella sits on the couch next to me, and I snuggle my girls close. This is my future, and I can't fucking wait to see what comes next.

Chapter 18

Stella

S O MUCH HAS CHANGED FOR Ada and me in the last week. Last Friday, Derrick dropped a bomb on me. In a way, so did Maverick. He loves us. I knew that, but I didn't know it went as deep as it does. It's been eight days, and he's never let a single one pass without telling us both. He's Da Da to Ada now. His face lights up every single time she says it.

I will forever be grateful for whatever higher power put this man in my path that day, or us into his, however you want to look at it. Maverick calls me angel, but let's be honest, he's our angel.

As far as Derrick goes, the document was legit. Maverick and I took it to Deacon, and he confirmed. Derrick has no rights where Ada is concerned. I feel sorry for him. He's missing out on knowing and loving the most amazing little girl. I think that one day, he's going to realize what he gave away so carelessly.

Then again, maybe he won't.

He should really look into having a vasectomy if he's so dead set against not having kids. It's not like I planned to get pregnant. It was my first time. I was covered. At least, I thought we were. All I know is that it was meant to be for me to be her mother, and if I'm being honest, I think it was meant to be that Ada and I ended up in Willow River as well.

This is where we found our family. This is where we belong. Even before Maverick turned my world upside down with his confession of love, I knew Willow River was home for us.

Turning off the light in the bathroom, I make my way down the hall to find Maverick and Ada. We're going to Orion's third birthday party today at Kincaid Central. I'm nervous because, as far as I am aware, his family doesn't know about us. Merrick moved out. He's been busy unpacking his new place.

My grandparents know. It's pretty obvious, considering I've spent every night here since the day he told me he loved me. Maverick was insistent his girls stay with him. I wasn't strong enough to say no. We've not technically moved in yet; we just keep bringing more stuff over and spending the night.

"We need to tell Mommy it's time to bring your bed home," Maverick is telling Ada.

I stop in the hallway so that I can listen in on their one-sided conversation.

"You have your own room here. It was Uncle Merrick's when he lived here, and now it's yours. Well, until Mommy and I find a bigger place. We need to have room for your brothers and sisters."

My smile is so big that I feel as though my face might crack. I love this man with everything inside me. I never knew love like this existed. It's the kind of love I read about. A man who is not afraid to show or tell how much he loves his lady, and in my case, his lady and her daughter.

Ada will grow up knowing what it's like to have two parents who love her to the ends of the earth, and that has tears burning in my eyes. I don't have time to cry or for my face to get red and blotchy. We have a birthday party to get to.

Inhaling a big breath, I slowly exhale and step into the living room.

"Are we ready?" I ask in a cheery voice.

"We're ready, right, Bug?" Maverick asks Ada. She's sitting on the floor at his feet, where he sits on the couch, playing with a truck he insisted she needed when we went to the grocery store last night. I didn't bother arguing with him. He probably would have just kissed me to shut me up—not that that's a bad thing. Damn, I should have complained.

"Let me double-check the diaper bag."

"Already done. We have extra diapers, wipes, toys, outfits, and a sippy cup full of milk. There are snacks in there, too, not that we'll need either one of those. We keep Kincaid Central stocked for the adults and the kids."

"Right. Okay. Oh, the gift."

"Already out in the truck."

"You're pretty handy to have around, you know that?" I tease.

He stands and slides his arm around my waist, his lips finding mine. "Good. That means you'll never leave me."

"I would never, Mav."

"I know." He smirks and kisses me again.

"Da Da." Ada stands and pulls at his jeans.

"Are you jealous, Bug?" he asks. "Come here." He bends and lifts her over his head. Her giggles fill the room. "Daddy's got lovin' for you too." He settles her on his hip and kisses her cheek. "Let's get your coat on so we can go to a birthday party."

Just from the tone of his voice, Ada knows something big is about to happen. She smiles and claps her hands.

"Two peas in a pod." I smile and shake my head at their antics.

"You expected anything less?" Maverick grins.

"Come on, you two." I slip into my jacket while Maverick wrestles Ada into hers and toss the diaper bag over my shoulder. I follow them out to the truck, making sure to lock the door behind me.

"Do they know?" I ask Maverick once we're on the road.

"Does who know what?" he asks.

"Your family. Do they know about us? That we're together?"

"Not officially. They all knew before I did." He brings our joined hands to his lips and kisses my knuckles.

"So... today?"

He glances over quickly before putting his eyes back on the road. "Today is just like any other day. We're going to my nephew's birthday party. I'll walk in there with my girls at my side. My family will accept that."

"I want them to be okay with this. With us. I work for Jordyn, and I love your family, every single one of them."

"Stella, angel, they already love you. You and our girl. Today is just them getting validation that they've been right this entire time. My brothers tried to tell me. My sisters-in-law kept giving me knowing looks. They expect this. They just expected it sooner. It took me a while to pull my head out of my a–behind," he corrects himself, glancing in the rearview mirror at Ada.

"I'm glad they were right."

He pulls into the lot and turns off the engine before he turns to me. "Me too, baby. Me too." He leans over, kissing me quickly.

"I'll grab our girl. Bug, are you ready to party?" he asks as he pushes open his door.

"I'll get the gift and the diaper bag." I smile as I speak. Life with Maverick will always be fun. There will be tough moments, but there is no doubt in my mind that this man will fight through each one of them with me.

Maverick pulls the door open and motions for me to walk in before him. I do, standing off to the side, waiting for him and Ada to join me.

"Hey, family!" he calls out.

Everyone stops and turns to face him. He links his arm around my waist, pulling me into his side. I move my arm behind him so Orion's gift doesn't get smashed.

"What's going on, Mav?" Merrick asks.

"I wasn't sure if y'all had met my future wife and my daughter?"

"It's about da—darn time!" Merrick rushes us. I step away so he can hug his brother, but to my surprise, I'm the one he wraps his arms around. "I knew he was in love with you," he whispers, just for me.

"Give me my granddaughter." Raymond takes Ada from Maverick and tosses a wink at me over his shoulder.

"Just like that?" I ask Maverick.

"Yeah, angel. Just like that." He takes my hand in his and pulls me into the crowd. We get hugs and slaps on the back with congratulations from his family.

"You've been holding out on me. All week!" Jordyn says, wrapping me in a hug.

"I'm sorry. I wasn't sure how we were handling this, and so much has happened."

"I need to hear it all." She gives me a pointed look.

"I promise. I won't leave out a single detail."

She points her index finger at me. "I'm watching you."

I laugh and nod, letting her know I intend to keep my promise.

"Hey," Alyssa says, taking a seat next to me at the table.

"Hi. How are you feeling?"

She rubs at her pregnant belly. "Excited." Her grin is infectious. "I've wanted this for so long, but I don't have to tell you what it's like to be in love with your best friend."

"You have a lifetime of friendship with Sterling," I remind her.

"Yeah, but he was still my best friend, and I fell in love with him." She shrugs as if the timeline of friendship makes no difference. Maybe it doesn't. What do I know?

She glances across the room where Sterling is holding Ada. He keeps offering her to Maverick and pulling her away. She laughs every time he does it.

"He's good with her."

"Yeah, they're all great dads."

"They are," I agree.

"So, I wanted to run something past you."

"Okay."

"Why don't you let Ada stay with us tonight? We could use the practice."

I chuckle. "Look around, Alyssa. I think you and Sterling are going to be just fine."

"Okay, then let us keep her so that you and Maverick can have some time together."

"Oh." I can feel my face heat. I'm a grown woman. This conversation shouldn't affect me.

"You don't need to do that."

"I know we don't. In fact, Sterling doesn't even know that I'm offering. Not that he'll mind. Look, I know what it's like to be in your shoes. To have the man you love finally love you back. Let us take her. Give you and Mav a night to... connect." She wags her eyebrows.

"Really, that's not necessary."

"Maybe not, but we'd like to do it, anyway."

"I've never been away from her overnight."

"We're family, Stella. I promise you she's in good hands. I can't promise you she won't be spoiled by the time my husband gives her back to you, though."

"That's a daily thing with Mav."

"Talk to Maverick, see what he thinks. The offer is open. Not just tonight, but anytime. You need a sitter, need a mom break, some kid-free sexy time, or for whatever reason, you know that you can call any of us, and we'll be happy to help."

"Thank you." I'm getting choked up, and I swallow back the emotion.

"Anytime. Go talk to your man and let me know. We'd love to have her." She stands and walks away.

I'm so lost in thought that I don't notice Maverick taking the seat she just left.

"What's going on?"

"What makes you think something is going on?"

"I know my wife."

I smile. "Not your wife." I hold up my bare ring finger.

"I'm going to fix that, but first, tell me what's wrong."

"Nothing is wrong. Alyssa and I were just chatting. She actually offered to keep Ada tonight to give us some time alone."

"That was nice of her."

"She told me to talk to you about it and let her know."

"How do you feel about it?"

"I've never left her overnight."

"Then we won't."

"But I know that's not realistic. I know she'll be safe with them. They're your family."

"Our family," he corrects me.

"What are you thinking?"

"I'm thinking that I don't have a strong preference either way. I'm still going to be buried balls deep inside your pussy when we get home later."

"Mav!"

He laughs. "Really, angel, I'm deferring to you on this. If you're not ready, that's okay. She's our daughter." He shrugs. "She should be with us, but I also know that her aunts and uncles want to spend time with her. As the kids get older, I'm sure they're going to be asking for sleepovers."

"I'm sure."

He leans in and presses his lips to mine. "Your call, Stel."

"While I appreciate the offer, I don't want to confuse her. We went from staying at my grandparents' place to staying at yours. Maybe next time?"

"Yeah, that way she'll be used to the fact that my place is home."

"What?"

"The two of you are moving in. We'll work on finding our forever home to raise our family, but for now, you're moving in. In the meantime, Merrick's old room will be Ada's."

"Are you sure that you want us to move in with you?" I don't know why I ask. I know the answer. I guess old habits die hard.

He laughs. Not just ha-ha funny, but full-on belly-shaking, head-tilted-back laughter. "Yeah, angel, I want my girls to move in with me. What do you think this week has been?"

I shrug. "I don't know. New relationship getting acquainted and stuff?"

"Nope. You're moving in. We'll go tell your grandparents tomorrow, or tonight when we leave here if you want."

This is my future. I'll never question his intentions again. Maverick and I are forever, and I'm ready to start our future together. "Tomorrow is fine. I kinda want that other thing you mentioned tonight."

"What's that?" He smirks. He leans closer, placing his lips next to my ear. "You want my cock buried balls deep in that pussy?"

I cross my legs to alleviate the ache between my thighs from his words. "Yes. That."

"Anything you want, angel."

I thank Alyssa and Sterling for the offer and explain my reasoning, reassuring them that I know my daughter would be safe and well cared for with them. We say goodbye to the birthday boy and head home.

Home.

Maverick Kincaid is my home.

"She's sound asleep," I say, climbing into bed beside Maverick. "I think she was happy to be back in her bed."

"We should have moved it over here last weekend."

"She's been sleeping fine. It helps that she played so hard today."

"Yeah, she's got some rowdy cousins."

"They're all great kids."

"I know, but that doesn't mean they're not rowdy. It's our fault. We all corrupted Blakely. Now she's the leader of the pack as the oldest."

"Stop." I push at his shoulder, snuggling further beneath the covers.

"Hey, I only speak the truth, and why are you so far away?"

"This is a big-ass bed, Kincaid."

"Poor excuse," he grumbles. Instead of moving me next to him, he comes to me, wrapping me in his arms, throwing his leg over mine. "Much better."

"And here all along you've been saying that Ada was the snuggle bug."

"I only snuggle with my girls, and my nieces and nephews. No other snuggling going on here." As he says the words, he slides his hand under his T-shirt that I'm wearing. I've discovered that I love sleeping in them. They're big and comfortable, and they smell like him. "I've got a promise to keep," he says, slipping his hand beneath the waistband of my panties.

"I love your promises."

"These are in the way." The next thing I know, he's tugging my panties over my thighs and tossing them over his shoulder. "Now, I can feast." He drops down and buries his face between my thighs.

I comb my hands in his hair, holding on for the ride that I know he's going to take me on. Every night since last Friday, he's done this. He gets his fill, then makes slow love to me. I love that, but I want him unhinged. Like our first night together. I love when he's slow and tender, but I want all sides of him, and tonight I intend to take what I need from him.

He slides a digit inside while his mouth clamps down over my clit, and I bite down on my bottom lip to muffle my cry of ecstasy.

I'm struggling to catch my breath, but I know I need to move. Rolling over, I settle on all fours and look over my shoulder at him. "I need more."

He grins. "My girl wants to play."

"I love everything we've done together, but tonight, I need more. I need it all."

"Say no more, future Mrs. Kincaid." He grips my hips and pulls my ass into his crotch. I can feel his hard cock. I rock my hips, needing him. "I need a condom, minx." He smacks my ass, and I let out a low groan of satisfaction. "This is going to be fast, Stel. I want you so much, and with this fine ass offered to me, I can't hold back."

"You've been holding back."

"Making love to you isn't holding back. I wanted to give you the sweet. I know your experience is limited. I wanted to give you time to decide what you want."

"This is what I want. Now. Please."

"Grip the pillow, face down." I do as he says. I hear the wrapper of the condom tear, and then he's there, the head of his hard cock pushing inside me. "Fuck, Stel." He doesn't stop until he's fully seated his hips resting against my ass.

"I'm gonna fuck you now, angel. Just remember when I'm fucking you, I'm also loving you." With that, he pulls back and slams back in. I hold on tightly to the pillow and take everything he's giving me.

Each thrust grows harder. Faster. His grip on my hips is so tight, it's painful, and I love it. I love knowing I'm the reason he's losing control.

Tingles race down my spine, and I know I'm close. With each stroke, the sensation of release draws near. I bury my face in the pillow and let out a scream as the most intense orgasm of my life takes control of my body. Wave after wave of powerful pleasure rolls through my body. My pussy is throbbing.

"There she is," Maverick pants. "My good girl." His hips buck, and then he stills. He grunts as he leans over, resting his chest against my back.

"I love you," he whispers huskily.

"I love you too," I pant. "I love you" doesn't seem like enough, but I don't know how else to declare what he means to me. This man is my soul.

He moves away and I miss the heat of his body wrapped around mine. "I'll be right back."

I flop back on the bed. I know he's going to take care of me, because that's who he is. It's what he likes to do, and I love him for that reason and so many more.

Sure enough, a few moments later, he's tapping my knee, placing a warm cloth over me, cleaning me up as best he can before climbing into bed next to me. He wraps me in his arms, one of his legs thrown over mine.

I fall asleep cuddled by my man with a smile on my face.

Maverick

I T'S BEEN A LITTLE OVER two months since the day I realized that Stella and Ada were my future. Ten weeks of coming home to them after a long day, and now that I'm laid off, I spend all day with my daughter, and greet my wife when she gets home from work.

I love every fucking minute of it.

There is only one thing I would change, and that's their last names. I want to adopt Ada. I want her to be mine, not only in my heart but in the eyes of the law. I want them both tied to me in all ways possible.

They are my family.

"I think that's it," Stella says. She's been digging presents for the nieces and nephews out from under our Christmas tree for the last half hour. "There are still a lot of presents under that tree." She gives me a pointed look.

"What? She doesn't know about S-a-n-t-a yet." I spell out the name, making Stella laugh.

"Maverick. Our house is too small for all of this. Her room is already bursting at the seams."

"Well, it's a good thing we're buying a bigger place." We found a house we both fell in love with. It's just down the road from Orrin and Jade, which will be nice to be so close to family. What my future bride doesn't know is that I signed the papers last week, and got the keys. The owners gave us immediate occupancy. It took some effort and a lot of help from my brothers, but I'm about to pull off some major surprises for my girls.

"That's not the point, Kincaid." She sighs heavily.

"Daddy's gotta spoil his little girl. It's in the dad contract."

"What dad contract?"

"Oh, it's top-secret stuff. Only dads know about it."

"Then why are you telling me about it?" She's barely containing her laughter.

"Because I love you, and I tell you everything." I lean down and press my lips to hers. "I'll get these loaded in the van."

"I never thought I'd see the day when Maverick Kincaid drove a minivan."

"I'm a family man. Ain't no shame in my game, Stel. I make that minivan look damn good."

She grins and shakes her head.

Last month, I finally convinced her it was time for a new car. We both want more kids, and hers wasn't going to last much longer. I did the best that I could, having my brother make it as safe as possible, but she was long overdue. I tried to get her to buy an SUV, but she said that a minivan made more sense with all the kids in the family, and the ones we want to have.

I relented when we found the Honda Odyssey. This thing is sweet. A good sound system, all-wheel drive, automatic doors, and even a vacuum for messes the kids make. I was sold, and now, here I am, a minivan dad and living my best life.

Hitting the automatic back gate button on the key fob, I start loading the presents. I remember the days when it was just Blakely. Our family is rapidly growing, and I love it. I know my parents are thrilled as well. They got Ada this year, and Alyssa and Jordyn are both expecting. I'm sure they won't be the only ones. It seems like someone in the family is always pregnant these days.

It takes me two more trips to get all of the gifts loaded. "The car's warm," I tell Stella.

"Okay. Let me wrangle Ada into her coat, and we'll head out."

"I'll get her. Just grab the diaper bag, and I'll meet you out there."

"Okay." She picks up the diaper bag and stops. I know she's mentally going through her checklist to make sure she's remembered to pack extra everything. Stella is always prepared. "The fudge."

"Already in the van. I put it on the floorboard of the back seat."

"Thanks, babe." She tilts her head up for a kiss, and I oblige her. There will never be a time when I will refuse to kiss this woman. I don't care where we are or who is around to witness.

Once she's bundled up and out the door, I scoop Ada up in my arms, and we race down the hall to her room. I quickly change her into the outfit I hid in her closet. I pat my pocket, making sure I have what I need, before making funny faces at her while getting her into her coat. I rush to the door, making sure it's locked before acting like nothing happened and loading her into her seat.

"Ready?" I ask Stella, sliding behind the wheel.

"Yeah." Her eyes are sparkling with happiness. "I always wanted a big family Christmas."

"You're about to get that and more, angel."

"I'm ready for all of it."

If she only knew.

Walking up behind Stella, I wrap my arms around her waist, resting my chin on her shoulder.

"Today has been everything, Maverick." She turns to glance at me. "I can't believe my grandparents are here."

"They're family."

"I love you." Her voice cracks.

"I love you too." It's time. I wait for the nerves to take over, but nothing. My heart is not even racing. That's because I know we're solid. I know she's going to love her gifts, and I know that this is the first of many Christmases we're going to spend just like this. Who knows? Maybe next year, Ada will have a sibling to open presents with.

"I have some presents for you."

"What? I thought we were going to open gifts at home tomorrow."

"We are. But I have some with me today too."

"Maverick! That's not fair. I didn't bring yours."

"I know, angel. That's how I wanted it to happen." I pull away from her, taking her hand in mine and leading her toward the massive Christmas tree in the corner of the room. Jordyn and Ramsey went a little crazy with the décor, but even I can admit this place looks incredible. The kids were all wide-eyed at the massive tree.

"Open this one first." I hand her a small box that I hid under the tree yesterday. I haven't told anyone in my family about my plans for tonight. My brothers think all the action will come when we leave here tonight.

"Thank you." She leans up and kisses my cheek.

"Babe, you haven't even opened it yet. You might hate it."

"I could never hate anything you give me." She looks down at the box. "It's too pretty to open."

"Just open it, Stel."

"Okay." She's smiling as she carefully removes the bow and then the paper. When she pulls the lid off the small box, her breath hitches. "Maverick, it's beautiful."

I take the box from her hands and pull the necklace out of the box. "This key represents the key to my heart. You are the sole owner." I nod for her to turn around, and she does.

"Diamonds. Maverick, this is too much."

"Nothing will ever be too much when it comes to showing you how much I love you."

"Stop. You can't make me cry with everyone here." She turns her back to the crowd that's still not paying us a bit of attention. Apparently, we're old news now that we're officially a couple.

"Okay. The next one." I dig behind the tree and find the second box I hid. It's similar in size to the first.

"The necklace is more than enough."

"Not even close, angel. Open it."

She nods and carefully unwraps this box the same way she did the first. When she opens it, she finds another key, this time a real one.

"What's this?"

"That is the key to our new home. I closed on it last week. This key is the key to our forever." I wrap my arms around her waist. "You have the key to my heart and the key to our forever. Basically, you have everything I am in the palm of your hands, well, minus our daughter, who's busy playing with her cousins."

Her eyes well with tears. "This is to the house?"

"Yeah. I wanted to surprise you."

"Maverick." She shakes her head, the emotion too much. "This is like a fairy tale." She offers me a watery smile.

"Not quite, but it's our story."

"Thank you for my gifts. Thank you for choosing us."

"You have one more gift."

"Maverick, no. This is already way too much."

"Technically, the house is for all three of us. That's not much of a gift."

"You gave me your forever, Maverick Kincaid. That's a big damn deal."

"Well, then, let me give you your last one."

She shakes her head. The smile playing on her lips tells me she's happy. That's all I ever want, for my girls to be happy. "I know you well enough to know arguing won't do me any good."

"You're learning, angel," I tease. I drop a kiss on her forehead. "Stay here. I want our girl to be here for this one." I turn and stalk toward Rushton, who's holding Ada. "Hey, Bug." Her face lights up.

"Dad, Dad," she calls out as she reaches for me.

I take her from my brother and kiss her cheek. "It's showtime," I tell my daughter.

"Wait." Rushton's mouth drops open. "Does that mean what I think it means?"

"Yeah, I'm doing it here."

Rushton grins. "I'll spread the word." He moves to start telling our family quietly what's about to go down.

"Okay, Ada, this is what we talked about. I'm going to take your sweater off so that Mommy can read your shirt. We're going to ask if she will marry me so that I can be your daddy in every way. You still on board, kid?" I ask her.

"Dad." She gives me a sloppy kiss.

"That's my girl." I slow my steps, giving Rushton and the rest of the family time to clue in to what's going on. I pause and pull off Ada's sweater. I toss it over the back of the couch and grin when I read what it says. Thankfully, Stella is talking to Crosby. I know she beelined it over to Stella to offer a distraction. I love my family.

Work hard. Love harder. We're damn good at both.

"There's Mommy," I tell Ada once we reach Stella.

"Hey, sweetie." Ada reaches for her mom, and Stella takes her into her arms. "You having a good day?" she asks.

Ada pulls at her shirt.

I watch as Stella realizes our daughter is in nothing but a thin long-sleeve onesie and that the cute Christmas sweater she was wearing when we arrived is now nowhere to be found. I watch as her eyes read the words I have memorized.

Mommy, marry Daddy so we can all have the same last name. It's the best I could come up with. I started to say something about adoption, but she's mine no matter what the law says. I went with changing the last name instead, capturing both of my girls at once.

Pulling the ring out of my pocket, I fall to one knee. My heart is beating steadily, my hands aren't sweating, and I couldn't care less about the audience surrounding us.

All that matters at the moment are my girls.

"Maverick." Stella's voice breaks as she tears her eyes away from Ada's shirt. Her gaze seeks me out, but all she finds is our family standing by waiting with bated breath for me to ask her.

"I love my girls," I say, my voice loud and clear. I want the world to know what these two mean to me. "I want forever with both of you. You have the key to my heart. You have the key to our forever, and you are literally holding a piece of my heart in your hands at this very moment. Stella, will you do me the incredible honor of taking my last name? I want to be Ada's daddy in the eyes of the law, and I want to be your husband. Will you marry me?"

She's nodding before I'm finished with my speech that I've practiced over and over for the last several weeks. "Yes." Tears rush down her cheeks.

"No cwy," Ada says, her voice showing she's starting to get upset.

I stand quickly, slide the ring on Stella's finger, and kiss the hell out of her, wrapping my arms around both of them. The room erupts in cheers and Stella laughs.

"We did it, Bug. Mommy said yes." I take our daughter from her mother and lift her into the air over my head. She giggles, and the sound fills my soul.

I get it now. I get how my brothers have altered their world for their wives and kids. This feeling, knowing they're mine forever. It's overwhelming and the most amazing rush I've ever felt in my life.

My family.

We're swarmed by her grandparents and my side of the family for hugs, handshakes, and congratulations. My mom takes Ada and puts her sweater back on her. It's perfectly warm in the room, but that's what moms do. They worry and fuss. As a new dad, I'm learning that I do a lot of that too.

We spend another couple of hours with the family. When all the kids start to get tuckered out, we all start loading up to head home because Santa is coming tonight. Once we're loaded up in the van, we head home, but not the home we left to come here. Our new home.

"Oh, are we driving by the new house?" Stella asks. She shimmies in her seat, and I can feel the excitement rolling off her in waves.

"Yeah." It's not a lie. We are driving by. We're also stopping, but she'll find that out soon enough.

Ten minutes later, we're pulling into our new driveway. I hit the garage door opener on the van and pull inside.

"Are we going in?" Stella asks.

"Yeah, I thought we might as well check it out."

"Eep!" She rushes to remove her seat belt and climbs out of the van.

I take my time and grab Ada, who fell asleep on the drive. "Go on in," I tell Stella. I follow along behind her. When we get inside, I hit the lights, and she walks around the kitchen. I leave her there to move to the living room. I hit the switch for the gas fireplace, and the one next to it that turns on the outlet the Christmas tree is plugged into.

"What?" Stella turns to look where the lights are coming from.

The house is an open concept. The living room, kitchen, and dining room are one huge area, so there was definitely no hiding the lights. At least she hasn't noticed the tree until now.

"Merry Christmas, angel."

She peers around the room. She eyes the air mattress on the floor, covered with blankets. "When did you do this?"

"I had some help. My brothers helped me make it happen."

"Maverick, this is perfect. Wait, are we staying here tonight?"

"Yeah, I thought we could have a little family campout by the light of the fire and the Christmas tree."

"What about the gifts under the tree at home?" She worries her bottom lip.

As if the house is bugged, and he knows it's his cue, headlights hit the living room window. "Like I said, I had some help."

A few minutes later, Merrick knocks on the door. He's got a huge box in his hand when he steps inside. "Ho, ho, ho," he sings.

"Really? Merrick Kincaid, I love you." Stella rushes to him and gives him a side hug before he has a chance to set the box of gifts down.

"Um, Stel, I think you have the wrong brother." He grins down at her.

"Stop." She laughs, swatting his arm playfully.

"That's my twin, baby. In case you needed a reminder." I lay Ada down on the air mattress. "I'm going to get another load."

When I make it back inside the house, Merrick is unloading his box of gifts under the tree. I do the same, and my heart feels so full it might actually burst from the love overflowing inside me.

"Thank you, Mer." I feel myself getting choked up just a little.

My twin pulls me into a hug. "Love you, Mav." He steps away and taps his chest. He doesn't need to say it for me to understand. He feels it. He can feel the love inside my heart for my family, not just Stella and Ada, but for my brothers, their wives, kids, and our parents. I'm so fucking lucky. It's a scary twin thing that we don't talk about much, but it's there, and I can see it in his eyes. He feels it.

"Your day is coming, Mer."

He nods. "I'm looking forward to it." With that, he hugs Stella, bends and kisses Ada on the head as she's sleeping, and leaves us to enjoy our first night and our first Christmas in our new home.

Stella

"WHAT DO YOU MEAN, IT'S our engagement party? We've only been officially engaged for a week." My hands are on my hips as I process what my fiancé just told me. We're headed to Kincaid Central later tonight to celebrate New Year's Eve with the family, but apparently, it's also doubling as our engagement party.

Maverick shrugs. "I knew you were going to say yes. We did a pre-proposal, remember? It's just low-key, Stel, nothing to worry about." He's acting as if this is no big deal, but it's a big deal. He planned a party for us.

I love the way he loves me. The way he loves us.

Nothing this man does is low-key. "I remember, Mav, but an engagement party? Really? We already live together. Is this really necessary?" I already know he's going to say that it's absolutely necessary.

I try to hide my grin. This is what life is going to be like with Maverick, and I'm here for it. All of it. Every over-the-top thing he wants to toss my way, I'm all in.

"It's absolutely necessary." He's nodding, a look of sheer determination on his face. He thinks he has to convince me, but I'm already convinced. If Maverick is there, so am I. It's as simple as that.

Brooks sits in the recliner, his body shaking with quiet laughter.

"What? Don't tell me you agree with him?" I ask my future brother-in-law. He stopped by to help Maverick move some shelving from the old house to this one. We're pretty much fully moved. The garage shelving was the last missing piece. It's been a busy week, but I admit it's nice to have so much family that's more than willing to jump in and help us. They're better than any moving company. Hands-down.

The day after Christmas, the family arrived with boxes, rolls of tape, and, as Blakely reminded me, arm porn to do the heavy lifting. We were packed and moved out the same day. All hands on deck. We had beds put together and rooms roughly set up by the time we went to bed that night.

"This guy—" Brooks points at Maverick, trying to compose himself through his laughter, "—once said he wasn't ever going to have an engagement party." He smiles at his little brother. "Changes things, doesn't it?" he says to Maverick.

Maverick nods, a serious expression on his face. "I didn't understand it then."

"Understand what?"

Maverick turns toward me, and his eyes soften. "Love, angel. I didn't understand that when you find your forever, you do anything you can think of to put a smile on her face." He looks like he wants to say more, but a rambunctious little girl interrupts him.

"Daddy!" Ada comes running toward Maverick, carrying her beloved ladybug.

He lifts her into his arms. "Have you been good for Mommy?" he asks.

She nods. "Good." She offers the ladybug to him, and he kisses it just like he always does.

"Ada, come see Uncle Brooks before I have to leave." Maverick hands her over, and Brooks tickles her sides as she squirms on his lap. "Are you ready for the party tonight? All your aunts, uncles, and cousins will be there, and Grandma and Grandpa."

His family has not only accepted me, but Ada too. They treat her just like all the other Kincaid grandkids. To them, and to us, she's Maverick's daughter. That's enough for them. If anything, they might love on her a little harder than the others just to show me and Maverick that she's one of them. That we both are. I've never felt so loved.

There was a time in my life when I felt like it would just be Ada and me. My parents want nothing to do with me. To them, I ruined my life. To me, I enhanced it. Being her mom is the greatest thing I've ever done.

"Par-tay." Ada nods, mimicking Brooks. She's been doing a lot more of that lately.

"That's right." Brooks hugs her tightly. "I'll see you later, kiddo." He puts her on her feet, and she scurries to the corner of the living room where her play kitchen set is, which Santa brought her. By Santa, I mean her daddy, who didn't even tell me he was getting it for her. I woke up on Christmas morning, and it was just there, sitting next to the tree.

This man, he goes out of his way to spoil us, to see the smiles on our faces. I'll never be able to love him enough for everything he's given us, but I'm going to try for every day of forever.

"You better put on your par-tay shoes, Momma," Brooks tells me, saying party like Ada did. He's smirking.

All I can do is shake my head and smile. "We'll be there," I tell him. Even if it wasn't also my engagement party, we would be there. Family is everything. I know what it's like to be a part of one that never wanted you, so you can bet your ass I'm going to be present in the one that chose me.

"Humor him," Brooks says, his voice low only for me. "He's really excited."

"I know. I am, too, but hijacking the family party?"

"Kills two birds with one stone. We'd all be at both, regardless." He hugs me and calls out his goodbye to Maverick and Ada.

"Are you mad?" Maverick asks from where he's sitting on the floor, pretending to eat a plastic banana that Ada handed him.

How can I ever be mad at this man? "No. I'm not mad. I just feel bad we're taking over the New Year's celebration."

Maverick shrugs. "They'd all be at both, regardless."

I smile when he recites Brooks's earlier words to me. "Yeah," I agree. Looks like I have an engagement party to get ready for.

"Wow," I say, walking into Kincaid Central. The entire place is decorated. There are enlarged pictures of Maverick, Ada, and me, some with his family and some just the three of us. There are also a few from our first trip to Sunflower Park. There are fairy lights strung overhead and so many other decorations I can't take them all in at once.

"When did you get these pictures blown up?"

"Oh, that was Sterling. He did something similar with Alyssa, and they thought it would be a nice touch."

"It's perfect." He leads me to a table with desserts. There's a cake decorated in black and gold with a topper that reads, *Kiss me at midnight*. There are cupcakes decorated in gold and black as well. Some have plastic wedding rings; some have miniature black top hats that say *Happy New Year*. There are some with our initials M&S on a stick and others that read, *She said yes!* It's over the top and perfect. I couldn't have done it better myself.

"When did you have time to do all of this in the last week?"

"About that." Maverick grins as he scratches the back of his neck.

"There's my niece." Archer takes Ada into his arms and rushes off with her.

"Well?" I ask Maverick.

"I started planning a while ago."

"What's a while ago?"

"After our pre-proposal. I knew you were going to say yes. You'd already said yes, so I kind of started putting things into motion."

"How did you pull this off without me knowing?"

"My sisters-in-law, my mom, your grandma. All the ladies were onboard. I told them the things I wanted, and they told me it was too much, and I told them I wanted it anyway, and they made it happen." He doesn't look even a little bit sorry for it either.

"It's great, Mav. Thank you."

"Oh, there's more. This is just the basics."

"There is so much attention to detail to incorporate both parties. How can this only be the basics?"

"You'll see," he says cryptically. He kisses me quickly, but I'm being pulled away by Alyssa and Jordyn.

"Should you ladies be tugging on me like that? It might send you both into labor," I tease.

"Stop." Alyssa giggles, holding her belly. She's only got a few more weeks to go before we get to meet her little one. She and Sterling decided to be surprised. Jordyn and Ryder did, too, so we're all on pins and needles, waiting on the arrival of their little ones.

"Do you love it?" Jordyn asks.

"I do. It's a little much." I chuckle.

"We tried to tell him," Ramsey says, joining us. "He was insistent."

"He's too much." I'm smiling so big my face hurts.

"We knew he would be like this. We told him when he falls, he's going to fall hard."

"He's definitely over the top."

Ramsey waves me off. "Let him. That's Maverick's love language. He's always been a little extra in... well, everything," she says, and we all laugh at her reasoning. She's not wrong.

The conversation turns to their pregnancies, and Ramsey tells us that she and Deacon are trying for another baby. Eventually, the other ladies join us. We're all sitting at the long kitchen table chatting. The men are off doing who knows what. I've learned that the brothers are a pack. It doesn't matter what one is doing, the others are all in. From moving to putting together baby furniture to New Year's and engagement parties. They're by each other's sides, no matter what.

At a few minutes before midnight, Maverick announces that there's about to be a show. Not sure what he's talking about, we bundle up the kids that aren't already fast asleep, and step outside on the back patio where the grill and firepit are.

We're all huddled together when Maverick comes to stand by us and wraps me in his arms. "Bug, Daddy is so glad you're still awake."

"She took a power nap and is ready to party again," I tell him. I know it's all the excitement and noise that's keeping her up. The only two that are crashed are Caden and Beckham. I think those boys could sleep through anything.

"Ready for the show?" he asks.

"What is it?"

"You'll see."

"Count it down!" Declan calls out.

Together, we call back. "Ten, nine, eight, seven, six, five, four, three, two, one." Fireworks explode into the sky.

Merrick, Declan, Sterling, Rushton, and Archer whoop and cheer as they light more. Maverick has Ada in his arms. She's not sure about the noise, but he holds her close and points to the sky.

"See, Bug, so pretty," he tells her.

I'm looking up at the sky when a firework explodes into a heart, and the next, an engagement ring. "What?" I whip my head around to look at Maverick. "How did you pull this off? It must have cost a fortune."

"No. Ramsey and Jordyn were already planning this. I just hijacked with a few specialized fireworks that we added to the mix. It wasn't that much, angel."

I stare back up at the night sky in time to see a firework explode into an angel halo. Tears spring to my eyes, and I don't fight them. I move to stand on the other side of Maverick so that I can curl into his chest.

I love this man.

I love the life we're building.

Forever won't be long enough.

Maverick

T ODAY IS FEBRUARY FOURTEENTH.

Today is also my wedding day.

Is it cliché to get married on the one day a year that was created to celebrate love? Maybe. Do I care? Not in the slightest. What I care about is the fact that Stella is going to be my wife.

"How you feeling, son?" Dad asks.

"Ready to get this show on the road," I confess.

He nods and grins. He knew the answer before he asked. My dad has always had the ability to read each of us.

"I can still remember the day I married your mother. I was the same way. No nerves, just impatience. I knew she was the one for me."

"Yeah," I agree. "It's right here." I tap my chest. "I never understood the hype until I met Stel." I chuckle.

"You wouldn't," he concurs. "It's not something you believe in until you experience it."

"And being a dad—best thing ever."

Dad laughs. "Why do you think your mother and I did it so many times?"

"I don't think I can talk Stel into eight more," I tell him.

"One of you is bound to have twins. You and Merrick are the most likely candidates since you're twins."

"That would be awesome. I hope one of us, any of us, has a set of twins."

"Yeah." Dad nods thoughtfully. "That would be cool. Your mother would be thrilled."

There's a knock on the door, and Merrick enters. "What's up?"

"Thanks for coming." I reach down and pick up the two small, wrapped boxes. "Can you take these to Stel and Ada? Oh, and this." I reach into the pocket of my jacket and pull out an envelope and hand it to him.

"Do I get to read it?" he asks. He's joking, but I still give him an "are you fucking kidding me" look. He laughs. "I'm going to stick around while she at least opens these. It's only fair since I helped pick them out."

"I don't care, as long as Stel is okay with it." I wonder if I can have him record her reaction? Nah, I better not push my luck. No one wants to piss their wife off on their wedding day. Not that she would be mad, but still. I can imagine her face when she opens them, anyway. I don't need a video to see tears in those big blue eyes.

"Oh, she will be. Your girls love me."

"They loved me first," I fire back as his laughter follows him out of the room.

"You know he's just messing with you," Dad tells me.

"I know. Just wait until his wedding day. I'm going to double the pain-in-the-ass efforts."

Dad doesn't reply. He's used to our antics.

"I'm proud of you, son."

"Thanks, Dad. I'm proud of myself too. She's the best, and Ada, that little bug wormed her way into my heart instantly."

My phone vibrates. Pulling it out of my pocket, I see a message from my group text with my brothers.

Orrin:	Our baby bro is getting married.
Merrick:	Hey! Technically, I'm the baby. He was born four minutes before me.
Brooks:	Aw, Mer, you're our baby brother too.
Rushton:	You think Stella will notice if I cut the cake? Just a small piece.
Archer:	I want cake.
Ryder:	You know Mav splurged for steak for dinner, right?
Deacon:	I expected nothing but over the top for Maverick.
Sterling:	If anyone is getting cake, it's me. My wife is due to give birth in a week. I need all the cake.
Ryder:	Oh, yeah, mine is seven weeks away. I should be behind Sterling for cake.

Me:	Fuck you, assholes. It's my wedding day. Sterling and Archer, stay away from the cake, and Deacon, remember that when you're sinking your teeth into a juicy rib eye after the ceremony.
Merrick:	I'm his twin and errand boy today. I should get first dibs on cake and steak.
Orrin:	We love you, brother.

I smile down at my phone. I know what they're doing. They think I'm nervous, and they're trying to help. I'm not nervous. I'm excited, eager, and so damn thankful for my girls, but no nerves.

Me:	I'm good, fellas. I'm ready to make them mine in all the ways. I appreciate the effort.

My phone pings eight times, and I don't have to look to see what each message says. I already know.

Love harder.

"All right," Merrick says, coming into the room like a banshee. "Stella cried and told me it's your fault if she's late getting to the altar because she has to fix her makeup. Baby Ada smiled and said 'pretty.' I helped her put it on, even though Stella said she was too little."

"And you're going to show me the picture you took of my daughter, right? I know you won't show me Stella."

"Oh, I took pictures of both, but yeah, you only get to see Ada." He pulls out his phone and taps at the screen. "Look at her." He turns his phone so that I can see.

I stare at my little girl. She's in a white dress with a pink bow around her waist and matching pink shoes. Around her neck is the necklace I bought her to match her mom's. They're cheap, nothing over-the-top expensive. I knew Stella would have a fit if I spent too much on something Ada could break or lose. It's a small *K* charm. Luckily, she's not one of those kids who puts everything in her mouth. She will bring you every tiny piece of anything she finds. Rocks, lint, crumbs, you name it. They don't go in her mouth, but she brings them to you.

Stella's is made of diamonds to match the key I gave her at Christmas. I know my wife will get the meaning. She has my heart, my forever, and now, my last name. They both do.

"Oh, I took a video." Merrick pulls his phone back and taps the screen before turning it back to me. "Say hi to Daddy." His voice fills the room.

"Daddy, pwetty." Ada points at her necklace.

I'm man enough to admit I have to swallow back my emotions. I couldn't love that little girl more if it were my blood flowing through her veins.

"Let me see," Dad says. Merrick shows him the picture and replays the video.

"You can see Stella. She's hot."

"Mer," I warn him. He chuckles and ignores me.

"You have a beautiful family, Maverick."

"Thanks, Dad."

"I gave her the letter, but I didn't stick around for her to read it. She did give me this to give you though." He hands me an envelope.

"Do you want us to step out?" Dad asks.

"No. It's fine." I walk to the couch in the room and sit down. Carefully, I open the envelope and pull out the papers. I read them three times to make sure I'm seeing them correctly.

"Mav?" Merrick asks. I feel his hand on my shoulder. It's that twin thing again. "Tell me."

I can't speak. I can't form the words of what the papers in my hands mean to me. Instead, I shake my head and hand him the papers.

"Damn," Merrick mutters as he reads them over. He clears his throat, but I can still hear the emotion when he says. "She's living by that family motto already."

"What is it?" Dad asks.

I swallow hard. I'm on the verge of letting tears fall. I feel so many emotions. Happiness, gratefulness, elation, and I don't know how to process each one.

Clearing my throat, I answer him, "Adoption papers." I look up and see my dad with tears in his eyes. "She's giving me my little girl."

I stand as my dad heads my way, and he wraps me up in a tight hug. We don't say a word as I hold on to the man who taught me how to love. He taught all of us.

"Make room," Merrick says.

The next thing I know, his arms are around both of us, and we're all laughing, happiness overflowing in our hearts.

I'm getting married to the love of my life.

I'm Ada's dad in all the ways that matter.

Today is officially the best day of my life.

I'm standing at the altar with all my brothers and Deacon. I know it's a lot, but I wanted them all up here with me. Besides, I made a promise to all of them that when I got married, I'd do it up big.

I don't know what's bigger than all my brothers and Deacon standing up with me.

That made us short a person on Stella's side, so Piper offered to stand in. Stella was ecstatic. Piper is Palmer and Deacon's sister. We don't see much of her anymore. She's been busy with life and her daughter. Her husband was transferred to the Atlanta Fire Department. It's only an hour's drive, but it's a lot when you have kids, activities, jobs, and everything else that comes with adulting.

The music starts, and the doors open. Did I mention that all my nieces and nephews are in the wedding as well? What can I say? It's a family affair. When it's Ada's turn, she sees me, and takes off running as fast as her little legs will carry her. I bend down and scoop her up into my arms.

"Daddy pwetty," she says, pointing to her necklace.

"Daddy loves you, Bug." I kiss her cheek.

"Wub you."

Damn this kid, she has my heart feeling all soft and squishy inside my chest. I hold her the rest of the time. When Stella appears, she takes my breath away.

"Mommy pwetty!"

Everyone laughs. Not that there's a lot of people in the audience. They're all in the wedding.

When Stella reaches me, I try to hand Ada off to Merrick, but she's not having it. She circles her arms around my neck, and that's perfectly fine with me. I hold her in one hand and reach out to Stella with the other. She takes it with both of hers.

I don't remember much about the ceremony. My daughter rests her head on my shoulder like she always does and snuggles close. My gaze never leaves my wife's. I speak where I'm supposed to, but I don't really hear anything until I've slipped the wedding band on her finger, and I'm told that I can kiss my bride.

"Come here, angel." I slide my free hand behind her neck and pull her into a kiss. Our first kiss as husband and wife. One I'll remember for as long as I live.

Stella

TODAY IS MY BABY GIRL'S second birthday. It looks very different from her first. Today, we're surrounded by family and surrounded by love. Maverick and I have been married for five months, and it's been bliss. Every day I fall more in love with him.

Today, my husband is up to his usual antics. He was insistent that we have a big family bash for Ada's second birthday. That part I was fine with. It's the bounce house, the balloon animals, and face painting I tried to dial him back on. It's no use.

The bounce house is part of her gift because, let's be honest, our girl has way too many toys. The balloon animals and the face painting are a husband-and-wife duo from Harris. They were fairly inexpensive for two hours of their time, and when Maverick gave me those puppy-dog eyes, I gave in.

Who am I to stop him from showing our daughter love? This is Maverick. It's who he is, and I've embraced that. Not to mention his smile is just as big as Ada's and the rest of the kids'.

"Do they ever grow up?" Jordyn asks. She's holding her thirteen-week-old son, Finn.

"I'm thinking that's a no," I reply.

"No, to what?" Alyssa asks. She plops down on the couch next to Jordyn with Ivy, her nineteen-week-old daughter, in her arms.

"They never grow up." I nod toward our husbands.

"Nope. But that's part of their charm," Alyssa says, smiling down at Ivy.

"How are you both feeling?" I ask them.

"Great," they say at the same time, making each other laugh. We've all grown close, as close as sisters can be.

"You ready for another one?" Jordyn asks me.

She must read something on my face. "Stella?"

"I can't tell you before I tell him," I confess without actually confessing.

Jordyn and Alyssa offer me matching grins. "When?"

"Today. I took the test last week. I scrambled to find what I needed to tell him."

"How far along are you?" Jordyn asks.

I shrug. "I'm not sure. I'm two weeks late. I was a week late when I took the test last week. I have an appointment next week."

"You said you had a doctor's appointment but didn't say what for."

"Yeah, I told Mav it was my woman's check-up, and he bought it." I smile, thinking about my husband. I know he's going to be out of his mind, excited about this news. "I wanted to make sure he could be there with me. He didn't ask why."

"Yeah." Alyssa smiles. "They never do. We ask, and they're there. All of them are like that."

"How are you going to tell him?" Jordyn asks.

"Well, I copied his move. I bought Ada a tank top. She's wearing it under her T-shirt."

"Do it now," Alyssa says excitedly. "I cannot wait to see his reaction."

"I don't want to take away from Ada's day."

"Stella, honey, she's two. She doesn't understand, and the other kids will keep on playing. It's not going to faze them. Tell him," Jordyn insists.

Before I can answer, Ada comes rushing over. "Mommy, milk."

"I can take her." Maverick appears. "You ladies enjoy your chat."

"Babe, she's getting hot. Why don't you take that T-shirt off her? She has a tank top on underneath."

"Got it." Maverick walks away to get our girl something to drink.

"We should follow him," Alyssa says.

"He'll find me," I assure them. "We'll know exactly when he reads it."

"What does it say, anyway?" Jordyn asks.

"This birthday girl is going to be a big sister."

"Aw," Jordyn and Alyssa say at the same time.

"No. Way!" Maverick's voice is loud, and everything stops around us. "Stella."

I turn to face him and work hard to keep my face neutral. "Mav?"

"Angel, can you read this for me?" He rushes toward me with Ada in his arms. She's bouncing on his hip, thinking it's a game, and laughing like she always does when she's with her daddy.

"Oh, that, yeah. It says this birthday girl is going to be a big sister."

"This one?" he asks, pointing at Ada. "This birthday girl?"

"Yeah, I mean, she's wearing the shirt, right?" I'm trying really hard not to laugh. It's the hope I see in his eyes that helps me keep it at bay.

"This is our daughter."

This time I do laugh. "Yep. Last I checked."

"That means we're having a baby."

"We are." I smile as tears fill my eyes. The look on his face, it's priceless and one that I'll always remember.

Ada squirms to get down, so he places her on her feet as he moves in closer to me. His hands cup my cheeks. "We're having a baby?"

"Baby number two." Tears well in my eyes.

I don't know what I expected, but it's not Maverick dropping to his knees, kissing my belly over my shirt. "I love you so much, baby. You, your mommy, and your big sister." He stands and pulls me into a hug. "How?" he asks.

"Um, babe, that's not a conversation for little ears."

He chuckles. "That's not what I meant. I know *how*. What I don't know is how I can love something so much when I've just learned of its existence?"

My heart melts, as do the hearts of every woman in the room. "Maverick Kincaid, you're one in a million."

"We're having a baby!" he shouts. Everyone cheers. They've watched it all go down but remained silent until Maverick yells it loud enough that I'm certain all of Willow River now knows our news.

He kisses me. Not just any kiss. It's slow and deep and definitely not appropriate for our two-year-old daughter's birthday party, but that doesn't stop me from kissing him back with everything I've got. "Mav, we should move out of the way of little eyes." I finally manage to find my bearings and remember exactly where we are.

"We should stay here in this spot. Let them see what love looks like. They have lots of examples, but ours, it's one for the books, Stel."

Maverick

"**Y**OU KNOW," ORRIN SAYS WITH a smirk on his face. "I remember a time when you said that you would never have a gender reveal."

"Something about just tossing out the gender to everyone and omitting the party," Rushton chimes in.

I smile and nod. I remember the conversation, and just like with everything else they did once they found the loves of their lives, I didn't understand. "Sounds about right," I admit.

"And here we are," Sterling quips.

"Not that we expected anything less," Archer chimes in. "This is Mav we're talking about."

"You just had to one up all of us, didn't you?" Brooks laughs.

"Hold up now," Merrick chimes in. "I haven't had my chance."

"Something you're not telling us, brother?" Declan asks.

"You have been quiet today," Deacon adds.

"Nothing to tell, but I'm still unattached, so don't go giving Mav the keys to the kingdom of best gender reveal."

"Uh, best of everything, brother. You were at my engagement party and my wedding. You know I pulled out all the stops."

"I don't know," Orrin speaks up. "You two have that crazy twin thing you do sometimes. I think Mer can be some stiff competition."

"It's not like any of you get a do-over." Merrick chuckles. "I'm the last to find my wife." He shrugs, but I can see the mischief in his eyes.

"Fine, when you find her, and you want to go over the top, you call me."

"I have my own ideas."

"Sounds to me like you might be making some plans," Brooks tells him.

"Nah, but after watching the nine of you get married, it's easy to know what I want and what I don't," Merrick tells him.

"I thought that too, but when it happens, it changes you."

"What he said." Rushton holds up his bottle of water and salutes me.

"That's what you all keep telling me. I guess one day I'll know for sure."

"So, when are we getting this party started?" Sterling asks.

I look across the room at my wife. She's got her hands over her baby belly, and smiling at something my mom just said.

"We might as well do it now. I'm starving, and honestly, waiting is killing me." Clapping Archer on the shoulder, I walk away, heading toward my wife.

"Daddy!" Ada rushes me, and I scoop her into my arms.

"Hey, Bug, are you ready to find out if we're having a brother or a sister?"

"Sister." She's been absolute in her guess every time I ask her.

"All right then, let's go get Mommy and find out." We walk to where the ladies are standing under the giant balloon arch I insisted we needed. I also made sure Ada had a shirt that declares her the big sister. We have blue and pink everything. I went overboard with napkins, plates, cupcakes, balloons, little, tiny diaper pins for games, and tablecloths. My wife let me. Kincaid Central looks like baby central, and I love it. I can't wait to find out what we're having. We had the doctor write it down and put it in an envelope, and we gave it to Jordyn. She helped with all of this and is of the same frame of mind in going over the top. Stella didn't have that with Ada, and I want to give my wife the world.

"Ready to do this?" I ask her.

"Yep. Jordyn!" she calls out.

My sister-in-law grins and grabs two large dark gray balloons and heads our way. "Are we ready?"

"Weady!" Ada tells her aunt.

"Come to Uncle Mer." Merrick steps up and takes my daughter. She smiles and wraps her arms around his neck. It took some time, but she's used to the fact that Uncle Mer looks just like Daddy.

"Bring it in people!" Archer calls out. Everyone does as he asks; we're all anxious to know the gender of the next baby Kincaid.

"Okay, so Mav and Stel, the two of you each get a pin. All you have to do is pop your balloons at the same time. We're going to count you down from five." Jordyn's smile is almost blinding.

"Come on, angel, we've got this." Taking my wife by the hand, we move to stand in the middle of the balloon arch. Jordyn hands us each a massive gray balloon and a pin to pop them with.

"Here we go!" Jordyn says excitedly.

"Five. Four. Three. Two. One." They count us down. I pop my balloon and pink confetti falls all around me. I close my eyes, and take in the moment that I'm having another little girl. I open them quickly to kiss my wife, and freeze. Stella is standing with a shocked expression on her face, and she's covered in blue confetti.

"Stel?"

"Mav?"

We both turn to look at Jordyn. "Twins!" she yells excitedly.

Twins.

We're having twins.

One boy.

One girl.

Holy shit!

I knew this was a possibility. I mean, I'm a twin, but none of my brothers have had twins. I just assumed it would be one baby. *Two babies!*

My arms wrap around my wife, and I hold her close. "Two babies, angel."

"Twins. Mav. We're having twins!"

"Bug!" I call out for my daughter, not letting go of my wife. Merrick brings her to me, and the emotion I see in his eyes has me swallowing back my own.

"Go to Daddy, Ada," he says. As soon as she's in my arms, he hugs all three of us tightly.

He feels this.

He can feel the overwhelming joy and love coursing through my veins right now.

"Love you, Mav."

"Love you too."

Merrick steps back and gives us a moment to tell Ada she's getting a brother and a sister. She cheers, and that's when our family descends.

Once we've passed out hugs, and my dad takes Ada to play with her cousins, I stand still holding my wife.

"We should go help clean up."

"No, we should stay right here."

"We're being rude, Mav." I can hear the smile in her voice, but I'm not willing to let her go just yet.

"Stay anyway, angel. I just want to hold you."

I feel her shoulders relax and I know that I have her. "I love you. I love our family, and I—fuck, Stel, I can't even put into words what I feel right now. Two more babies to love."

She pulls back just far enough to look up at me. "That's okay, Mav. I plan to stay right here." She places her hand over my heart. "This, the way it's beating, racing beneath my palm tells me everything I need to know."

"Looks like Mav might have loved a little harder than the rest of us," one of my brothers calls out.

The room erupts into laughter. As I smile down at my wife. 'Love harder' I mouth, and she mouths it back.

This is my forever.

Thank YOU

for taking the time to read **Stay Anyway**.
I hope you loved Maverick and Stella's story.

We have one Kincaid brother left!
You can preorder Merrick's story now
Stay Real
kayleeryan.com/books/stay-real/

Never miss a new release:
Newsletter Sign-up

Be the first to hear about free content, new releases, cover
reveals, sales, and more.
kayleeryan.com/subscribe/

Discover more about Kaylee's books here
kayleeryan.com/books/

Did you know that Orrin Kincaid has his own story?
Grab ***Stay Always*** for free
kayleeryan.com/books/stay-always/

Start the Riggins Brothers Series for FREE.
Download ***Play by Play*** now
kayleeryan.com/books/play-by-play/

More from KAYLEE RYAN

With You Series:

Anywhere with You | More with You | Everything with You

Soul Serenade Series:

Emphatic | Assured | Definite | Insistent

Southern Heart Series:

Southern Pleasure | Southern Desire

Southern Attraction | Southern Devotion

Unexpected Arrivals Series

Unexpected Reality |Unexpected Fight | Unexpected Fall

Unexpected Bond | Unexpected Odds

Riggins Brothers Series:

Play by Play | Layer by Layer | Piece by Piece

Kiss by Kiss | Touch by Touch | Beat by Beat

Out of Reach Series:

Beyond the Bases | Beyond the Game

Beyond the Play | Beyond the Team

Entangled Hearts Duet:

Agony | Bliss

More from KAYLEE RYAN

Standalone Titles:

Tempting Tatum | Unwrapping Tatum | Levitate

Just Say When | I Just Want You | Reminding Avery

Hey, Whiskey | Pull You Through | Remedy

The Difference | Trust the Push | Forever After All

Misconception | Never with Me

Cocky Hero Club:

Lucky Bastard

Mason Creek Series:

Perfect Embrace

Kincaid Brothers Series:

Stay Always | Stay Over | Stay Forever

Stay Tonight | Stay Together | Stay Wild

Stay Present | Stay Anyway | Stay Real

Everlasting Ink Series:

Does He Know? | Is This Love?

More from KAYLEE RYAN

Co-written with Lacey Black:

Fair Lakes Series:

It's Not Over | Just Getting Started

Can't Fight It

Standalone Titles:

Boy Trouble | Home to You

Beneath the Fallen Stars | Tell Me A Story

Co-writing as Rebel Shaw with Lacey Black:

Royal | Crying Shame | Watch and Learn

Acknowledgments

There are so many people who are involved in the publishing process. I write the words, but I rely on my team of editors, proofreaders, and beta readers to help me make each book the best that it can be.

Those mentioned above are not the only members of my team. I have photographers, models, cover designers, formatters, bloggers, graphic designers, author friends, my PA, and so many more. I could not do this without these people.

And then there are my readers. If you're reading this, thank you. Your support means everything. Thank you for spending your hard-earned money on my words, and taking the time to read them. I appreciate you more than you know.

Special Thanks:

Becky Johnson, Hot Tree Editing.

Julie Deaton, Jo Thompson, and Jess Hodge, Proofreading

Sarah Book Cover Boutique – Cover Design

Sara Eirew – Photographer

Emily Wittig Designs – Special Edition Cover

Chasidy Renee – Personal Assistant

Jamie, Stacy, Lauren, Franci, and Erica

Bloggers, Bookstagrammers, and TikTokers

Lacey Black & Kelly Elliott

Stacy and Ms. Betty - Graphics

The entire Give Me Books Team

The entire Grey's Promotion Team

My fellow authors

And my amazing Readers

Much love,

Kaylee Ryan
AUTHOR

Made in United States
Orlando, FL
03 June 2024

47507822R00153